Also by Alexander McCall Smith

THE
TALENTED
MR. VARG

THE
TALENTED
MR. VARG

ÄLEXANDER McCALL SMITH

Älfred Ä. Knopf Canada

PUBLISHED BY ALFRED A. KNOPF CANADA

Copyright © 2020 Alexander McCall Smith

www.penguinrandomhouse.ca

Library and Archives Canada Cataloguing in Publication

Title: The talented Mr. Varg / Alexander McCall Smith.
Names: McCall Smith, Alexander, 1948- author.
Description: Series statement: A Detective Varg novel
Identifiers: Canadiana (print) 20190157062 |Canadiana (ebook) 20190157070 | ISBN 9780735280076 (hardcover) | ISBN 9780735280083 (HTML)
Classification: LCC PR6063.C326 T35 2020 | DDC 823/.914—dc23

Jacket images: (man) Marcus Davies/Millennium Images; (paw prints) Chinch/Shutterstock
Jacket design by Kelly Blair

Printed and bound in the United States of America

10 9 8 7 6 5 4 3 2 1

Penguin
Random House
KNOPF CANADA

This book is for Lance and Pauline Butler

THE
TALENTED
MR. VARG

Chapter One

ENLARGED PORES

Ulf Varg, of the Department of Sensitive Crimes, drove his silver-grey Saab through a landscape of short distances. He was heading for a psychotherapeutic day at a rural wellness centre, and the drive, he thought, was part of the therapy. Southern Sweden lay before him, parcelled out into farms that had been in the ownership of the same families for generations. Here and there, dots of white amidst the green, were the houses of the people who worked this land. They were settled people, of long memories and equally long jealousies, whose metaphorical horizons stopped where the sky met the land, which sometimes seemed only a stone's throw away; who had never gone anywhere very much, and who had no desire to do so.

He thought of the life these people led, which was so different from his own in Malmö. Nothing was particularly urgent here; nobody had targets to meet, or reports to write. There would be no talk of inputs and outputs and communicative objectives. Most people worked for themselves and no other; they knew what their neighbours would say, about any subject, as they had heard it all before, time upon time, and it was all as familiar as the weather. They knew, too, exactly who liked, or disliked, whom; they knew who was not be trusted; who had done what, years back, and what the consequences had been. It would be simple to be a policeman here, thought Ulf, as there were no secrets to speak of. You would know about crimes almost before they were committed, although there would be few of those. People here were law-abiding and conformist, leading lives that ran narrowly and correctly to the grave—and they knew where that grave would be, right next to those of their parents and their parents' parents.

Ulf opened his car window and took a deep breath: the country air bore notes of something floral—gorse, he thought, or the flowering trees of an orchard that ran beside the road. Trees were not his strong point, and Ulf could never remember which fruit tree was which, although he believed that he was now in apple-growing country—or was it peach? Whatever it might be, it was in blossom, a little later than usual, he had heard, because spring had been slow in Sweden that year. Everything had been slow, in fact, including promotion. Ulf had been told—unofficially—that he was in line for advancement within Malmö's Department of Sensitive Crimes, but that had been months ago and nothing had come of it since then.

It had been a bad idea to spend the anticipated rise in salary on the purchase of a new living-room suite, especially one that was upholstered in soft Florentine leather. It had been ruinously expensive, and when his salary remained obstinately the same, he had been obliged to transfer funds out of his savings account into his current account in order to cover the cost. Ulf hated doing that, as he had vowed not to touch his savings account until his sixtieth birthday, which was exactly twenty years away. Yet twenty years seemed such a long time, and he wondered whether he would still be around then.

Ulf was not one to dwell on such melancholy reflections about our human situation. There was a limit to what one could take on in life; his job was to protect people from others who would harm them in some way—to fight crime, even if at a rather odd end of the criminal spectrum. He could not do everything, he decided, and take all the troubles of the world on his shoulders. Who could? It was not that he was an uninvolved and irresponsible citizen, one of those who do not care about plastic bags. He was as careful as anyone to keep his ecological footprint as small as possible—apart from the Saab, of course, which ran on fossil fuel rather than electricity. If you took the Saab out of the equation, though, Ulf could hold his head high in the company of conservationists, including that of his colleague Erik, who went on and on about fishing stocks while at the same time doing his best every weekend to seek such fish as remained. Erik made much of his habit of returning to the water any fish he caught, but Ulf pointed out that these fish were traumatised and were possibly never the same again. "It's a big thing for a fish to be caught," he said to Erik. "Even if you put him back, that fish is bound to feel insecure."

Erik had simply dismissed his objection, although Ulf could tell that his remark had hit home. And that he immediately regretted, because it was only too easy to make somebody like Erik feel ill at ease. It was hard enough to be Erik, Ulf reflected, without having to fend off criticism from people like me. Ulf was a kind man, and even if Erik's talk about fish was trying, he would take care not to show it. He would listen patiently, and might even learn something—although that, he thought, was rather unlikely.

As he drove the Saab along that quiet country road, Ulf was not thinking about conservation and the long-term prospects of humanity so much as of an awkward issue that had arisen as a result of one of his recent cases. The Department of Sensitive Crimes usually steered clear of day-to-day offences, leaving those to the uniformed officers of the local police. From time to time, though, a particular political or social connotation to an otherwise mundane incident meant that it was diverted to the department. This was the case with a minor assault committed by a Lutheran clergyman, who had bloodied the nose of his victim one Saturday morning in full view of at least fifteen witnesses. That was unusual enough, as Lutheran ministers do not figure prominently in the criminal statistics, but what singled this out for the attentions of the Department of Sensitive Crimes was not so much the identity of the perpetrator of the assault, but that of the victim. The nose that had been the target of the assault belonged to the leader of a group of Rom travellers.

"Protected species," observed Ulf's colleague Carl.

"*Tattare,*" mused Erik, only to be sharply corrected by their colleague Anna, who rolled her eyes at the unfashionable, disparaging name. Anna, more than the others in the department, knew the contours of the permissible. "They are not Tartars, Erik," she said. "They are *Resande,* a travelling minority."

Ulf had defused the situation. "Erik is only referring to the insensitivity of others," he said. "He's drawing our attention to the sort of attitude that leads to incidents like this."

"Unless he deserved it," muttered Erik.

Ulf ignored this, looking instead at the photographs in the folder of the nose in question. These had been taken in the hospital emergency department, when the blood was still trickling out of the left nostril. In other respects, the nose appeared unexceptional, although Ulf noticed that the pores on either side of the curve of the nostril were slightly enlarged.

"There are odd little holes here," he said, getting up from his desk to hand the file to Anna, whose desk, one of four in the room, was closest to his. "Look at this poor man's skin."

Anna examined the photograph. "Enlarged pores," she said. "An oily complexion."

Carl looked up from a report he was writing. "Can anything be done about that?" he asked. "Sometimes when I look in the mirror—I mean, look closely at my nose—I see little pinpricks. I've wondered about them."

Anna nodded. "Same thing—and perfectly normal. You find them in places where the skin is naturally greasy. They act as a sort of drain."

Carl seemed interested. His hand went up to touch the skin around his nose. "And can you do anything about them?"

Anna handed the file back to Ulf. "Wash your face," she said. "Use a cleanser. And then, for special occasions, you can put an ice cube on them. It tightens the skin and will make your pores look smaller."

"Oh," said Carl. "Ice?"

"Yes," said Anna. "But the most important thing is to keep the skin clean. You don't wear make-up, I take it . . ."

Carl smiled. "Not yet."

Anna pointed out that some men did. "You can wear anything these days. There's that man in the café over the road—have you noticed him? He wears blusher—quite a lot of it. He'll have to be careful—he could get blocked pores if he doesn't remove the make-up carefully enough."

"Why does he wear the stuff?" asked Carl. "I can't imagine caking my face with chemicals."

"Because he wants to look his best," said Anna. "Most people, you know, don't look the way they'd like to. It's a bit sad, I suppose, but that's the way it is."

Ulf said, "Very strange." He was thinking of the case rather than cosmetics.

The assault on the traveller might have led to a swift and uncomplicated prosecution of the assailant were it not for the fact that not one of the fifteen witnesses was prepared to give evidence. Four of them said that they had been looking the other way at the time; five said that their eyes happened to be closed when the assault took place, one actually claiming to have been asleep; and the remainder said that they could not remember anything about the incident and that they very much doubted whether it had taken place at all. This left the victim and the Lutheran minister. The victim was clear as to what had happened: he had been attending to his own business in the town's public square when a stranger in clerical garb had walked up to him and punched him in the nose. This was purely because he was a traveller, he said. "We're used to the settled community treating us in this way. They resent our freedom."

For the minister's part, he claimed that he had been suddenly confronted by a complete stranger who became so animated in some unfathomable diatribe that he had banged his nose on a lamp-post. He had been so concerned about this unfortunate's injury that he had offered him his own handkerchief to mop up the blood. This offer had been spurned in a most ungracious way. Any allegation that he had assaulted this man was abhorrent and patently false. "Some people are terrible liars," the minister concluded. "Bless them, but they really have no shame at all. Not that I'm picking on any particular group, you'll understand."

Ulf suggested to the victim and the assailant that it might be best to let the whole thing be resolved through the extraction of a mutual apology. "When it's impossible for us to tell what actually happened," he explained, "then it is sometimes best to move on. There are different understandings of conflict—as in this case— and if both sides can see their way to patching things up . . ."

The victim's body language made it apparent that this suggestion was not going down well. He appeared to swell, his neck inflating in what looked like a dangerous build-up of pressure, and his eyes narrowing in fury. "So, a Rom nose counts for less than anybody else's," he hissed. "Is that what you're telling me?"

"I am not passing judgement on your nose," said Ulf calmly. "And all noses are equal as far as we're concerned—let me assure you of that."

"That's what you say," snapped the victim. "But when it comes to the crunch, it's a rather different story, isn't it?" His voice rose petulantly. He glared at Ulf, then he went on, "My nose is as Swedish as yours."

Ulf stared back. He was always irritated by aggression, and this man, he thought, was needlessly confrontational. At the same time, he was aware that he was dealing with a member of a minority disliked by so many. That must change your attitude. His reply was placatory. "Of course it is. I didn't say otherwise."

"But you want to let him off, don't you? Justified assault? Is that it?"

This stung Ulf. "Vili . . ." He trailed off, realising that he did not know the complainant's name. It was recorded in the file, but he did not have that to hand. It was a particularly unfortunate *lapsus memoriae,* given that he was being accused of discrimination. He remembered the name of the minister, but not of this man. "Vili . . ."

"See!" hissed the victim. "You can't even be bothered to learn my name."

Ulf swallowed hard. "I'm sorry." He remembered now, and wondered how he could have forgotten. Viligot Danior. "I'm sorry, Viligot. I'm very busy with all sorts of problems. Things come at me from every direction, and I sometimes find it difficult to master the details. What I want to say to you is this: I am not going to let this go. I understand how you feel, and I am determined that the minister should be held to account."

Viligot visibly relaxed. "Good. That is very good."

"And so I'm going to propose that we charge him. It will then be up to the magistrate to decide whom to believe. It will be one word against another, but we'll just have to hope that the court can work out who's telling the truth."

"Which is me," said Viligot hurriedly.

"If that's what you say," said Ulf, "then I shall believe you unless otherwise persuaded to the contrary. After all, you don't get a bloody nose from nowhere."

"Especially when there are no lamp-posts in the square in question," said Viligot.

Ulf thought for a moment. Then he smiled. "I think you have just convinced me," he said.

The court was similarly convinced, much to the annoyance of the defence when confronted with a photograph of the *locus* of the incident. Where, the minister was asked, was the lamp-post into which Viligot might have walked? After that, the minister's conviction was assured. He was fined and given a stern warning. "A man of the cloth has a particular duty of probity," the judge said. "And you have singularly failed in that duty."

Ulf felt that justice had been done. Viligot had been the victim of an unprovoked attack because he was a member of an unpopular section of the community. Ministers might be expected to be more tolerant than the average person, but presumably there were those amongst them who harboured vulgar prejudice and resentment. Still, it was a strange case, and Ulf was not entirely satisfied that he had got to the bottom of the matter.

That came later—barely half an hour after the end of the trial. As he left the courtroom to buy himself a cappuccino in a nearby coffee bar, Ulf was approached by one of the recalcitrant witnesses who had failed to see anything: the postman who had been passing, but looking the other way, at the time of the fracas.

"Ulf Varg," the postman said. "I hope you're satisfied."

Ulf gave the man a warning look. "And what do you mean by that?"

The postman was uncowed. "That man back there," he said, tossing his head contemptuously in the direction of the court building. "That Danior person . . ." The word *person* was spat out. "Do you know anything about him? Do you know what he does?"

Ulf shrugged. "I know he's a traveller, if that's what you mean. But those people have exactly the same rights as you and I, er . . ."

"Johansson."

"Well, Johansson, the law doesn't discriminate."

Johansson smiled. "Oh, I know that, Ulf. You don't have to tell me that. But do you know what Viligot Danior was doing? Do you know why the minister did what he did?"

Ulf stared at the postman, thinking of the reluctance of the witnesses—fifteen people who must have seen something. Fifteen! "I thought you didn't see anything."

"It's nothing to do with what I saw or didn't see," retorted the postman. "I'm talking about what Danior was up to. He and those sons of his. There are three of them. Nasty pieces of work, every one of them. Covered in tattoos."

Ulf waited.

"They steal tyres," said the postman. "We're a small town out there, Ulf, and we've all had tyres stolen from our cars. They arrived in our area, and next thing—surprise surprise—we started to lose our tyres. They just remove them—the wheels as well, some of the time."

"Danior does this, you say?"

The postman nodded.

Ulf frowned. "And the local police? What do they say about this?"

This brought a laugh from the postman. "They've been told not to lean on them. It's something to do with community sensitivity. They look the other way."

Like you, thought Ulf. And yet . . .

"So, Danior and his sons stole the minister's wheels. He has a Volvo—a nice car. But two of his wheels were removed, along with one other tyre, and the spare."

Ulf sighed. "And how did he know it was Danior?"

"Because he saw one of the sons doing it. He chased after him, but the boy jumped into a car and made himself scarce. So next time he came across Danior in the town, he lost his self-control and took a swing at him." The postman paused. "It could happen to anybody. Even you, you know—if you don't mind my saying it."

Ulf was silent. He imagined how he would feel if somebody stole the tyres of his Saab. And yet the whole point of having a system of justice was to prevent people from taking matters into their own hands and assaulting those who wronged them. That was the whole point. And yet . . .

He sighed again. Suddenly he felt tired, as if burdened by the whole edifice of the state and its rationale. "I'm sorry to hear that," he said. "But we can't have people assaulting others because of something they've done. We just can't."

The postman looked down at the ground. "I sometimes wonder what's happened to this country," he said.

Ulf looked at him. "I understand what you're saying."

"Do you?"

Ulf nodded. "It's not as simple as you think, Johansson. It just isn't."

And then it had become even more complicated. Three days previously, Ulf had returned home one evening to discover a note from his neighbour, Agnes Högfors. A large package had been left for him, she said, and she had taken delivery of it. It would be waiting for him when he came to collect Martin. Martin was Ulf's dog, who was looked after during the day by Agnes. She was particularly fond of him, as Martin was of her.

The package was crudely wrapped in plain brown paper. Ulf took it back to his flat where he discovered that it was a silver Saab grille, of the exact vintage and style for which he had been searching. His own grille had been damaged and needed replacing, and here was the exact part he needed.

There was a note. *Ulf Varg*, it read. *Thank you for standing up for me. You're an honest man, Ulf, and I thought you might like this. I noticed your car needed it. With thanks, Viligot.*

There were procedures for such things, and Ulf knew that he should immediately return the gift. He intended to do this, and the following day he drove out to the site where he had first interviewed Viligot: a caravan park outside the town in which the original offence had taken place. But there was no sign of Viligot, his sons, or indeed of anybody else.

"They've decamped, thank God," said a woman in the town when Ulf made enquiries. "Good riddance, we think." Then she added, "They've taken most of our tyres—and other bits and pieces from our cars."

Ulf felt himself blushing. The Saab grille had been stolen—and now it was in his car, sitting on the back seat, in full view of anybody who might walk past and glance through the window. He thanked the woman and drove back to his flat in Malmö. Once parked, he took the grille from the back seat and carried it into his flat. There was nobody about, but he felt that he was being watched from more than one window. He glanced upwards, and saw a movement at one of the neighbours' windows. There was now at least one witness to his handling of stolen goods.

He knew what he had to do. The manual of proper police conduct stated quite clearly that gifts from those with whom one had professional dealings were to be returned to the donor. In certain circumstances—such as where the gift was from a grateful member of the public who would be offended by its return—it could be kept, but only with the official permission of the Commissioner's department. When a gift was thought to be stolen property, then it should be handed in to a superior officer along with a report on the grounds for concluding that it was stolen. This had to be done within twenty-four hours of receiving the gift. Ulf had intended to do this, but it had slipped his mind. Now three days had elapsed and it was too late to do anything, unless his report falsified the time of his receiving the gift. And Ulf would not tell a deliberate lie, least of all on an official form.

Chapter Two

IN DEFENCE OF STEREOTYPES

From the roadside, the sign reading *The Inner You, this way* was barely visible. Ulf recognised his destination, though, from the photograph he had seen on the leaflet given to him by Dr. Svensson. This publication set out the activities of the centre, including the Saturday group session on "Untying Your Past" that Dr. Svensson recommended.

"We've made undoubted progress," the therapist said, "but sometimes it's useful to get a different perspective on things, and 'Untying Your Past' is conducted by a very good friend of mine, a German, Hans Ebke. He's practising in Stockholm now, but was highly thought of by the Max Planck Institute people down in Leipzig. Very highly."

Ulf was not sure whether they really had made much progress.

This uncertainty as to the benefits of the expensive sessions with the psychoanalyst might have prompted him to end his treatment, but an almost superstitious reluctance to sever the relationship had meant that it continued. And it was undoubtedly interesting, he had to admit, to delve into the depths of the subconscious mind—at least, he *sometimes* thought this was interesting. At other times he felt that the subconscious mind was capable of such a degree of banality that it might be best to leave it undisturbed, as one did with the other detritus of one's life. Ulf did not disclose these unsettling thoughts to Dr. Svensson; perhaps they would emerge, in due course, when dredged up on the psychoanalytical couch.

His colleague Anna was very dubious about Ulf's therapy. "Frankly, Ulf," she said, "I don't know why you bother with all that. You are the best-adjusted, most resolved person I know. And that includes me and Jo."

Jo was Anna's husband, a mild-mannered and largely unobtrusive anaesthetist. Dr. Svensson had identified him as Ulf's rival, but as far as Ulf was concerned—at least, as far as his conscious mind and super-ego were concerned—there were no grounds for rivalry, because Ulf had decided that he could never do anything about his attraction to Anna. She was a colleague and a married woman, and both of these considerations precluded any emotional entanglements between them. How could he even contemplate, he asked himself, doing anything to disturb Anna's settled life with her husband and her two daughters, both breaststroke champions and tipped for great things in the swimming world? How could he?

But here was Anna implicitly suggesting that she and her husband were less well adjusted and resolved than he was. Ulf doubted that: they were the progenitors of a perfect, two-child family; he, by contrast, was a single detective, living by himself, undergoing therapy and with a hearing-impaired dog.

"People do not want their friends to be successful," Dr. Svensson had once pointed out. "The success of a friend underlines our own failures. We don't want our friends to have more money than we do; nor more friends, for that matter. Envy, you see, Ulf, lies deep-rooted in our psyche."

"But if this envy is so pervasive," Ulf asked, "then does it mean we can never take satisfaction in the good fortune of anybody?"

"At one level we can experience such pleasure," replied Dr. Svensson. "But it will be superficial. Deep down, in the profundities, we do not welcome the advent of good fortune in the lives of others."

The profundities… Ulf pondered the expression. Dr. Svensson occasionally referred to profundities, but never fully explained where the profundities were. Ulf did not doubt, though, that they existed. He was aware of his profundities when he encountered some egregious instance of human cruelty; he felt a revulsion so intense that it sickened him to the stomach, and the stomach, he imagined, must be close to the profundities, if not their actual seat.

Did his profundities have anything to do with his attitude towards Anna's marriage? If he did not want her to be happy in that marriage, that might be simply a question of self-interest and a rational calculation as to what was best for him. Or was it because of the prompting of blind envy—because he himself had been widowed after so short a time? One part of him, he realised—his id—would very much welcome a rift between Anna and Jo, as it would open the way for it to succeed in its undoubted desire to start an affair with Anna. That was typical id—always concerned with animal satisfaction, with sexual drives, with hunger, with grasping and consuming. How much stronger, thought Ulf, was the position of those who denied the id its ambitions; who rose above the carnal, soared above it with their lofty high-mindedness. Of course, that was illusory. The ascetic, the saint, the self-denier, usually had their grubby secrets, their hidden appetites, their failures. The id was not to be put off so easily; it demanded attention and usually got it.

Hans Ebke might be able to throw some light on these matters, thought Ulf as he advanced up the long driveway that led to the Wholeness Centre. Yet Dr. Svensson had warned him that the day would involve group work, and Ulf was not sure that he wanted to share his feelings about Anna with a whole group of strangers. He had not even confided these feelings to Dr. Svensson, who was bound by a strict code of confidentiality, and was certainly unwilling to do so with people bound by no such obligation. And so, if envy came up, as it might well do, he could hardly admit to being afflicted by it because the obvious question that the other participants would wish to ask was: What are you envious about? He could hardly say, "I experience envy when I think about my attractive colleague who has two daughters and a husband who keeps putting people to sleep." Poor Jo, with his gases and masks and so on, and his terribly earnest manner, which some might call soporific; Ulf felt a certain sadness at the thought.

He parked the Saab in the small car park to the side of the house. Others had arrived before him, as there were already six cars parked there. Ulf surveyed the other vehicles, his detective's mind already trying to establish which was Dr. Ebke's car and which belonged to the patients. That assumed, of course, that Dr. Ebke would already have arrived—which he would have, beyond all shadow of a doubt. Dr. Ebke was German, Ulf had been told, and Ulf had yet to meet an unpunctual German. He himself was late—arriving about fifteen minutes after the time that had been stipulated in the letter from the Wholeness Centre secretariat. So Dr. Ebke would definitely be there. That left five cars, and according to the letter Ulf had received, there were four other participants. One of the cars, then, must belong to the centre's administrator— the person who had written the letter to Ulf confirming his registration. The names of the patients had been listed in an appendix to the letter, along with the short biographical notes they had all been asked to provide. These would be shared with the other participants, the letter had warned, and as a result people were told not to include any confidential matters that they did not want to be disclosed. Permission had been given to use a pseudonym, if one felt more comfortable with that, and when Ulf turned to the list, he saw that three of the others had taken up that offer.

Ulf had read the biographical notes with interest. There were two women and two men. The first woman on the list was called Henrietta. An asterisk next to the name indicated that this was a pseudonym.

"I am a wool buyer," wrote Henrietta in her note. "I am unmarried. I buy wool for textile companies. Sometimes I travel to Australia. I like tapestry, needlework, and salsa dancing." There was then a brief paragraph about her reasons for seeking psychotherapy. "I feel I owe it to myself," she wrote.

Ulf turned to the second entry. This was from Ebba, who, like Ulf, was not using a pseudonym but who did not give her second name. "I am Ebba," she wrote. "I have a job in a creative agency. I write advertising copy and also come up with marketing ideas—when these come to me! My problem is indecision, but I am working on it. This is the first time I will have been to a group encounter and I am really looking forward to it. Or am I?"

Ulf smiled.

Then there was Olaf, who confessed that he had been treated for some years for what he called "troubling impulses," and Peter, a pilot, who revealed that he had mild OCD, which he hoped to conquer before he embarked on further training to fly a new generation of jets. Would Peter *ever* be satisfied with pre-flight checks, or would he have to repeat them time and time again, until the control tower asked him if he ever intended to take off?

Ulf looked at the parked cars. None of them was a recent model, and, with the exception of one, they all looked sensible and unostentatious. The single car that stood out was a Porsche—and that had clearly seen better days. That obviously belonged to Peter, Ulf decided; a Porsche would not match the aesthetic sense of a wool buyer and appreciator of textiles, nor was it a car for an indecisive person. Ebba would drive the slowest of the cars, Ulf thought, as that would give her plenty of time to decide whether to turn left or right—no such deliberative time would be permitted by a Porsche. That meant that the small, underpowered Fiat, the car previously known by the affectionate soubriquet of the Fiat Bambino, would be Ebba's.

Besides the Porsche, there was one other German car, a Mercedes-Benz, and Ulf decided that this belonged to Dr. Ebke. If pressed, he would acknowledge that this might be considered a lazy assumption, based on stereotypes, but he had seen it so many times before, and should one sacrifice the defensible results of empirical observation on the altar of open-mindedness? Germans liked German cars. They just did. And they, in turn, used empirical observation to justify what might be seen by others as no more than shallow nationalistic preferences. German cars were well made and did not go wrong. The Germans knew that, and chose their cars on that basis.

So, the mid-range Mercedes-Benz parked second closest to the entrance would be Dr. Ebke's, the car parked closest to the entrance being that of the administrator, who would, of course, have arrived first in order to open up the building. That left two cars, one of which had tinted windows in the rear. That car belonged to one who had something to hide, and was therefore the car driven by Olaf, who had troubling impulses. Shame, it seemed, could dictate the choice of a car every bit as much as could pride. The final car could now be allocated to Henrietta. It was a Spanish car, a Seat . . . Salsa dancing, thought Ulf, which confirmed his diagnosis.

Inside, he found the participants gathered around Dr. Ebke, drinking a cup of coffee in the meeting room.

"A preliminary meet and greet," said Dr. Ebke, shaking Ulf's hand. "I thought we might get to know one another a bit before our first session." He paused. "Your bio, by the way, was very brief. There's nothing wrong with that, of course, but it was rather short, don't you think?"

"One doesn't want to burden people," said Ulf.

"No, of course not," said Dr. Ebke hurriedly. "But you didn't tell us what you do, did you?"

"Is that necessary?" asked Ulf.

Dr. Ebke took a sip of his coffee, fixing Ulf with an intense stare. "Our work defines us, don't you think?"

Ulf shrugged. "If we choose our work, yes. But don't you think many people are doing things they didn't choose to do? Don't you think that many people fall into their occupation because ... well, by chance, or even by heredity? Farmers are like that, I think. Farmers are farmers because their parents were farmers before them."

Dr. Ebke laughed. "I can see that you're going to keep me on my toes," he said. "But tell me, what *do* you do?"

Ulf did not reply immediately. There was something about Dr. Ebke's manner that irritated him. And what right had he to information that Ulf might choose not to impart?

"I'm an engineer." He had no idea why he said this, other than in an attempt to protect his privacy. It was childish, of course, but now that he had said it, he could hardly correct himself.

But that was not needed. "An engineer?" echoed Dr. Ebke. "How strange. I thought you were a detective."

Ulf stared at the therapist. "Then why did you ask? If you already knew, why did you ask me?"

The direct retort appeared to fluster Dr. Ebke, who suddenly looked pointedly at his watch. "My goodness," he said. "Look at the time. We must start." He rose to his feet. "We shall have plenty of time to talk later, Ulf."

Ulf watched as Dr. Ebke mustered the participants. A set of easy chairs had been arranged in a circle near the meeting-room window, and it was here that they all sat down and were formally introduced to one another by Dr. Ebke.

"Ulf will no doubt tell us more about himself later on," Dr. Ebke said when he got to Ulf. The therapist gave him a sideways glance as he said this, and Ulf looked away. He had decided that he was not going to like Dr. Ebke, but he would stick it out in deference to Dr. Svensson. It was a waste of a Saturday, he thought, but then what else would he have had to do? There was nothing, really—other than a longer than usual walk with Martin, perhaps, or a visit to his cousin, who had just had her second baby and was keen to show him off because he had been named after him. "Ulf is such a lovely name," said the cousin. "Both Otto and I thought it perfect." He would have to find a present for the young Ulf. What did one give a baby? He would choose something silver, he thought, and would have it inscribed: *Ulf from Ulf,* with the date. Mind you, silver was expensive—and there had been those costly new chairs. So perhaps young Ulf would get something made of pewter rather than silver—and a baby would never be able to tell the difference. Even the expense of the engraving could be cut down if he were to decide on *U from U,* or even just *U.*

Olaf said: "I want to share something with you. I've never talked to other people about this—never."

Dr. Ebke nodded encouragingly. "Well, Olaf," he said, "this is why we're here. The whole point of a group approach is to share the burden. That's what we call it: sharing the burden."

Henrietta said, "Yes. Yes. I've always believed that sharing the burden makes it lighter. It really does. That's been my experience, at least."

This appeared to please Dr. Ebke. "Henrietta is quite right, you know. It's always easier to carry something if you have others helping you. This applies to anything—a parcel, a rucksack ... anything."

Ulf frowned. How exactly could more than one person carry a rucksack? The whole point of a rucksack was that you strapped it onto your back. That was the way they were designed and it would be impossible, surely, to get two people into those straps. They would end up facing away from one another, with the rucksack suspended in between them, the straps entangled in their arms.

Olaf had more to say. "I know I should say what I have to say quickly—I mean now, as opposed to later."

Henrietta leaned forward. "Yes, Olaf. I want to hear. I really want to hear."

Olaf looked at her with concern. "Why?" he asked. "Why should you be so keen?"

Henrietta gave him a look of injured innocence. "Because we want to help you," she said. "That's why we're here—to help you with these improper impulses of yours."

Olaf turned to Dr. Ebke. "Improper? Who said anything about improper?"

Although the question had been addressed to Dr. Ebke, it was answered by Henrietta. "You did, Olaf. You told us about them in your bio."

"I didn't," protested Olaf. "I said I was troubled. I said: *troublesome thoughts.*"

"No, you didn't," interjected Peter. "Look, it's here." He extracted the administrator's letter from his pocket and unfolded it. "Yes, it says *troubling impulses.* See? Impulses, not thoughts."

Dr. Ebke raised a hand. "I don't think we should take an accusing tone with one another, everybody. The important thing is what Olaf says here—in our presence."

"I'd like to know the difference between an impulse and a thought," Peter interjected. "Is there one, do you think?"

"It's really a question of—" began Olaf.

Peter interrupted him. "I was asking Dr. Ebke," he said. "Not you."

Olaf looked injured. "You don't need to take that tone with me. It's my thoughts we were discussing."

"Your impulses," said Henrietta.

Ulf observed. He had his eye on Olaf and was wondering whether he had encountered him somewhere before—professionally. It would be a tricky matter, he thought, if one of these people started to talk about having done something criminal. Would he have to act? Would he have to suddenly extract his police ID card and say, "Enough group therapy—you're under arrest"? He tried not to stare too hard at Olaf, but the more he looked at him, the more he suspected that the conversation would have to be about impulses rather than thoughts—and it might not be an easy one.

But then Olaf rose to his feet. "I'm leaving, Dr. Ebke. I'm sorry, but I'm withdrawing."

"You're being impulsive," said Peter, and laughed. This brought a stern look of disapproval from Dr. Ebke.

"There's no call for levity," said the therapist. "And we must not laugh at one another. This is very, very serious."

Ulf tried not to laugh. He took out his handkerchief and blew his nose. That helped.

Dr. Ebke accompanied Olaf from the room, trying to dissuade him as he strode out. But Olaf, it seemed, was adamant in his decision to withdraw. From where he was sitting, Ulf had a good view through the window of the car park outside. He noticed with some satisfaction that Olaf went to the car with the shaded windows, climbed in, and drove off. He noted with even greater satisfaction that Dr. Ebke, who had accompanied Olaf out of the building, still pleading with him, now went to fetch something from his own car. And that, of course, was the Mercedes-Benz.

Ulf turned to Peter. "Do you drive that Porsche out there?" he asked.

Peter nodded. "Yes. Why do you ask?"

"It's a nice car," said Ulf appreciatively.

Of course you drive it, he thought. *Of course you do.*

After Olaf's departure, the atmosphere changed and the remainder of the session went smoothly enough. When Ulf's turn came to discuss his problems, he restricted himself to talking about the distress that he felt in having to deal with bad behaviour.

Since Dr. Ebke had revealed that Ulf was a detective, he was able to talk about the stresses of work. He warned the group, though, that he could not talk about any details, and that any remarks he made about his work would be at a high level of generality.

Henrietta followed Ulf. Her concern was self-knowledge, she said. "I know that I have reasons for the things I do," she explained. "But sometimes I ask myself: Why did I do that? I mean *that* rather than *that*. That's the really interesting question, I find. That's why I started seeing somebody. I didn't want therapy to solve any issues for me—I wanted it to show me what the issues are." She paused, looking in turn at each of the other members of the group. "Does that make sense to you?"

"Yes," said Peter. "You want to find out about yourself."

"Yes," Henrietta enthused. "How many of us really know ourselves—I mean, really know?"

The discussion of Henrietta's quest took about half an hour. At the end she seemed pleased with the result. "I feel as if I've really got into myself, you know. I feel that I understand a bit better what brought me here today. I see it in its context, I suppose. That makes a difference."

Then it was Peter, who spoke for more than twenty minutes on a domestic ritual he had to perform before he could leave the house. "I know this sounds absurd," he said, "but I have to take all my shirts out of the wardrobe and put them away again. Twice."

"What would happen if you didn't do that?" asked Henrietta.

"My plane would crash," Peter answered.

Ulf stared at him. Did airlines not have strict medical requirements? Was there not a psychiatric examination for pilots?

"Oh, I know that's ridiculous," said Peter. "I know what you think."

"It's superstitious behaviour," said Dr. Ebke. "It's very common. Many people have to perform little rituals or they think something dreadful will happen. We've all probably done that at one stage or another. You say to yourself, *If I don't do this, then something awful's going to happen.* It's simple superstition." He looked at Peter. "But here's an interesting thing: Talking about those beliefs to other people, shining a light on them, completely defuses them. They go away."

"So the dreaded thing never happens?" asked Henrietta.

"Never," said Dr. Ebke.

Peter looked relieved. "Good," he said. Then his face fell. "But it could happen, couldn't it?"

Dr. Ebke gave a reassuring smile. "Of course, anything can happen—anything at all. But if the feared event *did* happen in a case like this, it would be pure chance. It would not be a case of *post hoc ergo propter hoc.* In other words, there would be no causal link between the failure to perform a superstitious ritual and the occurrence of the dreaded event." He smiled again, tolerantly. "It would be no more than an act of what people used to call God."

Henrietta drew in her breath. "Used to . . ."

"I don't wish to lead us into theological discussion," said Dr. Ebke. "Our plates are full enough as it is."

Peter was clearly not convinced by the answer he had been given. "But *if* the dreaded event materialises, how would you know that it was not caused by the non-observance of what you call the ritual . . ."

"And which others might call a precaution," muttered Ulf.

"Yes. If I failed to take the precaution of taking out and putting away my shirts, and my plane came down, how would you know—in the firm sense of the word *know*—that this was not a result of my not doing what I always do? How would you?"

Dr. Ebke waved a hand dismissively. "I'd apply the normal rules of scientific causation—as we understand them. We know from experience that the folding of shirts has nothing—absolutely nothing—to do with aviation disasters." He looked at Peter, as if to challenge him. "I would have thought that with your training you would know that too." He paused. "I take it that you understand Bernoulli's Principle."

"Of course I do," Peter snapped. "I'm a qualified pilot."

"Then you rely on science, don't you?" Dr. Ebke retorted. "And your only hope of dealing with your OCD, if I may be permitted to say this, is through psychological intervention—and psychology is a branch of science."

Peter stared dumbly at the floor. "I suppose you're right."

Henrietta was sitting next to Peter, and now she reached out and laid a hand on his forearm. "We're all with you," she said in a voice barely above a whisper.

"Thank you," said Peter. "I try and try, you know. I try really hard."

Ulf felt a pang of sympathy. "Of course you do," he said. "And remember, we all have our problems. All of us. Even Dr. Ebke here—he'll have problems."

Henrietta seemed interested. "That's a point," she said. Turning to Dr. Ebke, she asked, "What *are* your problems, Dr. Ebke? Could we talk about those, do you think?"

Time passed quickly, and before they knew it it was five o'clock, and the meeting broke up. Ulf accompanied Ebba out into the car park, where they chatted briefly before she let herself into the Fiat Bambino. Ulf had found her the most interesting of the participants—Henrietta went on for far too long about herself and her personal quests, and Peter was simply too anxious to engage with in any meaningful way. Ebba, by contrast, spoke about her difficulties in a balanced and unindulgent way.

"I know that my problems are nothing compared to those of others," she had said. "It's just this inability to make up my mind. It's odd. It strikes at strange times—over comparatively small matters. Often not big things—just little decisions, such as whether to have one slice of toast or two. That sort of thing."

Dr. Ebke had led that discussion. He blamed Ebba's mother, who they had been told had been in charge of the nursing staff in a large teaching hospital. "I don't wish to disparage your mother in any way," he had said. "But she might well have been a perfectionist—in that position. And that might have led her—I'm not necessarily saying it did—but it *might* have led her to imposing very high standards on you. So, you can't choose because your mother's there, still looking over your shoulder."

Ebba listened carefully. "She lives in Finland now. Her second husband was a Finn."

Dr. Ebke smiled. "I didn't mean that she's there physically. I meant she's there as a presence." He looked at each member of the group in turn. "We are surrounded by presences, you know. They are always there. Our parents, our grandparents, and even more distant ancestors, handing on their psychological burden, their unresolved issues."

In the car park at the end of the day, Ulf said to Ebba, "Well, I hope you feel that was helpful."

She said that she did. "And you?" she asked.

"A bit. I suppose it was useful to talk to all of you about my feelings for my work."

She nodded. "I found what you had to say very interesting. Your job must be extraordinary—and put you under real stress at times. This department you work in—this Department of Sensible Crimes . . ."

"Sensitive," Ulf corrected her. "Department of Sensitive Crimes."

"Yes, of course. You must see some very distressing things."

"Sometimes," said Ulf. "But not very often. There's very little gore, if that's what you mean. We don't do murder and such things. If we see distress, it's usually over some very minor thing, some odd criminal activity that doesn't fit any of the big categories. It's all very polite stuff. Very Swedish. I don't think there's another Department of Sensitive Crimes anywhere in the world. It's just us."

He looked at her. She was an attractive woman, and she was of just the right age for him—mid-thirties, he thought, perhaps a touch older. He wondered whether it would be appropriate for him to suggest dinner, if she was going back to Malmö. He was not sure of the etiquette: If you met somebody suitable in a group therapy session, was it inherently coercive to invite her to dinner? One had to be so careful these days, when dating was a minefield for the unwary.

He started to say, "There's a new restaurant opened up. I was keen to give it a try and—"

Ebba cut him short. "I really must be on my way," she said, looking at her watch. "Nils is expecting me to pick something up on the way home. We share the cooking, and it's my turn tonight."

"Of course," said Ulf, sighing inwardly. People assured him there were plenty of unattached women and he would find no difficulty in meeting one, but all the women he met seemed to be attached. Anna was. Oh, Anna, if only you weren't so . . . so attached. If only . . . He wondered what Nils was like. They shared the cooking, Ebba had said, which meant that he was a considerate and helpful type. It would be a strong and stable relationship, he suspected; to imagine anything else was wishful thinking— fired by envy, perhaps.

He watched as she got into her car. He saw her put the key in the ignition and start the engine. Then she sat quite still, her hand poised over the gear lever. And he realised at that moment that she could not decide whether to engage a forward or reverse gear.

Chapter Three

MAFIA CEMENT

The following Monday, Ulf began his morning, as he always did, with a large cappuccino in the coffee bar opposite the Department of Sensitive Crimes. This bar was popular not only with the members of the department, but also with the staff of the offices in the immediate area: a pension fund, a firm of consultant engineers, a publishing company, and a firm that clearly did something significant, but nobody knew exactly what it was. This firm, Olafsson and Co., had a staff of about twenty people, all of whom seemed to dress in much the same style and, what was perhaps more surprising, looked rather like one another. Ulf and his colleagues referred to them as the Olafssonssons and occasionally tried, unsuccessfully, to engage them in conversation in the coffee bar. They were not rude, of course, but seemed to discourage enquiries as to their activities, which of course only whetted the interest of the Department of Sensitive Crimes.

"It's about time we investigated those people," Anna said one day. "They must be up to something."

"On what grounds?" asked Ulf. "We have to have a reason, wouldn't you say? You can't just investigate people because you don't know what they do."

Anna sighed. "Pity."

From the other side of the room, their colleague Erik joined in. "No smoke without fire," he said.

Ulf glanced at Anna. That was typical Erik: as if detective work could be based on adages. "But where's the smoke, Erik?" he asked.

Erik shrugged. "We could just call in on some pretext. We could say that it's a crime prevention visit—one of those advisory programmes HQ keeps going on about. Then, while we're talking about that, we could have a quick look round. We might find incriminating papers—you never know."

Ulf shook his head. "No, Erik. We can't do that. That would amount to using false pretences."

Carl intervened without looking up from his desk. "Gaining access to premises under false pretences is an offence. Penal code…I forget the number of the article, but it's there all right. Just an observation."

Erik returned to his papers. "It'll blow up in our faces," he muttered. "Then the press will be plastered with accusations that they were carrying on their illegal activities right under our noses. We'll look pretty stupid then, I can tell you."

Ulf was firm. "All right, but what will we look like if we're found doing something illegal?" He paused. "And even if we aren't found out, how will we *feel* if we do something that the book says *nej* to?"

Nobody spoke. Anna looked pointedly at Erik, but he remained unabashed. They each returned to what they had been doing before speculation on the Olafssonssons had begun.

There were no Olafssonssons in the café that morning when Ulf arrived. Some of the engineers, though, were huddled at a table, discussing the collapse of a bridge in Italy. Ulf had heard about this on the radio news, and now he caught references to sub-standard concrete and low-quality steel. The finger was pointing, one of the engineers suggested, at a firm of contractors in Calabria, said to be an arm of the 'Ndrangheta. "Not surprising," another remarked, "in view of the fact that their activities amount to almost three per cent of Italy's GDP."

Ulf was tempted to join in. Three per cent? He found it difficult to believe that a criminal organisation could penetrate a country to that extent. Three people in every hundred would be involved—full-time; if one could extrapolate the figures in that way. Three per cent! Of course, in Calabria itself the proportion of the population involved would be much higher than that, because that was where things were concentrated. So it might well be that thirty per cent of the population was implicated in organised crime—one in three people. And if you excluded children—or at least those children too young to assist their corrupt parents—then the figure could be even higher.

He looked about the café. There were perhaps fifteen people seated at the various tables or standing at the bar. If this were Calabria, then five of those might be Mafiosi, or the equivalent. That man standing near the display case in which the café kept its pastries, the one reading his copy of the *Sydsvenska Dagbladet*, would be on his way to committing an organised crime—and the newspaper he would be reading would be the *Camorra Chronicle* or the *Organised Times*.

He wondered whether this corrupt, sub-standard Mafia cement had found its way into any Swedish bridges. He had never heard of such a thing, yet wherever there was money to be made, there would be criminals, and many of these were only too willing to put the public at risk in pursuit of illicit gains. Human wickedness, thought Ulf, is both persistent and pervasive. You fought it, you did your best to deal with it in one place, and no sooner had you chopped off its head there than it reappeared, Gorgon-like, elsewhere. And here they were, just four of them in their rather small office, engaged in this losing battle; five, if you included poor Blomquist, who had been allocated to them but who was still in uniform and not a fully fledged detective. Ulf sighed; poor Blomquist.

Ulf picked up the newspaper that a previous customer had left lying on the table. It had been scribbled upon in ballpoint pen— a few meaningless figures in the margins, a telephone number, and then a note: *Tell Maria.* Tell her what? Ulf looked up at the ceiling. Was this note to self a rallying cry, designed to spur the writer into action? Perhaps Maria already suspected. Perhaps she already knew, because she had stumbled upon a previous annotation on a page of her husband's newspaper—just as, in fiction, a woman hears her lover mutter another woman's name in his sleep—and had waited for the confession that never came. Or did he simply want to remind himself or herself to let Maria—the cleaning lady—know that they would be away next week but that it would be appreciated if she unloaded the dishwasher. That was more likely, thought Ulf, because if the note had been intended as an exhortation, it would have read *Must tell Maria,* which was quite different in tone. The conclusion pleased him. He did not like to think that Maria was being deceived. This innocent interpretation meant that Maria was not in for a disappointment; one fewer personal world was about to be destroyed through the selfishness or inconstancy of another. That, at least, was cause for gratitude.

He began reading an item in the arts pages: an interview with an artist who was bemoaning the lack of commercial sponsorship for installation art—something that Ulf had always thought of as a mere random collection of objects. Ulf grimaced; art was his major interest, particularly nineteenth- and early twentieth-century Scandinavian painting. That inured him to the posturing of conceptual artists, but he still found it hard to believe that anybody would pay for the banal and impermanent. And where would one *put* installation art? If a commercial concern displayed it in the foyer of their office, it would be mistaken for office detritus and removed by the cleaners. That often happened to installation art, Ulf believed: some exorbitantly expensive collection of *objets trouvés* would be found to have been thrown away by cleaners who understandably failed to see how it could be anything but abandoned rubbish. People loved that, seeing the cleaners as the agents of common-sense aesthetics who spoke for the general public.

He sighed and turned the page. The arts modulated into football, which was a subject of no interest to him at all. Somebody had scored a goal, somewhere, and for some team, and the newspaper's sporting correspondent was analysing this momentous event in great detail. Ulf sighed again, and then looked up and saw that his colleague Anna had entered the café and was ordering her usual latte at the bar. She turned, caught his eye, and waved, mouthing the words *I'll be over in a mo*. Anna was always chatted to by the barista, who now leaned across the bar and whispered something to her. She made a gesture of understanding, and laughed dutifully. Ulf had seen these exchanges before and asked her about them. "He likes weak jokes," she said. "Vulgar ones, mostly. He thinks I find them funny."

"And do you?" Ulf had asked.

Anna had shaken her head. "Not really. One or two, perhaps, but then they're all about human misfortune, aren't they, and how much can you laugh about that? He's harmless enough, I suppose. A bit dim, but harmless."

"He never tells me any," Ulf observed.

"That's because you're a man. He wouldn't get the same thrill in telling you about a man who . . . Well, he just wouldn't. For a man to relate a risqué story to a woman is to intrude sexually. I'm not sure that men in general understand that."

Installation art, and football, and risqué anecdotes too were forgotten as Anna crossed the room towards Ulf's table. One of the engineers nodded to her as she passed, and she smiled at him.

"They seem pretty preoccupied with something," said Anna as she sat down.

"They've been talking about crumbling cement," said Ulf. "I've heard snippets. Apparently, the Mafia have been putting cheap cement into bridges—passing it off as the real stuff, whereas it's actually icing sugar."

"No!"

"Well, perhaps not icing sugar, but certainly not proper cement."

Anna looked in the direction of the engineers. "No wonder they're animated," she said. Then she turned her attention to Ulf. "Good weekend? You were off at some group therapy thing, weren't you?"

"Yes," said Ulf. "So-so. Some of it was interesting, but some not so much. One of the participants walked out within minutes; another one went on and on about nothing very much. And we had an obsessive-compulsive pilot."

Anna took a sip of her latte. "Ah. I won't ask you what you yourself talked about."

"Nothing very much."

She was not surprised. "I've never believed you need to go and see that shrink of yours, Dr. . . . Dr. . . ."

"Svensson."

"Yes, him. Anyway, I suppose it passes the time."

Ulf wanted to change the subject. He was generally unembarrassed by the fact that he had psychotherapy, except with Anna. It pleased him that she thought he did not need it, and it pleased him even more to know that she even felt that it made him more interesting.

"And you?" he asked. "How was your weekend? Were the girls swimming?"

Anna nodded. It seemed to Ulf that she was distracted by something. "They had a club night on Saturday. They each won a race: breaststroke and butterfly. Butterfly's rather hard on the deltoid muscles; it really pushes them. I thought they did very well."

Ulf congratulated her. "You must be proud of them, Anna. They'll be swimming for Sweden one of these days."

She acknowledged the compliment, but then frowned. "Yes, perhaps. Perhaps."

"I mean it," he said.

She was avoiding his gaze.

"And Jo?" he asked. "Was he working this weekend?"

She lifted her coffee cup to her lips. He saw it as an evasion. He waited.

She looked at him now. "Ulf, could I talk to you about something?"

"Of course. Anything." He felt his breathing shorten. There was something wrong, and Jo was the problem. He took an illicit thrill in this. Jo, the rival ... But then he said to himself, *No, I must not. I simply must not.* And so he said, "Is Jo all right? He's not ill, is he?"

She put down her cup. "Ulf, you know that Jo and I have a perfectly sound marriage. You know that?"

He tried not to show regret. "Yes, and I'm glad that's so, Anna."

"Thank you." She paused before continuing, "You see, I think that Jo might be seeing somebody. Might be—not is—might be."

Ulf caught his breath. "An affair?"

She nodded. She looked miserable now, and he struggled to stop himself from reaching out across the table for her hand.

"I know that there's nothing worse than the suspicious spouse—always looking for signs of infidelity, that sort of thing. But I have some evidence, or possible evidence, you see, and well, I'm eaten up by doubt ..."

"Evidence?"

"Yes." She looked at him pleadingly. "I was hoping you wouldn't ask what it is."

"I won't ask," he said quickly. "Not if you don't want me to."

"I don't, but then . . . Well, it's so ridiculous. Just ridiculous."

Ulf waited.

"I was doing the laundry," she began.

He looked away. He did not want to hear this sort of thing. Why were unfaithful husbands so stupid about all that? Because they normally weren't married to detectives—that's why.

She lowered her voice. "I was doing the laundry, and I found an earring in his boxer shorts."

Ulf could not dissemble. He spluttered over his coffee. "What? In what?"

Looking thoroughly miserable, Anna continued, "An earring in his boxers. Not one of mine. Too flashy for me. It had got caught up—the pin was in a seam. That's why it didn't fall out."

She looked at him, as if challenging him to laugh. "You can imagine how I felt."

"I certainly can," said Ulf. "But there could be some innocent explanation. After all, it's a very unusual thing to find in a pair of boxers." He paused. "It may have been on a chair, and he may have sat on it. You never know."

She shook her head. "No, I don't think so. And anyway, there's something else."

Ulf raised an eyebrow. "Oh, yes?"

"You know that thin man in the robbery squad? You know him? I'm on the public engagement committee with him. He wears those blue-tinted glasses. He lives a block away from us, as it happens."

Ulf remembered him vaguely. It had struck him that an ascetic-looking man with blue-tinted glasses was an unusual policeman to find in the robbery squad, a robust and rather tough group of officers.

"Well, he happened to remark," Anna went on, "that he had been reviewing CCTV footage taken from a camera near an ATM.

The machine had been fitted with some fraudulent device and they were looking at who used it. Well, he said to me, 'I saw Jo on screen a couple of hours ago. Or his double.' He seemed embarrassed, and something was obviously worrying him. And I was puzzled, of course, and since our committee meeting had been delayed, I went to his office and he wound things back. And there was a man with a woman. He had his arm around her waist as she went up to the ATM."

She stopped. Her voice had faltered towards the end of her account, and Ulf's heart had gone out to her. He did not want her to suffer. That was why he had denied himself for so long; why he had refused to contemplate ever giving her the slightest hint of what he felt; and all the time Jo, the anaesthetist of all things, the mild and soporific Jo, was going off to ATMs with another woman.

He found his voice. "I'm so sorry to hear this, Anna. I really am."

She looked at him directly. "The only thing, though, is that I'm not sure that it's him. These images are often blurred. This one is. They use low-definition cameras."

"So it may not have been him?"

"No, it may not."

Ulf asked about the earring. Could it have belonged to somebody else and then just fallen into the laundry basket?

Anna had thought about this. "We have—or had, rather—a lady who helped in the house two days a week. She used to wear flashy jewellery. She used to put clothes into the laundry basket. I did too."

Ulf smiled. "Well, there you are. It must be hers. Ask her."

"She's just gone back to Manila," said Anna. "She has her mother there, and a whole brood of children, I think. I have no idea how to contact her."

Ulf did not know what to say. He did not have to say anything, though, because Anna had a plan.

"The man and woman on the CCTV arrived at the cash machine by car," Anna continued. "The licence plate was obscured and we couldn't get a number. So all I have is the earring and the unsatisfactory CCTV images. That's not much, but it's enough to put real doubts in my mind." She hesitated. "I can't bring myself to do this; I—" She broke off. "I can't bring myself to *distrust* Jo."

Ulf thought that if anything lay at the heart of her request, it was distrust. Or did she want him to exonerate her husband? *Tell me what I want to hear;* that might be the unspoken request here, he thought.

She fixed him with a pleading stare, and he noticed, for the first time, that her eyes had flecks of green in them; green amongst the hazel. And a light; there was a light in them that you didn't see in other eyes. And her skin, the living tissue, was without blemish; it really was—except perhaps for that slight shading on the neck that might be shadow, anyway, rather than melanin. Because, thought Ulf, we're all composed of chemicals, of water, of melanin—which, oddly, he remembered by its chemical formula of $C_{18}H_{10}N_2O_4$—and a whole microbiome, a living city, inside us, which one did not really want to think too much about. One might fall for eyes but not for a microbiome . . . There were plenty of songs about the heart—but was there a single song about the fauna of the large intestine?

"Ulf?"

"Yes. Sorry."

"You were lost in thought."

"Was I? Perhaps I was."

The tension of the last few minutes, her pain at the disclosure, her anxiety, seemed to dissipate. "Sometimes," she said, "I see you with that expression your face and I wonder what's going on in your mind. Sometimes I do that, you know."

He was pleased to hear that she thought about him; it had never occurred to him that she should do so, because of her slightly distant manner. That, he had always assumed, was due to the fact that she had so much else to think about, particularly the running of two young girls, with their swimming, and their friendships, and their demands to be ferried here and there. Parents are taxi drivers, Ulf thought. Cooks, taxi drivers, personal care assistants, and bankers: the roles taken on by parents all as a result of the biological urge to perpetuate one's DNA. How strange. Did it affect him? He had not thought much about it, but now, quite unexpectantly, he asked himself: What if Anna and I were to have a child together? The very question excited him. He felt a wholly unfamiliar tenderness. He would take the child to swimming competitions and report back to her. But there was Jo. She had another life that had nothing to do with him and that he should do nothing—*nothing at all*—to break.

Her frown returned. "Would you do it for me?"

He struggled to free himself of the thought, the impermissible thought, of him and Anna together, with their child, so suddenly and unexpectedly conceived—or should he say *conceptualised*—within the last few seconds of fantasy.

"I'd do anything for you, Anna."

The words slipped out, and he was sure that they crossed the line he had drawn for himself. So he made light of it, and added rapidly, "I'd do anything for my friends—any of them." *Eros* became *agape*, an altogether safer presence.

"I know that. You're good to your friends. Poor Erik—you're so patient with him."

"Erik!" sighed Ulf.

Now came the expected request. "Would you find out? Would you find out what's going on? I need to know exactly who she is, and when Jo is seeing her. I need to know that—I don't know why, but I have to. Times, places. Anything else you find out." She looked away. "It's like taking a blood test to find out if you have something that's going to kill you."

He was shocked by the analogy. Anna's demise was inconceivable. It would be as if the sun itself were to be extinguished. And that, he suddenly thought, was the metaphor by which love might be measured: the sun. If that were the case, then it's just as well, he thought, that I'm Swedish, a northerner by birth, and accustomed to the half-light, because that is what I have chosen for myself. It was a moment of self-pity, a state that he did not approve of in others and did not like in himself. No, there was no point in thinking such thoughts: I am not in love with Anna because I have not allowed myself that. Love has to be willed; it does not come upon you without your complicity. And it was by this logic that he reached the resolution: Anna is a friend, that's all; a friend and colleague.

"If I gave you the evidence, would you find out for me, Ulf?"

For a few moments he said nothing. He did not want to do it, but he knew the answer he would give.

"Of course I will," he said.

He swallowed hard as she gave him an envelope. Inside this, he could feel the tiny shape of an earring.

Chapter Four

GENUINE IMITATION LEATHER

They left the coffee bar at the same time as the engineers, who were still talking about the instability of bridges. The barista gave Anna a wave and Ulf an involuntary frown. This young man was stuck behind the bar of the café, dispensing coffee under the supervision of the rather miserable owner: a woman lodged, as Anna would have it, in a permanent low-pressure zone. Anna resorted to weather metaphors in describing others, who were sunny, cloudy, tempestuous, or, in rare cases, hurricanes. I should be kinder to him, thought Ulf, and he gave the young man a smile—slightly forced, perhaps—which was rewarded with a curt nod of the head.

He and Anna walked across the road and entered the building in which the Department of Sensitive Crimes had its offices. They did not have much room—an outer office in which a receptionist sat and served them and three other police departments in the same building: fingerprints and DNA, commercial fraud, and transport. They were all semi-autonomous, being separated by the length of several city streets from the main police headquarters, a bustling building from which Ulf felt progressively more detached. Commercial fraud kept very much to themselves, and had the reputation of being aloof and stuck-up; certainly, they never deigned to talk to either transport or fingerprints and DNA, who got on well together and had perfectly civil relationships with Ulf's department. Comity, though, did not prevent others from speculating whether it was really necessary to have a Department of Sensitive Crimes at all. "All crime is sensitive," observed the head of transport. "I don't see why they should be given special offices and special treatment."

"My feelings exactly," said the head of supplies. "We're stretched enough as it is when it comes to putting officers on the streets. We don't need to give Varg and those cronies of his special treatment so he can go sniffing around ridiculous non-crimes. Breaches of etiquette, for the most part—not even crimes. What a waste of resources!"

This bureaucratic antipathy to the department usually manifested itself in no more than the occasional barbed comment. From time to time, though, it emerged from the shadows to become overt and obstructive. This sometimes took the form of special rules designed, as far as Ulf could make out, to frustrate the ability of the department to do its work.

Requisitioning supplies was one such area where this unhelpful attitude surfaced. Here the head of supplies had devised a scheme for this purpose that involved different procedures and forms for each department. Thus, if fingerprints and DNA wanted anything, from new stationery or pens to an official vehicle, they were required to apply for this on a form that was particular to that department, and the same applied to all the other branches of the force. The overwhelming majority of departments used a form that was identical in its wording, apart from the heading and the form number. This form was simple and straightforward, and merely required a brief description of the requested item or items, such as "ink, black" or "files, manila, open." The Department of Sensitive Crimes, though, had to apply on a form that was different from any of the others. The stated reason for this was the sensitive nature of its work.

It was when one examined the form that it became apparent how deep must have been the supplies division's animus for Ulf's department. A Byzantine bureaucrat, at the height of the Ottoman Empire, could hardly have devised a more opaque and convoluted system, nor one more inspired by the goal of obfuscation or even sabotage.

"I don't understand this system," Carl had said to Ulf when it was first foisted upon the department. "You see, we have these special forms, yes?"

"Yes, we do," said Ulf, looking at the handbook that had just been sent to each of them.

"Well," continued Carl, examining his own copy, "it says here that we aren't allowed to ask for anything by name: we have to use a code."

"So I see," said Ulf, trying to make sense of the explanatory notes in the handbook.

He passed the handbook over to Carl.

"If I want a new notebook, then," Carl continued, "I can't simply write *notebook* in the box that says 'Item requested'—I have to put a code number."

"So it would seem," said Ulf. "But it's not altogether clear where the codes are listed."

"Well, that's the thing," Carl said. "It says on page forty-five that the codes are confidential. And as far as I can see, we have no means of getting hold of them."

"Then I don't see how we can order anything," said Ulf.

"Exactly. There's a list of codes at the back, but the key to what they are is not available." Carl turned the pages of the handbook to get to the back. "Yes, here they are—a whole lot of numbers, but no indication of what they mean. So, I have no idea what a 254c is. Do you?"

Ulf shook his head. "Is there a 254a, or even b?" It was an old trick, he thought, to add superfluous letters. This made people feel there was something special about an otherwise humdrum item.

"No," Carl relied. "Nor is there a 253."

"Ridiculous," Ulf snorted. "They're trying to intimidate us—that's all."

Carl agreed. But he needed to order photocopying paper, as their machine had recently run out. The problem, though, was that he had no idea of the code for that item, and when he had called the supplies office, he had been told that codes were not available.

"What we need to do," suggested Ulf, "is this: We order a few items at random. Then, when we discover that they are not what we need, we return them and order some other number. Eventually they'll get so fed up with dealing with our returns and re-orders that they'll give us a proper list."

Carl agreed to this, and they picked out, quite at random, item 354/2/d. The relevant form was filled out and a tick was placed in the box marked *urgent*.

"Let's see what we get," said Ulf. "You never know—it might actually be photocopying paper."

The ticking of the urgent box seemed to work: three hours later, a small box arrived by motorcycle messenger from the supplies department. Ulf signed for this—three signatures were required, including one from a counter-signatory. Ulf wrote his name twice, and then wrote Carl's as well, imitating his signature skilfully. This was standard practice in the Department of Sensitive Crimes, where it had been agreed that everybody could use a colleague's signature in order to simplify matters; everybody except Erik, who as a filing clerk did not have signing authority.

"Absurd," Ulf said as he penned the three signatures. "Kafkaesque."

Carl and Anna watched closely as Ulf opened the package.

"It's not photocopying paper," Carl observed. "It's too small."

"It'll have to go straight back," said Anna.

Ulf removed the last layer of wrapping to reveal a dog lead.

He held it up. "This," he announced, "is a 354/2/d."

Carl burst out laughing. "So now we know. If you want photo-copying paper, don't request a 354/2/d."

Ulf examined the lead more closely. "It's a very good lead," he said. He strained to read the small print embossed on the lead. "Yes, this says 'Made in China.' Well, that's a surprise. That reminds me of the Leonard Cohen song—you know the one where he sings about Suzanne giving him some oranges that come all the way from China. I've often wondered about that. But anyway, this also says . . ." Again he strained to read. "'Genuine imitation leather.'"

This brought a chuckle from Anna. "How can—"

Ulf interrupted her. "No, don't be so cynical. What that means is that the manufacturers have made a real effort—a genuine effort—to imitate leather. It refers to their *bona fides*. These people are not trying to fool anybody—this is a *real* attempt to imitate leather."

Erik looked up from his desk. "Why does supplies have dog leads? Didn't we get rid of our dogs a few years ago?"

Ulf considered this. Erik was right about the abolition of the dog department. A few years earlier, the Commissioner had announced that the police would no longer be using dogs for public order duties on the grounds that dogs gave the wrong impression. Police forces who used dogs presented newspaper photographers with a classic opportunity to portray the forces of law and order as repressive—with a snarling dog lunging on the lead, a Swedish policeman might look to all intents and purposes like a figure from a liberally minded person's nightmare. The announcement had attracted derision from outside the force as well as within. From outside, amongst the politicians who had criticised it was Ulf's own brother, Björn Varg, leader of the Moderate Extremists. Björn had issued a press release saying that more money should be spent on training more dogs to bite more people—"but only those who deserve it, of course." That was a typical Moderate Extremist position, Ulf had noted, rather to his embarrassment.

His brother, though, had taken matters further. "If the Commissioner feels that it sends the wrong message to have large German shepherd dogs or Dobermans on the force, then why not compromise by having less aggressive dogs. Poodles, perhaps. Or even dachshunds. There are many dogs who do not convey quite the same threat as do our current police dogs."

It was a *reductio ad absurdum* that brought a smile to many police faces, as well as to those of members of the public. "There's a limit to how touchy-feely a police force can get," Carl complained. "Either we're a police *force,* or we're a police *advisory unit,* or some such non-forceful thing. In the final analysis, you have to use *force,* and you'll never be able to wish that out of existence."

Ulf remembered this as he considered Erik's comment. Yes, the dog unit had been abolished, but he had a feeling that there were still police dogs somewhere. Perhaps in plain clothes—CID dogs … He smiled at the ridiculous thought.

"Something tickling you?" asked Anna.

Ulf told her. "I was just thinking of how one might use police dogs in plain clothes. Disguised as something else? A cat? A sheep or goat, perhaps—that suddenly started barking and gave the game away."

Anna made a dismissive gesture but was clearly amused. She loved Ulf's sense of humour and his occasional flight of fancy. Most men were so literal—and most women too, come to think of it. It was so refreshing to listen to somebody who could see the ridiculous possibilities in the most prosaic of situations. And Ulf did that, whereas Jo was so serious about everything.

And then Ulf remembered. "The airport," he said.

Carl looked puzzled. "What about the airport?"

"We still have dogs there. Sniffer dogs—I spoke to one of their handlers the other day."

That solved the mystery of why supplies should have dog leads, but it did not, of course, answer the question of what they should now do with the lead. Anna reminded them of their plans to confound the system. "Send it back," she said.

"Yes," said Ulf. "I shall. I'll drop them a note to inform them that we were under the impression that we had a dog, but actually do not."

"They don't have a sense of humour in supplies," warned Anna. "I've met them. They're a very grim bunch. Pale, troglodytic set-up."

"I'll just send it back," said Ulf, tucking the lead into the pocket of his jacket. He would do that later, when he had the time, which he did not have right then. A message had just flashed up on his screen informing him that there was a woman in reception who wanted to see him. She would not state her business, said the receptionist, nor would she give her name, but she was insisting on seeing Ulf and nobody else.

"I shall be in the interview room," Ulf typed. "Give me five minutes."

The woman had been shown into the interview room by the time Ulf arrived. She was sitting in what Anna had labelled the "guest chair" and was staring at the sole picture on the wall. This was a reproduction of a *plein-air* painting by Anders Zorn of three female bathers, unclad in one case and wispily attired in the other two. The picture had been bought by Ulf on a visit to the Gothenburg Museum of Art and had been the subject of a vote before its hanging. "I have no objection to it," Anna pronounced. "I don't consider this to be an objectification of the female form."

Carl had his doubts. "But is it the sort of picture we should display in an interview room? Bear in mind some of the characters we have to talk to in there. It could . . ."

They waited.

"It could what, Carl?" Anna prompted eventually.

Carl blushed. He had a prudish streak, Ulf had noticed. In a way this seemed out of time, as most people now seemed indifferent to the constraints of the past, as demonstrated by their casual use of strong language.

"It could fire them up," muttered Carl.

Anna giggled. "Really, Carl! Look at what people can get online at the click of a mouse. Do you really think they'd get hot under the collar over a nineteenth-century bathing scene?"

Ulf was unwilling to force anybody to accept his choice of painting. "I don't mind," he said. "If you don't want it, I'll take it home. We can get something more mainstream, if you like. Perhaps a print of *The Scream*. That'll settle our more jumpy guests."

Anna, though, was strongly in favour of the Zorn. "I positively want it," she said. "It's a gentle image, and isn't that what we want? Don't we want our guests to feel secure?"

"So that they open up to us?" asked Ulf.

"Exactly." She paused. "I suggest we vote. That's what they did at those art academies, did they not? When they were deciding what pictures to hang?"

Ulf confirmed this. His interest in Scandinavian art embraced the history of its outsiders, and the way in which recognition was granted or denied.

"Then I vote that we put it up," said Anna.

She looked at Ulf.

"I really don't want Carl to feel uncomfortable," he said. "It's all very well wanting our interviewees to feel secure—but what about us?"

Carl raised a hand. "I vote to hang it," he said. "I'm persuaded."

"Then that's a unanimous vote," Anna said. "The painting goes up."

Erik was not consulted. Being in charge of filing and clerical matters, he was deemed not to have a vote—nor a voice—in many departmental matters. Nor was any approach made to Blomquist, who was only on secondment to the department. Being from the uniformed branch anyway, he was not consulted on anything and had never been added to circulation lists. Ulf had wanted to put him on these lists but had encountered surprising opposition from the overall head of criminal investigation, a deputy commissioner, to whom he answered directly. "I'm not keen on having people foisted on us," he confessed to Ulf. "I know that Blomquist seems to have caught Ahlbörg's eye, but I really can't stand the man, and I don't want him to put down roots, so to speak."

Ulf had spoken in his favour. "He may go on a bit," he conceded. "But . . ."

"He certainly does," said the deputy commissioner. "And then some."

"He's actually rather well informed," Ulf continued.

"About what?" snapped the deputy commissioner. "About the price of children's vests? About the latest developments in vitamin therapy? About all sorts of arcane nonsense, if you ask me."

Ulf hesitated. The deputy commissioner was not one with whom one disagreed too vocally. But he had never felt comfortable about people being blocked in their careers simply because they were trying company.

"Blomquist was very useful on a number of investigations," he ventured. "He seems to have a nose for the solution to a tricky problem. It's almost as if he stumbles upon it by chance."

The deputy commissioner made a dismissive noise. Ulf and Anna had once tried to analyse this noise, and had decided it was best rendered as "Phlaw." Now he said "Phlaw" and shook his head. "You can't stumble on things," he said. "A conclusion either has identifiable premises or it's no more than a hunch. Surely you appreciate that, Varg. You've always struck me as being a very rational person."

But now Ulf entered the room and gave a start as he recognised Ebba. She turned round and smiled. "I was admiring the painting. It's Zorn, isn't it? I've always liked them—Zorn and Carl Fredrik Hill."

Ulf was pleased to discover that she knew about art.

"Yes," he said. "It is Zorn." And then he added, "People sometimes express surprise that a police office should have paintings. They find it odd."

"I don't," Ebba said. "I think that all public buildings should have at least some art in them. And anyway, you're not an ordinary police department, are you?"

"No," said Ulf. "Not really. We have a rather particular brief." He paused. "It's good to see you. But is this a private visit or a professional one? Sorry to ask, but we have to log our visitors in and out."

She answered quickly. "It's professional."

He felt a certain disappointment. But then she had mentioned her partner, and he had concluded that there was no possibility of anything else.

He sat down. "Well, then, what can I do for you?"

She took a while to reply. Then, hesitantly, and in a lowered voice, she said, "I have a partner, you know."

He nodded. "You mentioned him. Nils—or I think that was the name you gave."

She seemed surprised that he should recall the detail. "I suppose you're trained to remember things," she said. "I forget names almost instantly, but I imagine that would be no good in your line of work."

Ulf laughed. "No, it wouldn't. We could hardly say we're looking for ... what was his name again? I don't think that would work."

"My partner is Nils Personn-Cederström."

She stared at Ulf as she gave the name, and he thought: She expects a reaction. But why? Should he react to the name, which was a fairly typical upper-class Swedish name? Cederströms appeared frequently in the social pages of the magazine that Ulf read in his dentist's waiting room. They attended parties and openings and one of them, he thought, had been a diplomat in an important mission overseas. But Nils Personn-Cederström? And then he remembered. Of course: Nils Personn-Cederström was that writer who had been so heavily featured in the press over the last decade or so. "The Swedish Hemingway," they called him.

"*The* Nils Cederström?" he asked.

She lowered her eyes. "Yes."

Ulf was impressed. "He's very well known, isn't he? Not only here, of course, but in Germany, America, Britain . . . They love his books, I'm told."

She acknowledged the compliment with an inclination of her head. "He writes very well, yes."

Ulf was trying to remember what he had read about Cederström. Yes, that was it: Cederström was a bad boy—a heavy drinker, a brawler, a ladies' man. An unpleasant possibility suggested itself: Cederström's violence had a domestic side to it.

"Has your partner been abusive?" he asked gently.

She was quick to respond. "No, definitely not. Nothing like that. In this case he's the victim—that's what I've come to see you about."

"Victim of?"

"Blackmail. I discovered he's been making confidential payments to somebody. He was very cagey about it, and I challenged him. I said: 'Are you being blackmailed?' He didn't say anything, but I could tell that my instinct was correct. He looked very guilty."

Ulf sat back in his chair. "May I ask: Why is he not here to make the complaint?"

Ebba looked uncomfortable. "Because he hasn't admitted that he's been blackmailed. I found out about the payments going out of his account. But he won't tell me anything about them. And there's more: even if he admitted to being blackmailed, he wouldn't want anything done about it."

"And may I ask why?" Of course Ulf thought he knew the answer to that: in many cases victims of blackmail would never dream of going to the police because they did not want to reveal the secret that the blackmailer had discovered.

"I think it's because he doesn't want any publicity," she said. "Nils is famous—as you know. Famous people often prefer to avoid publicity if they possibly can."

"Or sometimes they seek it," Ulf pointed out. "Remember poor Princess Di. She would phone journalists to tell them she didn't want any publicity. Odd, that."

"I don't think Nils is like that," said Ebba. "He just isn't." She paused. "I'm the one who wants something done. I'm the one who wants to stop this blackmailer, whoever he is."

"Very well," said Ulf. "But our policy is usually to avoid looking into something if the victim doesn't want it."

Ebba shifted in her seat. "But you must sometimes investigate cases like that. What about domestic abuse cases? The victims are sometimes very unwilling to make a complaint—or so I've heard."

Ulf knew what she meant. In his earlier days on the force, he had dealt with any number of those—and he had always found it difficult to restrain himself. The husband—and it was usually the husband—would be there in the background, grinning with immunity, while the frightened wife stuck to the story he had fed her. No, her husband had not been violent; no, her injuries were caused by a fall on the stairs—or, in the case of the less imaginative, an awkward door handle. Ulf had seethed; he hated bullies, and he would dearly have loved to see the offending husband being confronted by one of his colleagues, Stig, who had briefly been Sweden's middleweight boxing champion. Stig, of course, was completely non-violent, except in the ring, and rather disappointed a few of his rougher colleagues who were not averse to what they called "gentle persuasion," usually exerted against anti-social teenagers—the graffiti sprayers, the racist bullies, the vandals—who needed the guidance they had never had from their usually absent fathers. Ulf would never endorse such tactics.

"Domestic abuse is difficult," he said. "We know it goes on— and sometimes in fairly subtle ways—but there are times we don't get the co-operation we need. We're prepared to go ahead and press charges in the more serious cases, although it's almost impossible to get a conviction without the victim being prepared to speak up."

Ebba sighed. "The world is an imperfect place, isn't it?"

"Deeply imperfect," agreed Ulf.

Ebba thought of something. "Is it always the husband?"

"Almost always," he said. "But I did have one case in which a man was at the receiving end. The neighbours called us after they heard a din next door. We went along and found this poor man with a black eye the size of a large plum and clearly very upset. I remember seeing his hands trembling. He was a professional saxophonist—quite a good one, in fact . . ." He stopped himself. He should not have given that detail, as it might amount to a breach of confidentiality—there were not all that many well-known saxophonists in Sweden.

Ebba interpreted his hesitation correctly. "Don't worry, you haven't said anything that enables me to identify him." She paused. "And I'm discreet." She paused again. "I take it that you are? In your job, I mean. You won't—"

He interrupted her. "I assure you I am—that little lapse then was unintended and rarely happens; I promise you."

She seemed satisfied. "Well, as I said, Nils is being blackmailed. He's as good as admitted it."

"Yes, but we would need proof to do something about it. Do you have any proof?"

She looked impatient. "Isn't what I say proof enough?"

Ulf told her that he completely believed her, but there would have to be something in addition to her statement. "We need legally admissible proof," he said.

"Can't you find it? Isn't that your job?"

Ulf did not reply immediately. He had attended a meeting of senior officers recently at which they had discussed the issue of how the statistics of uninvestigated crimes were being subjected to political scrutiny. In particular, questions were being asked by his brother Björn's party, the Moderate Extremists. They were vocal on law and order, and had been making comments in the press about how the police were usurping the role of the prosecutors and the courts by deciding which crimes to act upon. It could be embarrassing if Ulf were to be revealed as one of those officers who had failed to act on so serious a crime as blackmail.

He made his decision. "All right. I'll look into it."

"Good. And thank you."

"I'll need some details and . . ." He looked at her inquisitively. "You do know, don't you, that I should know what the threat is? In other words, I need to know what the blackmailer has on your partner. What if that's a crime? What if the blackmailer knows something that could land Nils in trouble with the police . . . with us?"

Ebba replied immediately. "Impossible. Completely impossible."

"But there must be something—even if it's not a crime."

"I don't care. Nothing shocks me."

Ulf considered this. If what he vaguely remembered reading about Nils Cederström were true, then perhaps Ebba was right and indeed nothing about him would shock her. Perhaps that was it: some people loved people in spite of everything.

"Can you put me in touch with some of his friends?" he asked. "That will be a starting point."

"You won't mention the blackmail to them?"

"No. I'll phrase it as a routine enquiry—a request for information on a collateral matter, perhaps." Ulf looked away briefly; he did not like subterfuge, but it was sometimes necessary. Ends and means, he thought—there were occasions when the ends justified the means, no matter what the purists said. "That sort of thing. I could always say that Nils is being considered for a public appointment." He looked away again; the more descriptive one became of an untruth, the more unacceptable it seemed. So he added, "Perhaps not that."

She started to rise to her feet. "You've been very kind," she said. "I appreciate kindness."

As he saw her out, he thought: she claims to appreciate kindness, and yet she lives with somebody who sounds very much the opposite. That was odd; although, on reflection, if you lived with nastiness then you might well hanker after kindness wherever you saw it. That must be it, he decided: kind men were the opposite of the sort of man to whom, for reasons of apathy or fear, she found herself bound.

Chapter Five

THE SWEDISH–RUSSIAN WAR

Ulf returned to his flat slightly later than usual that evening. During the afternoon he had attended a training course that had overrun its timetable by a good forty minutes, with the result that many of the officers taking part had left in a state of irritation. Traffic usually built up in the early evening, and many of those participating in the course would be late home as a result of those extra forty minutes—an unfortunate outcome, given the course title, "Coping with Stress in the Workplace."

"I wish they'd just leave us alone to get on with it," complained Lennart Pålsson. Lennart and Ulf were old friends, although their careers had gone in very different directions. If Ulf was in the relative backwater of sensitive crimes, Lennart was at the cutting edge, being second-in-command of the anti-terrorism department. "Why do they have to keep counselling us about this, that, and the next thing?"

"I suppose they feel they have to do something," said Ulf. "Everybody's under pressure to do something these days. If you don't do something, you'll be accused of doing nothing."

Lennart sighed. Ulf was right; the pressure was relentless. "We had that psychologist pestering us the other day. You know the one with the moustache? He came round to talk to us about PTSD. He kept asking me if I was all right. He never gives up, that man."

"And were you?"

Lennart sighed again. "I'm fine." He stared at Ulf. "Come on, Ulf, look at me. Do I look as if there's anything wrong? Do I look . . . haunted, perhaps? Bags under the eyes? Twitching?"

"Not overtly. But who knows what's going on underneath, Lennart?" He smiled. Lennart was undoubtedly robust, but then he reminded himself that appearances could be deceptive—of course they could. "Actually, Lennart, how a person looks may have nothing to do with what's inside. Remember that workshop we had on preconceptions?"

Lennart shook his head. "That one was voluntary. I decided that it was not for me."

Ulf laughed. "Thereby illustrating the proposition."

Lennart took a moment to take the point. He grinned wryly. "Perhaps."

"But I do sympathise with you," Ulf said. "Those psychologists . . ."

"That guy is obsessed," Lennart continued. "He was determined to get us to confess to nightmares. Honestly, he went on and on. He implied that there was something wrong with us if we didn't experience an adverse reaction to what we see. Whereas we see it quite simply: we have a job to do. There are a bunch of desperadoes determined to blow other people up in order to make their point. Our job is to stop them. Simple. I have no issues with that, and I accept that in the process I might witness disturbing things . . ."

Ulf raised a finger. "Disturbing. There you are, Lennart. That's the point."

"*Potentially* disturbing, then. But not necessarily to us. That's our job. It's the same with firefighters. They see unpleasant things sometimes, but they go back to the station and support one another. They know it's their job and they have to do it. They don't feel they have to go off sick after each call-out—until the psychologist comes along and tells them they should."

Ulf was not so sure. And yet Lennart did the job and should know how he felt. "There are always the weaker brethren," Ulf said mildly. "Not all of us are tough, Lennart."

"No," said Lennart. "But we're getting softer and softer, Ulf. Tell somebody they're weak and they'll be weak. Expect them to be strong, and that's what they'll be."

Ulf thought about this on his way home, stuck in a traffic jam that had built up as a result of the overturning of an articulated transporter. Cardboard boxes had spilled from the back of this vehicle and had broken open, the contents strewn across the road. For a few moments Ulf felt horror as he saw the bodies amongst the boxes, until he realised that the transporter's load had been made up of store-window mannequins. Here and there complete models lay prone, while plastic arms and legs had detached themselves from torsos and littered the roadside. He smiled at his mistake, but wondered what he would have felt had the bodies been real; or rather, what Lennart might have felt.

Traffic policemen were already at the scene and the road was already half cleared. He saw one policeman pick up a plastic leg and toss it out of the way, into a ditch. He was laughing as he did so, which made Ulf feel uncomfortable. Surely something like this should make one think, rather than laugh.

By the time he parked the Saab in its allocated place beside his apartment building, he had decided that Lennart was wrong. We were all weak, no matter how strong we thought we were, and if over-enthusiastic psychologists came to probe, we should be open to their ministrations. Yet it was easy for him to say that, he told himself: he was not remotely at risk of PTSD, at least not in the Department of Sensitive Crimes, where they rarely encountered anything violent. Of course, there had been that case involving

Hampus, the dwarf who had stabbed his victim in the back of the knee, but that was unusual, and the injury had been a minor one. Nobody liked to be stabbed, it was true, but if one is going to be stabbed, then the back of the knee is one of the less traumatic places for this to happen.

He went first to the flat of his neighbour, Mrs. Högfors, to collect Martin. Mrs. Högfors sometimes returned Martin so that he would be in when Ulf arrived home from work, but on this occasion, having been warned that he might be late, she had kept him.

Martin greeted Ulf enthusiastically, barking and running round in increasingly tight circles.

"I read somewhere that dogs believe that when their owners leave the house they're leaving forever," Mrs. Högfors said, watching Martin with amusement. "Look—he's overjoyed to be proved wrong."

Ulf bent down to pat Martin, in an effort to calm him. "They're strange creatures, aren't they?"

"We'll never know what goes on in their heads," said Mrs. Högfors. "They clearly entertain plenty of thoughts, but heaven knows what they are."

Martin stopped running round, and sat expectantly in front of Ulf.

"I have just this moment put on a pot of coffee," Mrs. Högfors said. "Would you care for a cup?"

Ulf accepted. He was keen to get back into his own flat and kick off his shoes, but he did not want Mrs. Högfors to feel he was taking advantage of her. If she unstintingly gave Martin hours of her time during the day, then the least he could do was allocate fifteen minutes to having coffee with her. Besides, he enjoyed her conversation, which was unpredictable in its direction. Mrs. Högfors was, in most matters, completely out of date, having stopped reading the daily newspapers fifteen years previously and having been impervious, it seemed to Ulf, to most major developments of the late twentieth century, let alone those of the earlier decades of the twenty-first.

Now, as they made their way into her living room, she let slip a remark that was surprising, even by her standards: a reference to President Nixon, as if he still occupied the White House. It could be a slip of the tongue, Ulf thought, or it could be an example of a deeper chronological problem—it was hard to tell.

"Of course, Nixon's dead," Ulf said casually.

Mrs. Högfors seemed unperturbed. "Some of these people never really retire, you know."

"That's true," Ulf conceded. "But I'd suggest that once one actually dies, it does tend to put a stop to political activity."

The gentle irony escaped Mrs. Högfors. "I never really took to him," she mused. "Nor to that other one. You know the one I mean?"

"Possibly," said Ulf.

Mrs. Högfors shook her head. "Högfors . . ."—she always referred to her late husband by his surname—"Högfors found an awful lot of politicians distasteful. He thought it ridiculous that people should claim to be able to run the country when they hadn't run so much as a corner shop. These career politicians—Högfors never approved of them."

Ulf smiled. "I know what your . . . what Högfors meant. I think you should have a bit of experience before you presume to tell others what to do."

As Ulf expected, that was what Mrs. Högfors wanted to hear. "Exactly," she said. "Högfors was writing about that precise matter when he died. It was an unfinished essay, and he hadn't decided where he wanted it published."

"Did he write a great deal?" asked Ulf.

"Oh yes. Nobody would publish what he wrote, I'm sorry to say." She looked away, her expression one of regret. "He was ahead of his time, I think."

"And a prophet is never honoured in his own country," Ulf added.

"He wrote a whole book on the Swedish–Russian War," Mrs. Högfors continued. "He was very suspicious of the Russians, you know."

"I recall your telling me that," said Ulf.

Mrs. Högfors sighed. "And he was right to be," she said. "The moment you stop watching the Russians, they make a move. That's the way they operate. They watch you very carefully, and the moment you let down your guard, they make their move."

Ulf nodded silently. They had talked about the Russians before, and he did not wish to bring the subject up again. Yet he felt that she was right—the Russians *did* behave that way; the Russians *were* up to something.

Mrs. Högfors leaned forward to impart a confidence. "I'll tell you something, Mr. Varg," she said, her voice lowered. "I wasn't going to mention this, because I know how it sounds."

Ulf waited.

"You see, some people might say—if they heard what I'm going to tell you—that I'm just a silly old woman with a bee in her bonnet. They think that way, you know. After you get to a certain age, people look at you and think, Whatever she says, it's likely to be rubbish."

"Oh, I don't know, Mrs. Högfors. I'm sure people don't think that way about you."

But she was not convinced. "No, it's true, Mr. Varg. When you get to your more mature years, you become invisible to certain people. They just don't look at you. They think—if they bother to think about you at all—they think, Oh, that's just another elderly person. That's what they think. And they don't actually *look* at you, you know. They look *through* you, and that's different."

Ulf made a gesture to signal his disagreement, although once again he thought that what she said was probably true. And perhaps, by dismissing her argument—even for the best of motives—he was himself doing precisely what she was complaining of: he was not listening, which was, after all, a form of looking through somebody.

Mrs. Högfors had more to say. "I was talking to a friend who goes regularly to America, Mr. Varg. She has a daughter who married an American doctor—some sort of orthopaedic specialist. He makes very tall people shorter, apparently, or very short people a bit longer—I forget which." She waved a hand airily, to show it hardly mattered. "But this friend of mine regularly goes off to see her daughter in Florida, in a place called Boca Raton. Funny name, that, but there you are. And she told me that in America, elderly people have got fed up with people not noticing them and have created these places where everybody is over a certain age. Everybody. And they don't allow young people to live there—except to be policemen and nurses and so on."

Ulf thought: no teenagers. Perhaps there was a case for such places; but he quickly corrected himself. It was only too easy to think uncharitable thoughts, but we had to remember that we had all been teenagers once.

"And they have everything they want," Mrs. Högfors continued, "including lectures on every subject under the sun and dances and calisthenics classes for after they've finished dancing. And Pilates too—they all do Pilates over there, you know."

Ulf said that he thought this must be very enjoyable for everybody, although it was a pity, was it not, that there should be such segregation. "Surely it's more natural for us all to live together—like the Italians, who love to have three generations under the same roof if at all possible."

Mrs. Högfors thought about this. "True," she said. "And, of course, there's Japan, isn't there? They don't look through elderly people, do they? They bow to them and listen very seriously to what they have to say. They respect wisdom, you see." She paused.

"But that's not what I wanted to tell you about, Mr. Varg. I wanted to tell you about what happened in the park, when I took Martin for his walk the other day. I was going to mention it to you that very day, but I didn't."

Ulf looked down at Martin, who was sitting on Mrs. Högfors's blue Chinese rug, gazing up at him. The dog loved that rug, Ulf knew, and Mrs. Högfors had generously started referring to it as "Martin's rug."

"Martin and I were enjoying our walk. He had spotted a couple of squirrels and had seen them off very convincingly—but humanely, you know: Martin never actually bites a squirrel. He warns them, and they scamper off."

Ulf smiled. "He's good that way. I've always thought of Martin as a pacifist. I know that's unusual for a dog, but I've always thought he doesn't like violence." He smiled again, as the thought occurred to him that dogs probably reflected their owners' attitudes. South American dogs were perhaps a bit excitable; French dogs were fussy about their food; and Swiss dogs never got involved in other dogs' scraps. Would it be possible ever to test such a theory? Psychologists engaged in all sorts of weird and wonderful research—there must be somebody who would look at this particular hypothesis, absurd though it sounded.

"Martin is a very sympathetic dog," said Mrs. Högfors. "You're right about that. Anyway, he and I were on our walk, and we passed two men sitting on a bench. They looked perfectly respectable, and appeared to be doing no more than having a conversation in the sun. But when I came within earshot, I was able to hear that they were speaking Russian. It's unmistakable, that language— unless they're talking something like Serbian, but you can always tell Serbians by the shape of their heads and I don't think these were Serbs."

Ulf listened politely.

"So, Mrs. Högfors—these two men, these Russians . . ."

Mrs. Högfors resumed. "I didn't think very much about it, other than to register that they were Russians. I don't disapprove of *all* Russians, Mr. Varg. I am not one of those people who are prejudiced. I wouldn't want you to think that."

Ulf assured her that no such thought had crossed his mind.

"But the interesting thing," she went on, "is that as we approached the bench—the path led that way, you see—Martin began to bristle. You'll know how he does that—the hairs along his back stand up a bit, like one of those ridgeback dogs you occasionally see. It was like that. And then he started to growl. Not loudly—just a low growl. It was a sort of warning, I suppose."

She looked at Ulf to gauge his reaction. "You don't think I'm imagining this, do you?"

Ulf shook his head. "Of course not, Mrs. Högfors."

Now came the challenge. "Why do you think he did that, Mr. Varg? You tell me if you think you can explain it. Because Martin could not possibly have heard them speaking a strange language—his deafness would have prevented that, wouldn't it? And so why did he bristle and growl? I'll tell you what I think: I think he could tell. Dogs can—they can sense things that we can't. They pick up feelings, vibrations—call them what you will—that we don't notice."

"And Martin sensed something unusual, you think?"

"Yes."

Ulf looked down at Martin, who, returning his stare, moved his tail in a half-hearted wag.

"I'm not sure, Mrs. Högfors," said Ulf. "It could be that Martin took his cue from you. He might have sensed that you were hostile to—"

She interrupted him. "But I'm not hostile to Russians, Mr. Varg. I'm cautious when it comes to Russians because there is every reason to be. I'm cautious because the Russians are up to something.

That's all. But I fully accept that there are some Russians who are innocent, or who should at least be given the benefit of the doubt. I accept that. But the fact remains that the Russians have always been up to something. As Högfors said of the Swedish–Russian War, we didn't start that . . ."

Ulf closed his eyes. No. That simply was not true, and his soul, still the soul of one committed to the upholding of the truth, rebelled at the blatant falsehood. He opened his eyes again, and saw that Mrs. Högfors seemed to be expecting a challenge.

"Well, we didn't," she said. "You hear all sorts of accusations about that, but most of them are completely absurd."

Ulf looked down at Martin. The dog, sensing human disagreement, as dogs often can do, looked back, first at Ulf and then at Mrs. Högfors. It seemed that he was uncertain as to whom to believe: a dog expects cohesion in the pack, and this sort of thing is unsettling.

"I really don't think the Russians were entirely to blame for that particular episode, Mrs. Högfors," he began. "We mustn't lose sight of the truth, even if it makes Sweden look less than perfect." That was a problem, he thought; we so want to be perfect that when we discover we aren't, there's a temptation to ignore the evidence. "We must admit there were rather a lot of people itching to have a go at the Russians—"

He was not allowed to finish.

"No," Mrs. Högfors interjected. "I'm afraid I must disagree, Mr. Varg. I really must."

Martin twitched. He did not like this. He could not hear the slightly raised voices, of course, but he could detect the change in body posture of these two central figures in his life. There was Ulf, his master, his father so to speak, and there was Mrs. Högfors, his carer, the feminine pole in his life, whom he loved with that unquestioning devotion of which dogs, uniquely, are capable.

Together these two humans were the sun that warmed his world, and sensing disharmony between them, Martin lowered his head and stared glumly at a fixed point on the floor.

"You have to accept, Mr. Varg," Mrs. Högfors lectured, "that the Russians attacked us on our border. They invaded." She paused briefly, but not long enough for Ulf to make a riposte. "They're great ones for violating other people's borders, the Russians. Show them a border and they violate it. It's a Pavlovian reaction on their part—and Pavlov, be it noted, was a Russian, I believe."

"Oh really, Mrs. Högfors," Ulf protested. "You can't—"

"Oh, I can, Mr. Varg. I can. Let us not forget Puumala, where the Russians struck their first blow. 1788. Let us not forget that infamous date."

Ulf laughed. "Oh, come now, Mrs. Högfors. Everybody knows that that was staged. It wasn't Russians at all—it was Swedes dressed up as Russians so that King Gustav would have an excuse to go to war. And everybody knows that he wanted a war to distract people from his domestic unpopularity. A common *casus belli,* don't you think? And Gustav was only human . . ." Perhaps if he portrayed Gustav as being much like others of his time, then Mrs. Högfors might take a more dispassionate view of his shortcomings.

Mrs. Högfors shook her head. "You believe the Russians about that? In spite of the fact that they tell such terrible lies?"

Ulf looked at his watch. It would be simpler to agree with Mrs. Högfors—to wind the whole thing down by saying that perhaps she was right about the Russians after all. The past was the past, and should one be raking over eighteenth-century coals here in the twenty-first century when there were surely so many more relevant things about which one might argue? There was really no doubt about that feigned attack at Puumala. The Swedes had been wearing Russian uniforms that had been specially made by the costume department at the Swedish Opera. The costumiers had been spotted making them, after all, and why would they be making Russian military uniforms when there was no opera on at the time that called for such outfits?

"That business about the opera and the uniforms," he said. "It's difficult to ignore, surely."

Mrs. Högfors was not having any of that: the Russian empress had much to answer for in that context. "Catherine was one to talk about opera," she snapped. "She wrote all those operas herself, and one of them, we might perhaps remember, was very insulting to Gustav. It made fun of him, and if that isn't provocation, I don't know what is. Imagine having somebody write an opera about you and you don't come out of it at all well. Who can blame Gustav for being angry? I certainly don't."

Ulf made his decision. "You're probably right, Mrs. Högfors," he said. "It was most unfortunate all round."

He felt that this formula should put the subject to bed—where it belonged. Things *were* unfortunate all round, whichever way you looked at them.

"Martin must be tired," said Ulf. "Perhaps I should get him home."

"He had a very good walk," said Mrs. Högfors. "He'll be looking forward to his dinner. I gave him one of those biscuits of his, but he hasn't had his main course."

Ulf thanked her. He felt in his pocket. The lead that he had obtained from the supplies department was still there. He took it out and showed it to Martin, who became animated and wagged his tail in response. Ulf thought: I must return this lead. I must. And that Saab grille too, while I'm about it.

Chapter Six

A BOOK FOR ALL TASTES

Ulf Varg bought most of his books at a gallery, the Malmö Konsthall, where the bookshop sold the art books that formed the bulk of his collection. He was proud of his library, a collection of volumes, double-stacked in places, that took up two full walls of his apartment and had begun to impinge on a third. The majority of his books were on painting and painters, reflecting his abiding passion for Scandinavian art, but he also had a small collection of travel and cookery books, as well as a shelf of assorted *krimis*. He read the *krimis* for pure entertainment; they amused him, sometimes to the point of open laughter, with their prolonged and sometimes absurd inaccuracy. None of them, he had noted, was written by an author with the slightest connection with crime, with the result that their portrayal of the life of detectives bore no relation, in Ulf's view at least, to the reality faced by him and his fellow detectives. Every so often, of course, a real policeman, or possibly a criminal defence lawyer, set out to write a book dealing with crime. These books would usually be rich in detail and accurate enough, but also tended to be clumsily written: policemen and lawyers may be good at detecting criminals or defending them, but that did not make them masters of prose.

These were *and then* books, as Ulf termed them: books in which the construction *and then* was used with breathless enthusiasm.

And then there were his cookery books, arranged on the shelf according to the nationality of the cuisine. A row of books on the culinary traditions of India spoke to Ulf's taste for curry and spiced foods in general; *The Kitchens of Kerala* was particularly well thumbed, as Ulf had always had a weakness for coconut. Next to it was *Pongal and Paniyaram: Culinary Adventures in Chennai,* not so obviously used but still far from untouched. Ulf disliked cabbage and doughballs, and so where Eastern Europe might have been there was a gap.

Now, standing outside Jens Bokhandel, a small bookshop no more than a few blocks away from the Department of Sensitive Crimes, he gazed at the display of books in the window. A book on wind energy, *Our Invisible Future,* sat on a small pedestal, next to several titles on climate change. *This book must be read by all those who use electricity,* pronounced a handwritten placard below the book. Ulf raised an eyebrow. He used electricity, and was well disposed towards green energy, but did *everyone* have to read this?

A sign on the front door said *Open, of course,* and Ulf entered. He had been in the shop once or twice before, and remembered buying an atlas for his nephew's birthday. He also recognised the man behind the desk—he was occasionally to be seen in the café opposite the office, reading the newspaper or immersed in a book. Now this man looked up when the bell attached to the front door rang. He studied Ulf, clearly trying to place him, and then did. He smiled. "Well, good morning . . . ," he said. He left a space for the name.

"Varg," said Ulf. "We see one another in the café."

The man smiled. "Of course. You're one of the people from over the road, aren't you? The police office—the Department of Strange Affairs, or whatever."

Ulf nodded. He had not planned to reveal that, but now that it was in the open there was no point trying to conceal it. "Sensitive Crimes," he corrected. "The Department of Sensitive Crimes."

"Ah, of course." The man rose from his chair and extended a hand to Ulf. "Torn Axelsson."

Ulf took Torn's hand. "Ulf. Ulf Varg."

Torn gestured to a chair beside the desk. "I could make you coffee, if you wish. It won't be as good as the stuff we get in the café, but . . ." He looked enquiringly at Ulf.

Ulf shook his head. "No thank you. I have to watch the number of cups I drink in the day. It mounts up, I find."

"Very wise," said Torn. "Caffeine is a double-edged sword. Keeps you awake, but makes you jumpy." He paused. "Are you after something particular? We can get you any title you like within twenty-four hours—as long as it's published in Sweden. Foreign books obviously take longer."

Ulf glanced at the books on the display table close to his chair. "I find it impossible to keep up with what's being published. I read the reviews, but it seems that publishers are churning them out."

"Tell me about it," sighed Torn. "They're publishing far too much. Then they complain if an individual title sells hardly any copies. 'Whose fault is that?' I say to them. And they look at me blankly. They obviously blame the public for not buying all their books."

Ulf smiled. "The public doesn't always do what people want it to do."

"Remember *Pravda?*" said Torn. "The Russian newspaper? They had the biggest circulation of any paper in the world, I think, but it was because people were forced to read it. There wasn't anything else—and presumably it was wise to have the odd copy of *Pravda* lying about, just in case."

"Those were the days," said Ulf. "The command economy."

Torn looked at him expectantly.

"Actually," said Ulf, "I haven't come to buy a book: I'm making enquiries."

Torn hesitated. "I see ... Well, I don't know whether I'll be able to help you with anything." He waved a hand vaguely. "I don't see much—sitting here. There could be a bank robbery outside and I probably wouldn't notice a thing."

"It's nothing to do with seeing anything," said Ulf. "I need information about an author."

Torn brightened. "Oh well, I might be able to help you there. What period? Nineteenth century? Twentieth?"

"Contemporary," said Ulf. "Somebody I gather you know—or so I'm told."

Torn looked doubtful. "I don't know many writers. Their books, of course, I know those—but I don't really move in literary circles. I never have."

"Nils Personn-Cederström," said Ulf.

Torn laughed. "Oh, Nils. Yes, well, I've known him for a long time. I think of him as a friend, I suppose, rather than as a writer." He paused, and his expression became grave. "Don't tell me that our bad boy has done something really bad." He shook his head. "I've often thought his lifestyle took him rather too close to the wind."

Ulf reassured him that Nils was not in trouble. "No, Nils is not accused of anything."

Torn seemed unconvinced. "No criminal charges? Then why are you ..." He did not finish, but looked at Ulf quizzically.

Ulf explained. "The fact that we ask questions about somebody is by no means an indication that the person we are interested in is in trouble. Of course, it often is, but I really can assure you that is not the case here. Nils is categorically *not* in trouble."

"So why are you asking about him?"

"Collateral enquiry," said Ulf. He had invented the term on the spot, but it sounded right to him. Perhaps he should embellish. "A collateral enquiry occurs when we need to know about somebody in order to investigate somebody else—if you see what I mean."

There was still a note of anxiety in Torn's voice. "So Nils is in the clear?"

"Definitely," said Ulf.

Torn appeared to relax. "You sure you won't have a cup of coffee? I have decaf, I think. I could dig it out."

"In that case," said Ulf, "I'll count it as a collateral cup."

Laughing again, Torn got up and went into the small kitchenette at the back of the shop. Ulf picked up a book that had been lying on Torn's desk—*Lolita Revisited*. He put it down. Then he picked it up again and opened it at random. He read a sentence or two and closed it.

Torn shouted out from the kitchenette, "Do you take milk? Because I don't have any."

"In that case," Ulf replied, "I don't."

There was another book on the desk. He turned his head to read the title, which was upside down—*Pretty: A Young Lady's Diary*. He looked away in discomfort. For all his years as a detective, Ulf still felt awkward about prying: it was like opening somebody's mouth and looking inside it, or asking them to take off their clothes. It was an intrusion. And yet he had to do it; it was for this that his monthly salary was paid into his Swedbank account.

Torn returned with two cups of coffee. "Javan," he said.

Ulf nodded. "I find that I can't tell the difference, and yet I suppose there is one. Colombian. Javan. West African. I suppose there are people who can tell."

"Hang on," said Torn. "I'll get you something to put your cup down on. There's a coaster somewhere here." He rummaged in his desk, putting his own cup on top of *Lolita Revisited*. "Here." He placed the coaster in front of Ulf. Ulf put down his cup; the coffee was too hot—people always made coffee too hot; it was something that everybody did, except Mrs. Högfors, who served it cold.

"Now then," said Torn. "Nils. What do you want to know?"

Ulf asked him when he and Nils had first met, a question that was answered with a shrug. "Heaven knows," said Torn. "We're contemporaries, you know. Born in the same year—same month, in fact. His birthday is ten days before mine. Something like that. We were at school together for years, and then his parents moved. They went over to Gothenburg when he was sixteen, I think—his father was something to do with shipping. We didn't see one another after that until Nils was in his twenties, I think."

"You were close friends as boys?" Ulf asked.

"Oh, yes. We ... what do kids say these days? We hung out."

Ulf nodded. "One is close to friends at that age. They mean so much, don't they?"

Torn looked thoughtful. "Close, yes, but also ... Well, you can have pretty intense disagreements too. I suppose that's always a risk with a passionate friendship. You feel everything so intensely."

Yes, thought Ulf, remembering his first betrayal, when he had discovered that he had not been invited to his friend's party. He had been fifteen at the time, and his friend Casper Berggren had inexplicably excluded him from his birthday party. He had been puzzled, and hurt, and only later had discovered that the reason for his exclusion had been Casper's interest in Elise Kjellsson, a girl who had confided to a girlfriend that she was keen on Ulf. In the gossipy world of teenagers, that news had soon got out, with the result that Casper realised that if he were to get anywhere with Elise, it would be better to have Ulf removed from the scene. Against this background, an invitation had gone out to Elise and none to Ulf. Casper did not know it, of course, but the only reason Elise accepted was that she imagined that Ulf would be there, he and Casper being known to be inseparable friends. In the event, Elise left the party early, having little interest in Casper's advances.

Ulf shunned Casper, and that was the end of the friendship, at least until they both turned eighteen and patched things up after Casper's father's accident. Harald Berggren was a telephone engineer who absent-mindedly put his metal ladder up against a live wire and was electrocuted on the spot. Ulf wrote a note of sympathy to Casper—the only one of his peers to do so. "Dear Casp," he wrote. "That's really bad luck about your dad. I'm really sad that this happened. Your friend, Ulf." It was enough to repair the friendship. Elise Kjellsson was no longer an issue: she still had a soft spot for Ulf, but only as a friend, as she had discovered that at heart she preferred girls. "Nothing personal," she said to Casper. "Boys are just, well, less interesting than girls. I'm not talking about you—well, actually I am, to tell the truth—but you know what I mean."

Ulf's train of thought meant that he did not hear what Torn had to say next. "I'm sorry," he said, "I was thinking of what you said about those intense teenage friendships."

"I said: We took up again in our twenties. We got in touch again."

"Yes. And since then?"

Torn was staring out of the window, past the book that everyone who used electricity had to read. "Since then? I see him from time to time. He drops in here."

"For books?" Ulf asked.

Torn hesitated. It was the briefest of hesitations, but Ulf noticed it.

"Sometimes."

Ulf took a sip of coffee. "What sort of thing does he read?"

Torn's gaze shifted. Now he looked at Ulf in a slightly bemused way. "Should a bookseller reveal his clients' preferences? I'm not sure about the ethics of that."

"I can't see the harm in it," said Ulf.

"He needs books for his research," said Torn. "He writes about . . .

well, you know the sort of thing Nils writes about—everybody does. Men doing tough things."

"I assumed that he did the things he wrote about," said Ulf. "I assumed that he actually went to the rough bars and got into fights and went big-game fishing in the Caribbean, and so on."

This amused Torn. "Yes, he does all of that. I don't know if you know his novel in which the hero is a shark fisherman on Antigua. You know that one?"

"And drinks?" said Ulf. "Catches sharks and drinks?"

"That's the one. Well, Nils went out there and lived with this guy in a shack, this shark fisherman. And they went out and caught sharks and drank rum—the works. It was all very carefully researched. But . . ."

Ulf waited.

". . . but he lives it, you know. He does these things because that's what he wants to do. That's what he's like."

Ulf reached for his coffee cup again. "I read an article on him recently. He was interviewed by somebody who described him as Ernest Hemingway and Norman Mailer rolled into one."

Torn grinned. "I read that too."

"And you agreed?"

"Yes, for the most part. He does all that stuff. But there's one big qualification. Nils is kind. He's the kindest man I know."

Ulf was taken aback. "Surely . . ."

"No, I mean it. Nils is very kind and considerate. He wouldn't hurt a fly. In fact . . ." Torn leaned forward, as if preparing to impart a confidence. "In fact, Nils is vegetarian. What do you think of that?"

It took Ulf a few moments to reply. There was nothing unusual about vegetarianism, which was hardly a matter of note. But then there were people whom one would not expect to be vegetarian. People who hunted or went big-game fishing, for example: How many of them would be vegetarian? "I wouldn't have guessed it—not with his reputation."

"Exactly. But he is. I get him books on vegetarian cuisine. He's very inventive in the kitchen."

"I find that quite difficult to imagine."

"So did I," said Torn. "I found it difficult to imagine until he invited me round for a meal. That must have been ten years ago or thereabouts. He'd just taken up with his new girlfriend, Ebba. She was out somewhere or other, and Nils had to make his own dinner. He rustled something up in the kitchen and it was delicious. Couscous and all sorts of spices. It was Lebanese, I think."

Ulf tried to imagine Nils Cederström in the kitchen, wearing an apron, rustling up a Lebanese meal. And he found himself wondering about the relationship between Torn and Nils. Was there something more than simple friendship? If that were the case, then possibilities opened up for blackmail. Attitudes had changed—fortunately—but there were still people who were protective of their sexual orientation and might wish to hide it. A novelist with a reputation for machismo might be just such a person, thought Ulf. Hemingway would not have been Hemingway—at least in the eyes of his readers—had his private life been less heterosexual. As Ulf thought of this possibility, the more likely it seemed.

He looked at Torn. "Do you mind my asking you something?"

Torn made an open gesture with his hands. "Fire away."

"Do you think that Nils might be gay?"

Torn's eyes widened. "Nils? Gay? Are you serious?"

Ulf felt he should justify the question. "It's just that sometimes a very macho façade can conceal something rather different—a more sensitive persona behind it." He paused, noticing Torn's increasingly amused expression. "But perhaps not; perhaps not in this case."

"Perhaps not indeed," said Torn. "In fact, most definitely not."

"No," said Ulf. "I see."

"Nils is not that way inclined," Torn said. "Not that he is in the slightest bit against such inclinations: he is very accepting. But he is very fond of women."

Ulf noticed the slightest hesitation before the word *women*. It was, he thought, as if Torn had been going to use a prefix, but thought better of it. He glanced again at the book under Torn's coffee cup: *Lolita Revisited*. Of course, booksellers had all sorts of books passing through their hands, and one could not read anything into what books were on their desk, but then, in one of those sudden moments of insight it became clear. The book was Torn's because he had put his coffee cup down on its cover: no bookseller would do that to a book that formed part of his stock for sale. A coffee cup ring on a cover would render a book unsaleable—at least as new stock.

That meant that Torn liked reading about Lolita, and that meant that he and Nils might—and it was only a possibility at this stage—just might share an enthusiasm for young girls. If ever there were grounds for blackmail, then that surely would be it.

He stared at Torn, who, noticing the intensity of Ulf's gaze, shifted slightly in his chair. Ulf noticed that, and knew immediately that he had reason to be suspicious.

Ulf made his decision. He would now apply pressure, by hint. Pressure by hint was often the best way of rattling the guilty, as it allowed full rein for their imagination.

"Do you and Nils share any . . ." He paused before continuing, ". . . any interests?"

"Interests?" asked Torn.

It's working, thought Ulf. There was something in Torn's manner that suggested he was now very much on his guard.

"Yes. Enthusiasms. Hobbies." Ulf watched, and then continued, "Common affections. Liking the same sort of people. That sort of thing."

Torn said nothing. He glanced at the book under his coffee cup and moved the cup slightly so as to obscure the title. Too late, thought Ulf.

"No," said Torn. "Well, yes and no. We both like motor racing—

watching, of course, not participating. And tennis. We sometimes see one another at the Swedish Open. But otherwise . . . No, nothing in particular."

"I see," said Ulf.

Torn glanced at his watch. "I'm really sorry," he said, "but I'm going to have to go. I have an appointment at the dentist."

"I'm sorry to hear that," said Ulf. "Toothache?"

"Yes," said Torn.

"Which tooth?" asked Ulf.

The question unnerved Torn. "At the back," he said grudgingly.

"The worst place," said Ulf. "Which dentist do you go to? It's so important to get a good one, I find."

Torn ignored the question. "So, if you don't mind . . ."

As well he might, thought Ulf; there is no dentist. "Of course not."

Chapter Seven

BLOMQUIST COMPLAINS

Ulf returned to the office. It was a more than usually quiet time: usually there would be at least two or three new matters reported to the Department of Sensitive Crimes each day, and although most of these were referred on to other departments on the grounds of lack of sensitivity, this process of triage was enough to keep everybody busy. Sometimes, however, nothing at all came in, and this was one such day: even Erik, who could usually find some filing task to busy himself with, was sitting at his desk perusing a fishing magazine, while Carl, engaged in a conversation with Anna on the other side of the room, was doodling on a notepad with a police-issue pencil.

Ulf's enquiry into the Cederström matter was not yet official. He had said nothing about it to Erik, who would immediately insist on opening a file on the case, a process that would involve all sorts of paperwork that Ulf felt was best avoided at this stage. Forms could always be filled in retrospectively, and if prosecution ever became a real possibility, the necessary bureaucratic formalities could easily be completed. He had talked to Anna about it, though, and he would in due course tell her about his conversation at the bookshop.

"I see we're busy," said Ulf, as he hung his raincoat on its peg behind the door.

Erik looked up from the article he was reading on brown trout. "No," he said. "We're not." Irony, Ulf had noted, was lost on Erik.

Ulf caught Anna's eye. "Nothing's come in?"

It was Carl who answered. "Nothing at all. That boy from the post room, you know the one with the tattoo on the side of his neck—a spider, I think, or a spider's web, something of that sort—he came in and was about to give us an envelope. Then he looked at the label again and saw that it was intended for Commercial Fraud. So he took it away."

Ulf shrugged. "Oh well . . ."

Erik joined in. "That tattoo . . . That young man with the spider on his neck . . ."

"Are you sure it's a spider?" asked Ulf. "The web motif is pretty popular."

"No, it's a spider," Erik said. "There's a bit of web in the background, but the main tattoo is a spider. I know that because I counted its legs while I was signing his delivery book. He bent down beside me to put the book on the desk and I had a good look. It's a spider with seven legs."

Ulf smiled. "Seven? Artistic licence perhaps?"

"He was short-changed," suggested Carl.

Anna laughed. "I simply cannot understand these people who cover themselves with tattoos. What on earth are they thinking about?"

"They think it makes them look better," Ulf said. "Tattoos are a matter of aesthetics. It's some people's idea of adornment."

"I know that," said Anna. "But I can't imagine allowing anybody to draw on my . . . on my body. I just can't."

Ulf, who had now seated himself at his desk, shot a glance across the room towards Anna. *Your body*, he thought. *Your body . . .* He brought himself up short. He was no callow schoolboy thinking lascivious thoughts; he was a grown man who knew better than to undress somebody mentally, especially since that some-body was a married woman, and a colleague.

Anna had more to say on tattoos. "Jo," she said, "had a patient the other day who was covered in tattoos. Apparently, it was head to foot. Everybody in the theatre had their eyes out on stalks, he said. Once Jo had put the patient under, they started to poke and prod at the designs, discussing their merits—or otherwise—like visitors to an art gallery. He said that they would have turned him over on the table to look at what was on the other side, but Jo stopped them as he said it would interfere with the patient's breathing."

Carl did not approve. "They shouldn't do that sort of thing," he muttered. "You're very vulnerable when you're under anaesthesia. You trust the doctor not to laugh at you."

Anna felt that she had to defend her husband's colleagues. "They're weren't laughing at him," she protested. "And had he been conscious he would probably have been perfectly happy to show them his designs. They're often proud of them, you know."

Carl remembered something. "A spider? I read something about that." He frowned as he recalled the details. "Yes, there was a young man over in Copenhagen who had a spider tattooed on his neck. It was quite a big one—a tarantula, or something like that. He didn't tell his girlfriend he was going to have it done—it was to be a surprise for her."

"This is going to end badly," said Anna.

Ulf agreed. "Stories about tattoos often do."

"And tarantulas," Anna added.

"Yes," Carl continued. "It ends even worse than you imagine."

Anna shrugged. "His fault. You should think long and hard before you get a tattoo. Think long and hard and then decide against it."

Carl, not liking to be interrupted, pursed his lips before continuing. "As I was saying, he planned it as a surprise for his girlfriend—and it was. It turned out that she was an arachnophobe. She screamed and created so much fuss that she ended up in hospital."

"And the relationship?" asked Ulf.

"It didn't look as if it was going to work," said Carl. "She started to hyperventilate when he came near her. So that was it. They split up."

Ulf looked at Anna. It could have been so different, if only he had met her before she met Jo. And that was pure chance: fate brought some together at the right time, and then she brought others together at the wrong time. He looked at Anna, and then looked away. This is your sentence, he thought. This is what you have to accept.

"There's a young woman in the coffee bar," said Anna, "who has an angel tattooed on her stomach. Right in the middle. When her T-shirt rides up, you can see it. An angel."

"Angels are a common motif," said Ulf. "People like angels."

"And believe in them," interjected Carl.

"Not really."

Carl shook his head. "No, they do. A very high proportion of the population actually believes in angels. There was something about it on the radio. They did a survey."

"Who did?" asked Erik. "People are always doing surveys to support their view. They all do it."

"This was independent," snapped Carl.

Erik was not convinced, but asked Carl what the survey purported to show.

"What I said it did," said Carl. "It showed that just over thirty per cent of people believe in angels. They actually believe they're there."

"Guardian angels?" asked Erik. "That sort of thing?"

"Yes," said Carl. "Proper angels with wings." He smiled. "Invisible, of course." But then he corrected himself. "Well, not entirely invisible. People claim to see them, and so they might be visible to some people even if invisible to ... to the rest of us."

Ulf wondered whether a claim by some to be able to see angels amounted to visibility. "Just because somebody says that he sees something doesn't mean that the thing exists."

Anna felt that this was all a discussion about language, rather than about angels. "The point is that some people think angels exist, and some don't. All of us in this room are agreed, though, that they don't, but if we went out into the street and asked passers-by what they thought ... well, we might be surprised."

Erik looked down at his magazine and turned a page—rather too deliberately, thought Ulf. Erik believes in angels, he said to himself. And he imagined Erik's guardian angel, who would be interested in fishing and who might perhaps offer advice about the best fly to use on a particular river, or about the location of shoals of fish invisible to the angler in the rowing boat but easily spotted by an angel hovering above the surface of the water. Angels, presumably, had good eyesight; rather like that of birds of prey, who, from a great height, could spot the smallest mouse scurrying about in the undergrowth.

He shook his head. The whole discussion was absurd. "I suggest we find something better to do than talk about angels," he said.

Anna looked at him peevishly. "Like what?"

Ulf shrugged. "Are all our reports up to date?"

Carl reached for a piece of paper on his desk. "There was a memo yesterday. It was addressed to me for some reason, but I was going to pass it on to you."

"About?" asked Ulf.

"About restructuring. It asks for views on restructuring."

Carl rose from his desk and brought a piece of paper over to Ulf. Ulf took it cautiously, as if it might be infected. Memos descended fairly regularly from the Commissioner's office, and they usually concealed an agenda. "Restructuring" was a current buzzword, having replaced "efficiency" and "skills development," terms that had been the subject of the last two reports that the Department of Sensitive Crimes had been requested to submit. Each of these reports had taken two months to write and had disappeared into the maw of the police department without any sign of ever having been read by anybody. That was almost always the case with departmental reports, Ulf thought: People wrote them and submitted them. They then sat unread on several high-level desks before they were removed for filing. So it was, he suspected, throughout bureaucracies everywhere: people filled in forms and wrote reports that were rarely scrutinised and almost never led to anything happening in the real world.

He was troubled that this memo on restructuring had been addressed to Carl. He was senior to Carl, and it should have come to him. Was there a message here? Was Carl going to be restructured upwards while he was due to be restructured downwards? Something like that had happened in the Department of Traffic and Public Order once, when the head of department found that his desk had been downsized overnight while that of his immediate junior had been correspondingly enlarged. The formal promotion of the junior had followed a few weeks later.

He thanked Carl. "I'll write something," he said, and then added, "Unless you were planning to . . ." He left the sentence unfinished. It was a direct assertion of seniority, allowing for challenge but making it quite clear that such challenge would not be welcome.

Carl's reply was unambiguous. "Definitely not," he said. "This is you, not me. They sent it to me by mistake—I'm pretty sure of that. There's nothing more to it than that."

"Use the last report," Anna suggested. "Simply delete 'efficiency' or whatever and insert 'restructuring.' That will save you a great deal of time."

Ulf acknowledged the wisdom of this advice. "Restructuring" would go away, just as "efficiency" and "skills development" had gone away. But hoops had to be jumped through in order for this to happen, and Ulf would have to do that. Then, because "skills development" had crossed his mind, he remembered that Blomquist had asked to see him and that he had suggested they meet in the café across the road that afternoon. He had not entered the commitment in his diary and remembered it just in time.

"I have to meet Blomquist," he said to Anna. "I almost forgot."

"People do that to him," said Anna. "He complained to me about it once. He bemoaned the fact that people never kept their appointments."

"Poor Blomquist," said Ulf. "He is, I suspect, one of those people who is much forgotten and much cancelled."

Carl smiled. He liked Blomquist but knew exactly what Ulf meant. There were some people who were destined to be cancelled, and Blomquist was definitely one of those.

"We must all remember," said Ulf, "that Blomquist is technically a member of this department."

"Allocated to us," said Carl. "That's what it says on his file. I've seen it. It says 'Allocated to the Department of Sensitive Crimes until further notice.' That's not the same as being a member of the department. There's a distinction, you know."

Ulf sighed. There were advantages to working within an organisation—you knew where you stood and you received a steady pay cheque at the end of each month—but there were also disadvantages. There were the rules and the jargon. There was the petty insistence on procedures that had been devised for a purpose long forgotten. There were the jealousies and the scheming. He had often wondered what his life would have been like had he never taken that fateful step of enrolling in the police. He could so easily have accepted the offer he had received of a teacher-training place and ended up teaching mathematics or geography in a high school somewhere. He could have enrolled on the art course he had looked at longingly and even now be showing his latest work in the galleries of Stockholm, or even Berlin. Or preparing a frugal lunch, from a can, in a garret somewhere, cold even in the middle of summer, squeezing each last drop of paint from the tube, reusing unsold canvases to paint new unsellable pictures. But happy, perhaps, and supported by some adoring young woman who would say to her friends, "Ulf's paintings are pure genius—the world will see that sooner or later."

Instead of which he was writing reports on restructuring, enquiring into the private affairs of others, and now facing the prospect of a cup of coffee with a semi-colleague who was hanging on to his position by his fingernails and who went on and on about diet and health and the latest remedy for the same old complaints of humanity.

He rose from his desk, glancing at Anna as he did so. She looked up and caught his glance, and smiled. It was a moment of pure bliss. Anna was everything. She was decency, courtesy, reliability, motherhood, Sweden, and love. All of that; all of that. And she was somebody else's. She was that too, perhaps above all those other things.

Blomquist was already there when Ulf arrived in the coffee bar. He had found a seat at one of the popular window tables, and seemed deeply immersed in a copy of the *Sydsvenska Dagbladet*. As Ulf came in, he looked up and folded the newspaper away. Two cups of coffee, freshly served and still steaming, were on the table.

"I took the liberty of ordering for you," said Blomquist as Ulf sat down opposite him.

Ulf was unsure about this. The gesture of ordering in advance for somebody who had yet to arrive implied a certain familiarity, and for a moment Ulf struggled with irritation. He almost said, "I suppose you know what I like, do you?" but did not, and thanked Blomquist instead. Ulf would never be rude to someone below him in the pecking order; he was always faultlessly polite to people who could not answer back. Just as he was prepared, when the situation required it, to be blunt with those above him.

Blomquist reached for his cup of coffee. "You know what they're saying about coffee now?" he said.

Ulf reached for his own cup. "Oh, they're always changing their advice, aren't they? I can never keep up."

"Well, I can," said Blomquist. "I have a file at home to store the cuttings. It's one of those concertina files—you know the sort? They expand."

Ulf nodded. Inwardly, he sighed.

"I've labelled the various sections," Blomquist continued. "Heart. Liver. Cancer. Skin. Free radicals. All the various categories."

Ulf took a sip of his coffee. From the corner of his eye he noticed that the young woman they had been talking about in the office—she of the angel on the stomach—was taking over from the unfriendly young barista, who was removing his blue striped apron, wiping his hands on it as he did so. His eyes wandered to the young woman's midriff, covered by a dusty pink blouse. Beneath that, he said to himself, is concealed an angel.

He decided to come to the point. "You wanted to see me," he said.

Blomquist inclined his head slightly. "That's correct."

Ulf waited. "So?"

Blomquist shifted in his seat. "It's a bit awkward."

"You can speak directly to me," said Ulf. "You don't have to worry. Anything you say to me will go no further."

Blomquist seemed grateful. "Oh, I know that, Varg. I know that you respect confidentiality."

"So what is it?" Ulf coaxed. "Problems at home?"

Blomquist was quick to deny this. "Oh no, nothing like that, although I suppose you get quite a bit of that—with your seniority. People must feel they can unburden themselves to you."

"Some feel that way," said Ulf. "Not many, but some do." He paused. "And I don't mind, you know. You can speak perfectly freely."

There was a silence that seemed to last for several minutes. Then Blomquist said, "I'm not happy in my work."

Ulf stared at the other man. This was a ubiquitous complaint. Nobody was happy, in his view, because the work they did was essentially unhappy work. Crime was a pathology—a failure—and how could anybody be happy when dealing day in, day out, with things of that nature?

"Do you feel you're in the wrong job?" Ulf asked. "A square peg in a round hole?"

Blomquist's answer came as a surprise. "Oh no, being a policeman is exactly what I want to be."

"Then why are you unhappy?"

Blomquist fiddled with his teaspoon. "Why is anybody unhappy? That's a question that I've often asked myself and . . ." His voice trailed off. The spoon with which he had been fiddling was slightly bent, and he was now trying to twist it back into shape.

"Uri Geller," said Ulf. "Remember him?"

Blomquist smiled. "The man who bent spoons by . . ."

"Sheer willpower. By concentrating and directing his thoughts to the spoon. Or so he claimed."

Blomquist made a dismissive gesture before placing the spoon back on the table. "I have no time for such things. It's all wishful thinking, isn't it? People want to find evidence of the paranormal, but they never do, do they? It's all smoke and mirrors."

Although he himself had created the diversion, Ulf now steered the conversation back to Blomquist's unhappiness. "So," he said, "you've never been able to answer the question of why anybody is unhappy. Where does that leave you in your own unhappiness? Unable to work out why you feel the way you feel? Unable to do anything about it?"

Blomquist shook his head. "Oh no. As far as I'm concerned, my unhappiness has a very obvious cause."

Ulf waited. A conversation with Blomquist was always like this, he reminded himself. It drifted off down unexpected alleys and then suddenly returned to the point. And when it did return, it often did so with remarkable clarity and insight. It was easy to underestimate Blomquist.

Blomquist leaned forward. "A lot of unhappiness is caused by diet," he said, lowering his voice as might one sharing a confidence. "People eat the wrong things, Varg."

Ulf agreed. "I'm sure they do."

"Too many carbohydrates," said Blomquist. "Far too many."

Ulf glanced at the neighbouring tables.

"Yes," whispered Blomquist. "Exactly. Look at them. Look at that woman over there. Look at her waist—if you can locate it. She has no waist, in fact. Carbohydrates, you see. That's a Danish pastry she's polishing off."

"You can't blame the Danes for everything," Ulf said.

Blomquist looked puzzled. "I don't," he said. "They have a carbohydrate problem, just as we do. All I'm saying is that people eat far too much starchy food—and far, far too much sugar." He paused, taking another look in the direction of the offending woman. "Sugar is the killer, Varg. Sugar is what does it."

"Kills you?"

"Yes. But it's the unhappiness that it causes that interests me. Sugar is a mood changer."

Ulf thought about this. It seemed to him that people who ate too much sugar seemed to be happy when indulging in their fatal passion for sweetness. It may be making them overweight; it may be rotting their teeth; but he was not sure that sugar made them unhappy. He expressed these doubts to Blomquist, who dismissed them summarily.

"Sugar leads to mood swings," he said. "And mood swings are intimately linked to unhappiness. There's a lot of research pointing to that. I could give you the references, if you like. You could look up the literature online. It's all there."

Ulf looked at the other man. Blomquist was well built, but not overweight, he thought. Was he eating too much sugar, though? Was that the cause of his unhappiness?

Ulf was direct. "Do you eat sugar, Blomquist? Is that why you're unhappy?"

Blomquist answered firmly. "Oh no. That's not the reason. Sugar consumption is undoubtedly the reason why so many people are unhappy, but that's not the case with me. I'm unhappy because I'm bored." He looked into Ulf's eyes. "I'm really bored, Varg. I'm desperately bored."

"With your work?" asked Ulf. "Have you gone stale?" It was easy for that to happen, he thought. If you did the same thing day after day—as so many did—then it was understandable that one became bored. But there was not much that he—or anybody—could do about that. Boredom was part and parcel of modern society, and would become even more so once the artificial intelligence revolution gained real traction.

But it was not staleness that was troubling Blomquist. The work itself was interesting enough, he said—when he was allowed to do it. The problem was that he was not being given a chance to do it.

"It's the others," Blomquist complained. "Whenever I ask them if there's anything I can do, they say that everything is being taken care of. They never give me anything to investigate. I don't have a single case at the moment—nothing at all. And that's the way it's been for weeks—months, even. Nothing."

Ulf shifted in his seat. This was his fault, he thought. He was technically head of the department, even if they worked on a collegiate basis. He had been party to the decision that Blomquist should work in a separate office, even though they might have been able to squeeze in another desk in their existing office had they tried. And having done that, having sent him up to the—and here he had to admit to himself he could not remember which floor Blomquist worked on—having sent him up to the nth floor, he should have ensured that work was allocated to him. But he had not, and now this poor man, a conscientious officer, for all his faults, was bringing his failure home to him.

"I'm very sorry, Blomquist," Ulf began. "I should have done more. In future—"

Blomquist interrupted him. "But it's not you, Varg. It's the others. Everybody really—but not you. They seem to take pleasure in messing me about. There's a man in personnel who keeps changing the location of my desk. I get into work and discover that I've been shifted from the third floor to the second. My actual desk—the physical desk itself—is moved, and this is done without my being informed. There's a note where my desk used to be, saying 'This desk has been relocated.' That's all."

Ulf was appalled. "Oh, Blomquist, I'm really sorry about that. There's no excuse for that sort of thing. It's harassment."

"I don't like to complain," said Blomquist. "I assure you, I'm not the sort to complain."

"Of course not," Ulf soothed him. "Anybody would feel upset by the sort of treatment you've been getting." He took a sip of his cooling coffee. "I shall speak to personnel. I shall speak to this man ... what's his name?"

"Frederickson."

"I shall speak to him. I shall tell him all that has to stop."

Blomquist looked relieved. "It would be a great help," he said.

Ulf made a quick decision. "And I have a case for you. I'm

involved in a very sensitive investigation at present on which I could use some help."

"I'm ready to assist," said Blomquist.

"When I say it's sensitive," Ulf warned, "I mean it's *very* sensitive. Complete discretion is required. The parties—or one of the parties, should I say—is very well known. We shall need to be very careful if we want to avoid being splashed all over the front pages of the newspapers."

"Sex?" asked Blomquist. "Is it a sexual case?"

"Possibly," Ulf replied. "It's blackmail, you see, and sex often lies at the heart of a blackmail case. But in this instance, I'm not too sure."

Blomquist picked up the teaspoon again and tried once again to twist it back into shape.

"Does the name Nils Personn-Cederström mean anything to you?" Ulf asked.

Blomquist abandoned the teaspoon, now considerably more misshapen than before. "Cederström?"

"Yes. It's one of those rather grand names."

"Cederström," muttered Blomquist. "Nils Cederström." And then, with sudden recognition, "Yes, it does."

"You've read his books?"

This brought a shaking of the head. "No. Does he write books? Interesting. Maybe he was searching for material when I found him."

Ulf looked at Blomquist expectantly. The missing information—the basis of the blackmail—was possibly going to be revealed. Once again, Blomquist was coming up with the answer. It had happened before.

"Yes, I had to speak to a Nils Cederström once. I remember the occasion very well. It was one of those times when you're pretty sure you know what's going on, but you have no proof. So you give a warning, hoping that it'll do the trick."

Ulf asked about the circumstances.

"It was when I was in charge of the market," Blomquist said. "You know the sort of thing that goes on down there. Stolen goods. That sort of thing."

"And that Hampus," Ulf added. "Remember him? The dwarf who stabbed somebody in the back of the knee."

Blomquist smiled. "Yes. I remember. Nice enough fellow. But this was nothing to do with him—or with stolen goods either. This was a bit murkier."

Blackmail always is, thought Ulf. It was as murky as it got.

"Young men," said Blomquist simply. "This Nils Cederström was sailing a bit close to the wind with young men. Seeking them out in the market. Talking to them very intensely. You'd never get any of them to make a complaint, of course. They were willing participants."

"Underage?"

Blomquist shook his head. "Not really. Barely legal, as they say. But the traders didn't like it. They said it was bad for business. He went for skateboarders, it seemed. Something about skateboards did it for him—you know how strange people can be, Varg."

Ulf asked how the warning had been received.

"Very well, as it happened," Blomquist replied. "I was surprised. Usually these types deny everything. They become very defensive. But not in the case of Nils Cederström. He listened to what I had to say and then said he was terribly sorry that he had been causing offence. He said that he was doing research and there was nothing more to it than that. He seemed rather taken aback that anybody should object to his having conversations with young men. That was the term he used: 'having conversations.'"

"That's one way of putting it," said Ulf.

"Of course, I didn't believe him," Blomquist continued. "I told him that I wasn't born yesterday, and that he should watch his step. He took that perfectly well. He just nodded and then gave me his word he would stay away. And he did."

"There were no further complaints?"

"No, none. That was the end of Nils Cederström, as far as I was concerned."

"I'll get back to you about this," Ulf said. "In the meantime, let me sort out that teaspoon."

Chapter Eight

DOG POLITICS

Martin was still with Mrs. Högfors when Ulf returned to his flat that evening. As Ulf parked the Saab, he looked up and saw the dog looking at him through his neighbour's kitchen window. Ulf waved, and Martin's head bobbed up and down in excitement. Ulf could not hear the barking through the glass, but he could imagine it, and smiled at the thought. Martin always gave him a hero's welcome on his return, as dogs so usually did with their owners, no matter what sort of person that owner was. Dogs did not discriminate: the meanest, most inadequate owner would be rewarded with the same canine loyalty, the same love, as the most conscientious and caring. Occasionally, of course, a dog gave up and turned against his owner, but that was only after the gravest provocation.

Mrs. Högfors had Martin ready for his evening walk. "I was going to take him myself," she said, "but I was listening to a programme on the radio and when I looked at the clock I saw it was too late." She sighed. "Where do the hours go, Mr. Varg? That's what I want to know: Where do the hours go?"

"And the days, Mrs. Högfors," said Ulf. "And the months, and the years."

Mrs. Högfors nodded in agreement. "And they go more quickly as you get older, don't they? Have you ever worked out why that should be, Mr. Varg?"

Ulf had read that it was something to do with memory. Time passed more slowly when we were filing away memories. When you were young, you did a lot of that because so many experiences were new to you; later, when you had seen it all before, you did not lay down the same volume of memories, and time, as a result, seemed different. He wondered how he should explain that to Mrs. Högfors. She was an intelligent woman, but she would sometimes worry away at a problem for rather long, and Ulf had to go out that night and could not spend too much time talking.

"It's complicated, Mrs. Högfors," he said.

"Undoubtedly. But do you think it's something to do with how much you've already experienced? Something to do with proportions?"

"Possibly, Mrs. Högfors. No doubt the psychologists could throw some light on it."

Ulf patted Martin on the head and took the lead that Mrs. Högfors had already attached to his collar.

"That's a very fine new lead you have, Mr. Varg," she remarked. "Did you look at what it says on it? 'Designed in Sweden; made in China.'"

"I didn't see that," said Ulf. "I suppose that's to make us feel better about not making anything. If you put 'Designed in Sweden,' then we feel that at least they've left us something to do. We may not be able to make anything any longer, but we can at least draw pictures of what we'd like other people to make for us."

"The world is a funny place," said Mrs. Högfors. "What with the Russians . . ."

Ulf looked pointedly at his watch. "I'm really going to have to dash, Mrs. Högfors. It's going to be a quick walk for Martin, and then I have to go off to see my brother. They've invited me for dinner."

Mrs. Högfors smiled. "I saw him on the television today. He was saying something about something or other."

"That's him," said Ulf. "The television people come to him for a quote on anything at all, and he usually obliges. He has a position on everything—no matter what." He paused. "He is a politician, I suppose, and that's what they have to do."

"I saw that the Moderate Extremists are doing quite well in the opinion polls," said Mrs. Högfors. "People seem to be ready for their message."

Ulf rolled his eyes. He did not agree with his brother's politics, and the thought that his share of the vote—traditionally a very small one—might become larger did not appeal. "I'd read the fine print very closely, but people don't, do they? They vote with their . . ." He did not complete the metaphor. Did people vote with their hearts rather than their heads? Or did they vote with their stomachs, on the basis that they always voted for those who offered them the most in the material sense. Ulf sometimes wondered whether the most effective political message might be something as simple as "Free sandwiches for all, for life." Who could resist the temptation to vote for that?

He thanked Mrs. Högfors for her dog-sitting and stepped out into the evening air. There was a small park nearby where he took Martin for his walks, and he now made his way there with Martin tugging enthusiastically at the lead. There were few people about, but there would always be one or two dog owners walking their dogs and these, almost without exception, knew one another. There was a strong convention, though, that one did not stop for conversation if the other person was looking straight ahead. That meant that the walk was a business-like one and there was no time for a chat. Looking about, though, was a sign that a chat, even if only a brief one, would be welcome. And once again there were conventions about the subjects that could be discussed. Dogs and their activities were the default topic, and every conversation should start with a nod in that direction. Then one might move on to veterinary bills, the weather, and finally what had been seen on television. Any discussion of politics was frowned upon, unless the political issue touched in any way upon the canine world. Thus, a recent proposal by a small political party, the Left Centrists, that dogs should be obliged to wear seat belts while travelling in their owners' cars had been much discussed by the frequenters of the park.

Ulf's position had been that this represented an excessive inter-ference in personal liberty. "The state should not intervene too much," he said. "There have to be corners of life where, in spite of there being good reasons for intervention, the state simply holds off. This is because excessive interference dilutes public support for really necessary measures."

That met with broad approval, although one or two of the dog owners looked slightly perplexed by the argument. One expressed the view that politicians should keep out of dogs' lives because none of them had a mandate to regulate what dogs did or did not do. "Did any dogs actually vote for these people?" he asked. "They did not. So what right do they have?"

Ulf had found that argument amusing, and had been about to laugh when he realised that its proponent was serious. And so Ulf strangled his laugh and it became a cough. "An interesting argu-ment," he said.

Having allowed Martin a brief sniff around the park, Ulf turned round for home. There was very little traffic on the nearby road, and so he decided to let the dog completely off the lead. Martin was well behaved and had good traffic sense. He had never been known to dash off into the road, as some dogs did, and was usu-ally content to trot beside Ulf, never getting ahead of him or falling behind. Ulf wondered why Martin should be so well behaved. A simple explanation might be that Martin was just a good dog—some dogs were just that—and that his deepest instinct was to obey. That was one possibility. The other was Martin, being intelligent as well as deaf, had worked out that the best way of dealing with his disability was to stick close to his owner and do whatever he wanted. That, Ulf thought, might be the canine equivalent of Kierkegaard's leap of faith: one did what supreme authority appeared to want to be done.

He looked down at Martin, who was trotting contentedly by his side. "You're a good dog, Martin," he said. But then, immediately realising that Martin could not hear him, he stopped, leaned down, and patted Martin on the head. "Good dog," he mouthed, and Martin, whose lip-reading had come on by leaps and bounds, seemed to understand. Wagging his tail, he looked up at Ulf and opened his mouth. No bark came, but Ulf was sure that he could see the mouth patterns of the word *woof*. He stopped himself: it was one thing for Martin to lip-read; it would be quite another thing for him to understand that his owner might do the same.

"Good dog," Ulf repeated, making sure that his lips were visible to Martin. "Good boy."

Once again, Martin wagged his tail, staring up at Ulf with the total, unquestioning attention that dogs give to those in authority over them. It was an attention that brought with it the promise of complete and unquestioning obedience. A good dog—and Martin was undoubtedly a good dog—did not question the demands made of him. If the defence of superior orders was only a qualified defence for humans in international criminal law, then for dogs, Ulf reflected, it would bring complete acquittal.

"Remarkable," Ulf muttered to himself. He wondered whether there were any other lip-reading dogs in Sweden. He doubted it, but then he reminded himself that when we thought we, or our issues, were unique, we were almost invariably wrong. Somewhere there would be someone with exactly our thoughts and concerns. Somewhere, even in Sweden perhaps, there would be another lip-reading dog—although when he came to think of it, Ulf doubted that. Perhaps there would be such a dog somewhere in America, in all its vastness, where the possibility of anything unusual or peculiar being replicated was close to certain. Such a dog might even belong to a middle-ranking detective, with an interest in the history of art, and a silver-grey Saab. No—that, surely, was highly unlikely. The more one particularised one's situation, the smaller the chance that in all of humanity there would be somebody who completely matched one's circumstances.

He looked down at Martin and sighed. Martin, like most dogs, was composed almost entirely of devotion. He lived for Ulf; that was his *raison d'être*, his purpose in life. And how many of us could find in ourselves a similar, single-minded purpose, fired and sustained by simple and unconditional love? Here and there, perhaps, a noble soul might aspire to such a goal, but for the rest of us life was a mixed bag of saliences. Love of others was in that mixture somewhere, but it rubbed shoulders with venality and selfishness and crude ambition. Such were our lives in this world, which we, unlike dogs, knew to be a flawed one.

Kitty Varg, the Colombian wife of Ulf's brother, Björn, opened her front door and smiled at Ulf standing before her. Rain had set in during his journey, and even the few yards between the taxi and the porch of the modest suburban house had made Ulf wet.

"You're soaking," said Kitty, brushing the raindrops off the shoulders of Ulf's jacket.

"I hadn't expected rain," Ulf said. "And this has been a bit of a downpour."

He looked over his shoulder at the evening sky, now an ominous shade of purple.

"Global warming," said Kitty. "They warned us, didn't they? They said it time and time again. And were people listening? They were not."

Ulf sighed as she ushered him into the entrance hall. "People don't like to hear other people say, 'Time's up.' Remember what it was like as a child? Adults would come and tell you to stop your play, because it was time for bed, or bath, or homework. We didn't like it then, and we don't like it now."

Kitty laughed. "Denial is wonderful, isn't it? It gives us a bit more time before the lights are switched out."

"Björn?" asked Ulf.

He had intended to ask whether Björn was back from Stockholm yet, but Kitty interpreted the question as an enquiry as to her husband's position on global warming.

"Oh, he believes in it."

Ulf frowned. "In what?"

"In global warming. He chaired the Moderate Extremists' working party on the subject. They endorsed everything the scientists have been saying." She gave Ulf a glance that seemed to be looking for sympathy. "It's one of their policies that I happen to support one hundred per cent."

Ulf knew what lay behind the look. Kitty did not enjoy politics. She had once confessed to Ulf that she would be overjoyed if Björn were to resign as leader of his party, but had accepted that this was unlikely. "It's food and drink to him," she said. "In Colombia we have an expression: 'What people do is what they want to do.' It's a very simple saying, but like most simple sayings, it says it all, doesn't it?"

Ulf smiled and reached out briefly to touch her arm. It was a gesture of solidarity. Being married to Björn, he suspected, was not much different from being his brother. It was the same long-term contract with one who was there but, in a subtle and seemingly immutable way, was not there. Ulf had known that from childhood, although he had not had the words then to articulate the feelings he had about his brother. He had somehow sensed Björn's absence, his abstraction from the now, the immediate, the place they were actually in. Only once, as a boy, had he given voice to how he felt, saying to Björn, "You live somewhere else, you know. Not here, as the rest of us do." And Björn had looked at him with bemusement and said, "How do you know where I live?" That had been the extent of their discussion, but Ulf had felt that his brother knew exactly what he meant.

Then, when Ulf was in his early twenties and had just completed his degree at Uppsala, he saw, in an exhibition in Paris, where he was spending a week with a French girlfriend, a picture entitled *The Separation of Brothers*. It was the work of an obscure French painter of the 1930s, a minor figure on the edge of the group of artists known as the Nabis. Like Vuillard and Bonnard, this painter had been an exponent of *intimisme,* and all four of his works were of domestic interiors. *The Separation of Brothers* showed two young men seated at a kitchen table, a loaf of bread and a bottle of wine before them. The space between them was empty, cavernous even on the small canvas that the artist had chosen for his study. Ulf had peered at it and then remarked to his girlfriend, "That's me and my brother. That's how it is." She had examined the painting and then slipped her arm into his, saying nothing but conveying comfort.

Ulf had been pleased when Björn had met Kitty. He had been concerned that his brother would have difficulty finding a partner, given his single-minded immersion in political life. All he ever wanted, Ulf thought, was to be behind the desk from which orders emanated. "You want to control things, don't you?" he had once accused his brother—to receive the disarming answer, "Yes, I do." When Björn introduced him to Kitty, Ulf had at first imagined that she had been chosen because she in some way would help his political career. Until he realised that she was Colombian— although she had lived in Sweden since the age of twelve—he had thought that she would be the daughter of a senior politician, of somebody who would be of help to Björn in his attempts to clamber up the political pole. He felt slightly guilty when he learned that she came from a completely apolitical background, being the daughter of a professor of psychiatry in Bogotá. Her parents had divorced when she was eleven, the reason for the divorce being her mother's affair with a Swedish diplomat. The diplomat had been recalled to Stockholm and Kitty's mother chose to follow him, to the dismay of the professor of psychiatry. He might have tried to prevent Kitty's being taken out of the country, but did not, judging it less traumatic for the young girl to move countries than to be separated from her mother, even if it meant that she would grow up in Sweden and he would rarely see her.

Ulf had taken to Kitty. When Kitty and Björn's engagement was announced, he had been pleased in one sense, but concerned in another. "Björn's very lucky to have found you," he said. "And I'm pleased for him—I really am. But . . ."

He had hesitated, but she had encouraged him to continue. "Is there somebody else?" she asked nervously.

"No," Ulf replied. "Nothing like that. It's just that I think Björn cares too much about politics."

Kitty laughed. "Lots of people are like that. They talk about politics all the time. I don't care."

"You don't care about politics?"

She frowned. "No, I wouldn't say that. All I'd say is that I don't care if people care, if you see what I mean."

Ulf had left it at that. He had expressed a doubt about Björn as marriage material, and that was the most he should do. In fact, he wondered whether he should have said anything at all—he did not think that Björn would be pleased if he knew.

But his instinct had been right. He did not think that Björn paid enough attention to Kitty. Nor did it occur to his brother that she might find the whole business of being married to a political party leader tiresome. Ulf knew that this was how Kitty felt, because she had told him as much.

"People think," she once said to Ulf, "that just because I'm married to Björn, I care about the party. They think that I walk, sleep, and eat party affairs as he does. But I don't. I'm bored with the Moderate Extremists and their constant complaining about this, that, and the next thing. Do these people not have a life? Don't they have other things to think about?"

"Have you spoken to him about it?" he asked.

She nodded. She looked sad. "Many times. But I don't think he takes it in. He says that he'll try to spend more time on other things—and I suppose he considers me to be one of those other things. But he doesn't."

She smiled at a memory. "You know what happened once? A journalist was coming to interview him for a profile piece in the papers. It was a big thing—an interview with the main Swedish news agency, which meant that the resulting article would end up . . ."

"Everywhere," said Ulf.

"Yes. In all the local papers, heaven knows where. All that." She paused. "Anyway, the party's press agent told him that the journalist would want to know about what he did with his time outside politics. That led to a major panic, because the answer to that question is, as you know, that Björn doesn't have a life outside politics. There *is* nothing. That's it.

"So he told the press agent that this was going to be a tricky issue, and the press agent said that he should take up a hobby—then and there—so that he could tell the journalist all about that. He recommended bird-watching, because that, apparently, is a very good hobby from the point of view of public trust."

Ulf smiled at this. Philately too, he thought. His dentist, Dr. Sjöberg, was a keen stamp collector, and Ulf had always felt reassured by this. It was, he thought, an entirely suitable hobby for a dentist.

"The public likes people who watch birds," Kitty continued,

"because they don't feel threatened by them. Yes, that's the way they look at things, it seems. There's a lot of research on this."

Ulf's smile broadened. Kitty often said *There's a lot of research on this* when advancing views on a wide range of matters. She never cited specific research, but referred to it in tones of respect, sometimes giving it a vague geographical provenance. Her supporting scientists might come from America, or, in the case of the more outré findings, more specifically from California. It was psychologists in California, for instance, to whom she attributed the research that showed that more than eighty per cent of men married women who reminded them of their mother. Ulf had questioned that. He thought that there was a lot of research pointing to the tendency of people in general, and not just men, to marry people who looked like themselves. Kitty had considered this gravely before giving her verdict that there might be something in that, and even as she spoke, Ulf reflected on the fact that Björn and Kitty did look remarkably similar, especially when regarded from a particular angle. And his own wife, who had left him for her hypnotist lover? Had she looked like him? Possibly, although he found it increasingly difficult to picture her in his mind's eye. Did the memory of how people looked fade with the passage of time, like an old photograph exposed over the years to the light? There might be research on that: there seemed to be research on just about everything else, including the question of what research there was on what subjects.

Ulf asked whether Björn had acted on his press agent's advice. "Did he take up ornithology?"

"For a day or two," Kitty replied. "He went out for an hour or so with a pair of binoculars and saw a few birds. But he didn't have a field guide and had no idea what he'd seen."

Ulf laughed. Björn had never been interested in nature when they were boys, and he was largely indifferent to animals. Martin had picked this up on the occasions that Björn had visited Ulf's flat. The dog had watched his master's brother with suspicion, occasionally growling *sotto voce*. "Your dog doesn't like me," Björn had said.

"Perhaps he disapproves of your politics," Ulf had suggested.

"Very funny," said Björn.

Now he looked at Kitty. This story of Björn's brief interest in bird-watching did not paint his brother in a good light. "Well," he said, "let's see. It might be that he'll make a bit more time for other things in future. Who knows?"

Kitty looked at her watch as she led Ulf through to the sitting room. "He said he'd be back by seven," she said. "But he hasn't phoned. Sometimes his meetings go on and on . . ."

"What meeting doesn't go on and on?" said Ulf. "And it doesn't matter. If he doesn't turn up, I can see him some other time." He paused. "My social diary is pretty empty."

He had not intended the remark to sound self-pitying, but that was how it seemed. And so he quickly added, "Not that I'm complaining. I like having free evenings."

Kitty poured him a drink. Ulf liked Scotch, and since Björn did not, there was always a virtually untouched bottle in the small drinks cabinet in a corner of the room. Ulf raised the glass to his lips and savoured the peaty smell. "This is an island whisky," he said. "Lovely."

Kitty wrinkled her nose in disgust. "Too medicinal for me," she said. "It reminds me of the stuff my father would put on cuts and grazes when I was a child."

Ulf glanced at the silver-framed photograph on the bookcase. That was her father, Dr. Antonio Xavier-Ortez, author of the small row of paperback books immediately behind the picture. This was his *oeuvre:* several collections of annotated case histories and a two-volume discussion of adolescent psychopathology, *The Adolescent Within.* Kitty had shown them to him with pride, handling each as an awestruck country priest might handle a relic left to him by a rich parishioner.

Kitty had related to him her father's life story. He had been born in Colombia but had been sent to university in Buenos Aires, funded by an uncle who had moved there from Bogotá. That was where he had come under the influence of Lacanian psychoanalysts, trained in Paris, and had developed the theories he was later to expand upon in *The Adolescent Within.*

He had not been happy in Buenos Aires, in spite of the professional opportunities it had given him. He returned to Bogotá, where he met Kitty's mother, a society beauty of simple tastes. Those tastes were simple because they were focused solely on money and cosmetics. Within a few months he realised his mistake in marrying her, but by then she was expecting Kitty and he was too principled a man to abandon her. When she started to have affairs, he turned an eye that was both blind and relieved, and when at last she left with her Swedish diplomat lover, he breathed a sigh of relief. He adored Kitty, of course, and would miss her, but he was unwilling to put her at the heart of a tug-of-love court case. He had been advised that he would win because the courts were loath to allow children to be taken out of the country, but he abstained nonetheless. "I knew you would do the right thing," said his wife. "I knew it all along, Antonio. That is why I married you in the first place—because I knew you would always do the right thing."

Now, as Ulf stood before the photograph of the late Dr. Xavier-Ortez, Kitty's father smiled back at him. Ulf's gaze wandered to the books behind the photograph, past *The Adolescent Within* to a small cluster of volumes with striking red spines and large title lettering. It took a moment or two for the titles themselves to register, but he suddenly realised that he was looking at a collection of the novels of Nils Cederström.

He reached forward and was taking one off the shelf when

Kitty looked over his shoulder. "Do you read him?" she asked. "Do you read Cederström?"

Ulf glanced at the title of the book in his hand: *Matador*. And there, below the title, was the strapline "Hard-drinking, hard-fighting, he was a man's man who loved the wrong woman."

Ulf smiled. "This isn't really my sort of thing."

Kitty shook her head. "Don't be too quick to dismiss him," she said. "He gets good reviews. He can write, you know."

"Oh, I know that," said Ulf. "He's won a lot of prizes. And they like him in America, I believe."

"That's because they're missing Hemingway," Kitty said. "He's Hemingway's spiritual successor, they say."

Ulf opened the book at random. "'He felt the pain shooting down his side,'" he read. "'The bull's horn had grazed the side of his ribcage . . .'" He looked up and winced. "Very uncomfortable, I'd say."

"Well, I enjoy them. I know that people say they're men's books, but I know a lot of women who like reading him."

"The attraction of the rough type?" Ulf suggested playfully.

Kitty laughed. "Women like men like that. People say they don't, but they're wrong. Give a woman a choice between reading about men who are in touch with their feminine side and men who fight bulls, and they'll go for the bullfighters any day. Sad, in a way, but there we are."

"Are you serious?" asked Ulf. "Because if you are, those men who have spent all that time making themselves into new men have been wasting their time. They won't get the approval they've hoped for."

He slipped the book back into its place on the shelf.

"We know him," said Kitty.

Ulf turned round sharply. "Cederström?"

"Yes. Nils. We've known him for years. Björn has been friendly with him for heaven knows how long. They met at a fishing lodge up north when a wealthy party member took Björn up there. They got on well and stayed in touch."

Ulf was listening attentively. "And his partner? Do you see much of her?"

Kitty nodded. "Yes, I do, as it happens. I rather like her, actually."

Ulf was silent. "I read somewhere that he's ... well, that he has a bit of a roving eye. Plenty of girlfriends. There was something about his having three children by different mistresses."

Kitty reacted to this with laughter. "That's nonsense. Complete nonsense." She hesitated. "Ebba—that's his partner—told me that she was one hundred per cent certain that Nils never so much as looked at another woman. She's quite definite about that."

Ulf frowned. If Nils, contrary to those press reports, never looked at women, was that because he had no interest in them? And was that because his interests lay elsewhere?

"And another thing," Kitty went on. "You know how they talk about his drinking? You've read about that? About those benders in Havana and places like that? Endless rum, and girls."

"I've seen something."

"Well, it's nonsense. I know for a fact that he's pretty abstemious. Ebba says that he likes dry sherry and that yellow Dutch stuff—you know, the egg drink."

"Advocaat?"

"Yes, that. He occasionally drinks that. But never to excess."

Ulf shook his head in disbelief. "Not what one would imagine," he said. "A bit ... how should one put it? Not very macho."

"But he isn't," said Kitty. "He's a new man, you know. Actually, he's always been a new man."

Ulf had a further question to ask. "Do you think he might be up to something?"

"Like what?"

Ulf shrugged. "Oh, something private."

Kitty thought for a moment. "There might be something," she said at last. "I know that they go to Grand Cayman from time to time. Every year, in fact. And why do people go to Grand Cayman?"

"Money," said Ulf.

"Precisely. Nils will have made a fair packet from the films they made of his books. Ebba once said something about how he hated paying taxes."

"Who doesn't?" asked Ulf.

"Oh, there are some who do it willingly. They show a sort of fatalism about it. That, or they make a big thing about how keen they are to pay for schools and hospitals and all the other things."

"But Nils is not one of those?"

Kitty shook her head. "Definitely not."

"Even to the extent of engaging in a bit of tax evasion?"

Kitty grinned. "If I suspect him of anything," she said, "it's that."

She was about to add something, but her mobile phone rang at that moment and she fumbled in her pocket to answer it. Ulf heard Björn's voice at the other end of the line. He was stuck in Stockholm, he said. He was very sorry. Could she pass on his apologies to Ulf—and could she tell him, too, that they would try to rearrange the dinner for two or three weeks hence when he was sure that he could be in Malmö? Ulf nodded his silent agreement as Kitty took the message; this was no surprise—Björn had done this time and time again, cancelling things, ever since they were six or seven, possibly even younger. Björn's operating principle, it seemed to Ulf, was clear enough: if something more interesting turns up, then cancel existing commitments, but always offer to reschedule. That was important, as Björn would not wish to be thought rude, or at least not egregiously so. Ulf knew what their father would have thought of that. He was old-fashioned, a man of firm standards, who claimed to know only three words of Latin—

pacta sunt servanda. "That means 'keep your word,' boys," he had said. Ulf was listening; Björn was not.

Kitty served dinner, a rack of lamb with new potatoes. Ulf did not stay for coffee afterwards. Caffeine kept him awake at night, and anyway, he was tired. He would return to the flat, where he would take Martin out for a brief walk round the block. Then he would read for a while, as he always did, falling asleep with the bedside light still on, the book by his side, his place lost, but always remembered the next morning when Martin scratched at the bedroom door to wake him up.

Chapter Nine

GARLIC DOES ITS WORK

S o, who exactly is this Dr. Dahlman?"
Ulf knew the answer that he should give to Blomquist's question. He knew that he should explain to him that Jo Dahlman, as well as being an anaesthetist, was the husband of their colleague Anna Bengtsdotter, and that the reason why they were opposite the main entrance to the Skåne University Hospital was that they were waiting for an opportunity to follow the doctor. He should have explained further that the reason for this interest in Dr. Dahlman was nothing to do with any criminal investigation, but was instead the desire to establish whether or not he was having an affair. In other words, this was, on the surface of things, a misuse of police resources.

Ulf knew that, of course, but had justified the investigation sufficiently to keep his conscience clear. Firstly, he was doing this in his own time, having arrived at work that morning two hours early to ensure that he would have completed his shift by the time he took up his position outside the hospital. As far as Blomquist was concerned, he was still officially on shift, but Ulf felt that his involvement was necessary in order to give him something to do. Blomquist had complained about being denied the opportunity to do anything, and if Ulf did not respond, then the other man's spirits would sink. And surely it was not in the interests of the department, or indeed the public, that Blomquist should be bored and frustrated; his involvement, then, in this informal and quite unofficial enquiry, was justified on the grounds of staff morale. But it was probably better, Ulf reasoned, that Blomquist should be kept in the dark about the investigation's true purpose, as it would do no good for him to think that his presence on the investigation was superfluous.

"I want to find out where he goes after work," said Ulf. "He may lead us to somebody we're interested in."

Blomquist fidgeted with the cuffs of his shirt. "You mean he's not a suspect?"

"No, he's not."

"But somebody he knows is? Is that what you're saying."

"Could be," said Ulf. And then he thought: This is wrong. I should not mislead Blomquist like this. This is quite wrong.

Ulf turned in the driver's seat of the silver-grey Saab. "Actually, Blomquist, I've been meaning to tell you. The story is a bit different, but I need your word—your solemn word—that you'll keep this strictly confidential. Do I have that?"

Blomquist looked pained. "Of course. Of course you do."

"It's important," said Ulf. "It's important because this involves a colleague."

Blomquist made a strange sucking sound through his front teeth. "Corruption?"

"No," said Ulf hurriedly. "Nothing like that." He looked down at his hands. "This Dr. Dahlman is married to Anna—our colleague Anna."

Blomquist said nothing. Then he began to smile. "It's a familiar story, isn't it? Everybody, but everybody, is having an affair. Everybody."

Ulf thought this an exaggeration. He wanted to challenge Blomquist; he wanted to say, "*Et tu, Brute?* Tell me about it."

But Blomquist was there first. "Except me, of course."

"Of course," said Ulf.

Blomquist looked thoughtful. "I must admit, I wouldn't know how to go about it. I'm bad at lying."

"Some affairs don't involve deception," Ulf said. "There are open relationships, I believe. People give one another their freedom."

Blomquist sighed. "I'm not in an open relationship."

"But it seems to me you're happy enough."

Blomquist nodded. "Yes. We have a happy enough marriage." He looked at Ulf. "I'm very sorry about what happened to you, Varg."

Ulf thanked him.

"It would be good if . . ."

Ulf nodded. "Who knows? I might meet somebody. I wouldn't mind if I did."

"But you're not trying?"

Ulf thought: Am I trying? No, and the reason for that is that I am allowing myself to be in love with Anna. I know there is no future in that, and yet I allow it. "Not at the moment," he said.

"So there's nobody?"

He looked at Blomquist with annoyance. It was none of his business. "No, there's nobody," he said.

They lapsed into silence. On the other side of the road, a small group of people emerged from the hospital. One or two of them peeled off; the others continued down the road. Medical students, thought Ulf. An ambulance went past, slowly, not engaged in an urgent mission.

"I went to see the doctor the other day," Blomquist said suddenly.

"Oh yes?"

"I had one of those blood-sugar tests—you know, the ones that look at what your blood-sugar levels are over three months."

"Interesting," said Ulf.

"Yes. Very."

"And?"

"And he was pleasantly surprised," said Blomquist. "My blood sugars were within the normal range."

Ulf drummed his fingers against the steering wheel. It was not a conscious gesture, and when he realised that he was doing it, he stopped himself.

"You see," Blomquist continued, "we all eat far too many carbohydrates."

Ulf nodded. This was the second of Blomquist's general observations: people had affairs and ate carbohydrates. If only they were less given to these things, then …

"I'll give you an example," Blomquist went on. "I was at the airport the other day, seeing off my aunt. She's the one who goes to Florida—I think I've told you about her?" He paused. "Have I?"

"I think so," said Ulf. He remembered Blomquist saying something about Florida once, and it may have been to do with his aunt.

Blomquist drew in a breath. "Her husband was a swimming pool engineer. He started off in a small way—I suspect he was probably not much more than a handyman who happened to fix pools, but then he acquired his own business. It did rather well. They expanded into Norway and then Holland, believe it or not. The Dutch like swimming pools, you know."

"Oh yes?"

"Yes. You'd think they'd have swimming pools stitched up themselves, what with all their experience in creating polders and building canals and what have you, but it turned out there was plenty of room for his firm down there. So they set up in Holland and did quite well."

"Amsterdam?"

"Eindhoven to begin with. Then they moved to Amsterdam. Have you ever been there, Varg?"

Ulf shook his head. "I like their electric razors, though," he said. He thought that Blomquist was drawing him in somehow—drawing him into his strange world of rambling association. Electric razors, aunts, Florida, carbohydrates . . . In Blomquist's company it was so easy to drift off into these Proustian realms.

Blomquist became animated. "Oh yes," he exclaimed. "Those razors. I have one. It's waterproof, you know. Well, you can't put the whole thing in the water—you wouldn't put the body bit—but you can certainly put the heads under the tap. They have a tap symbol on them, you see, and that's how you tell whether your electric razor is waterproof or not."

Ulf suggested that the main body unit was waterproof too. "I think the whole thing is sealed," he said. "Otherwise water would get into the works and it would short out."

Blomquist considered this for a moment. Then he responded, "Possibly, possibly. But in general I think you should err on the side of caution with things that claim to be waterproof. I don't think the manufacturers intend you to take things too far. Splash-proof might be a better term to use, don't you think?"

"Perhaps."

"And you have to be particularly careful with salt-water," Blomquist said. "Salt-water and electronics don't mix. They just don't. The slightest bit of salt-water in the works and that's it."

"Yes, salt . . ."

Blomquist remembered something. "This aunt of mine—you know the one who—"

"Goes to Florida . . ."

"Yes, her. Well, I'll tell you something about her, Varg. You'll like this story. She has an iPad—or, rather, she *had* an iPad. She used this for emails to her daughter, who lives in Stockholm. She's married to a Pole—a rather nice man, actually, who is some sort of osteopath or chiropractic, or whatever. I never know the difference between these people, but he's one of those characters who manipulate you if you have a sore back. One of those. Anyway, my aunt uses this iPad to stay in touch with her daughter—my cousin, of course. She took it with her to Florida, as she always does, and she was sitting in a café one day and she dropped the iPad into the sea, which was right there. The café was on a sort of deck, right over the sea."

"That would not have done it much good," said Ulf.

"No, it didn't. It sank right down and there was nothing she could do."

Ulf wondered whether that was the end of the story. It was difficult to see what sequel there could be, and as it happened there was none. Yet, how had they got on to the subject? He looked at his watch, and at that moment Dr. Dahlman emerged from the front of the hospital, glanced up at the sky, and began to walk down the street.

"We can talk about your aunt later on," said Ulf. "That's our man over there."

Ulf reflected on the fact that he could not remember the last time he had followed somebody on foot. He felt vaguely self-conscious about it, imagining that it would be obvious to any observer, even if not to Jo Dahlman himself. Of course, following a quarry along the street, keeping sufficient distance between pursuer and pursued, readily lent itself to fantasy, and for a moment Ulf imagined himself in some Eastern European landscape, in some Cold War drama, following a defector or double agent, in the eternal cat-and-mouse game of espionage. Such things still happened, no doubt, played out by others, in new settings, because there were still secrets that people kept from others. In human affairs, so little changed; new enmities replaced old; the children of rivals re-enacted their parents' battles; nothing much changed in the human script.

Dr. Dahlman seemed unhurried, with the result that Ulf and Blomquist had to saunter rather than stride. It was important, Ulf explained, that he should not be spotted, as he had met Jo Dahlman on several occasions and would probably be recognised. "It's going to be over to you," he said to Blomquist. "I'll have to hang back."

Blomquist nodded. "There are a few bars down there," he said. "He's probably going to meet his lover there."

"If he has a lover," said Ulf. "We don't know that yet."

"Oh, he'll have a lover," said Blomquist. "No smoke without fire." He paused. "I take it that Anna found some evidence."

Ulf drew in his breath. Blomquist had a habit of working out what was what with uncanny accuracy. "Yes," he said. "She did."

"Probably something left behind after an assignation," mused Blomquist. "An item of jewellery, perhaps. Underwear."

Ulf threw a sideways glance at the policeman. Jewellery *in* underwear, he thought, but how was Blomquist to know that?

Blomquist touched Ulf's arm. "Slow down," he said. "He's going to make a call."

Dr. Dahlman had stopped and could be seen extracting his mobile from his jacket pocket. Blomquist turned to face Ulf and addressed him, gesticulating as if they were engaged in an animated conversation.

"Always check the packet for carbohydrate content," he said. And then, under his breath, "Act, Varg. Act in case he looks this way."

Ulf made an indeterminate gesture. "Carbohydrates?"

"Yes," said Blomquist, watching as Dr. Dahlman put the phone to his ear.

"Packages should give information on the number of grams of carbohydrate in every hundred grams," Blomquist went on. "Fifty or sixty grams is high. Fifteen is better, if you're trying to cut down on carbs." He paused. "He's putting his mobile away. He's found out where she is. She'll be waiting for him."

"You seem pretty sure, Blomquist," Ulf said.

"It's obvious," Blomquist retorted, with the air of one who was pointing out something self-evident. He pointed to a side street, a few yards on from where Dr. Dahlman had been standing. "He'll be heading for that bar down there. I know the place. Booths. Candles. Ideal place to meet a lover." He smiled, then added, "Garlic may not be everybody's idea of the ideal accompaniment to romance."

Ulf looked puzzled. "Garlic?"

Andersens was a beer and garlic bar, known for its range of ales and its garlic-flavoured snacks. Everything served in the bar was laced with garlic: the beer, the martinis, the nuts, the burgers served from the small, garlicky kitchen at the rear of the building— all of these had generous quantities of garlic added to them. Ordering two beers, Ulf noticed the copious pinch of chopped garlic floating at the top of the glass. "I hope you like garlic, Blomquist," he said, passing the drink to his companion.

I need not have asked, Ulf said to himself, as Blomquist launched into a litany of praise for the benefits of the odiferous allium.

"There's more and more evidence," Blomquist began, "that points to the benefits of eating raw garlic. It lowers blood pressure, you know, but also protects against cancer. Had you heard about that?"

Ulf shook his head.

"The Chinese have recently shown that if you eat a clove of raw garlic twice a week, you are at far lower risk of lung cancer."

"Really?"

"Yes. And it's good for fungal infections. It's been used to treat that for, well, for centuries, I believe."

Ulf took a sip of his garlicky beer. It was not unpleasant, the garlic imparting a sharp taste, rather like that of lime or lemon.

The Mexicans added lime to their beer, did they not? He took a further sip; yes, it was a bit like a Mexican beer.

"Fungal infections can be difficult," said Blomquist. "Lots of people have them under their toenails. The fungus gets in and can be quite hard to shift. It's because it's warm and damp down there—if you wear socks. It's not so bad if you wear sandals—the air can circulate, you see."

Ulf looked out over the bar. At the other end of the room, Dr. Dahlman had taken a seat in a booth. A young woman with short cropped hair had joined him. As Ulf watched them, he saw the woman lean forward and give the doctor a lingering kiss. It has been so easy, Ulf thought. He had found out what he needed to find out, and it had been so very simple.

"I had a fungal infection in my toenail a year or two ago," Blomquist said. "They can give you pills for it, of course, but you have to take them for months—for some reason. The drug's called terbinafine, I think."

Ulf was watching Dr. Dahlman. He had a hand on top of the table, and now it moved towards the young woman's hand. He felt his heart beating within him. There was no doubt about it now: Jo Dahlman was having an affair, and that meant that Anna . . . He stopped himself. This was not why he had agreed to do this; he had offered because she had implored him to find out what she feared and dreaded. And the news that he would have to impart to her would cause her immense distress; he hated the thought of that. If only he hadn't offered.

Blomquist had more to say about fungal infections. "I don't like taking medicines for months and months," he said. "I know some people have to do that, but I'm not keen. So when the doctor offered me this drug for my toenails, I said, 'I'd prefer not, doctor.' And he said, 'Well, that drug is much better than any topical application—you know, that stuff you paint on the nails. That's not so effective, they say.' I knew that, but I said, 'Well, I'd like to see what I can achieve with garlic.' And you know what? He laughed. He said, 'That's old wives' stuff.' He actually said that."

Ulf said the first thing that came into his head, which was, "Doctors shouldn't laugh at garlic."

Blomquist vigorously agreed. "You're absolutely right, Varg. They shouldn't. And now that there are all these studies, even more so."

"Did it work?" asked Ulf. "Did it sort out your fungal infection?"

Blomquist shook his head. "No, it didn't, as it happened. But there are differences in the way in which people respond to these things. I might just be one of those who are insensitive to the active ingredient—who knows?"

Blomquist now nodded at a passing waitress. She stopped, put down her tray, and kissed him on each cheek.

"This is Marie," said Blomquist.

"You two know one another?" said Ulf, responding to the waitress's handshake.

"We were at school together," said Marie. "Remember that, Blommy?"

Blomquist laughed. "A long, long time ago." He leaned towards her. "Do you know that couple over there? Last booth on the right?"

She glanced in the direction of Dr. Dahlman and the young woman. "They're regulars," she said. "They're in here once or twice a week. I think he's a doctor from the hospital. Somebody said he was a surgeon."

"And her?"

Marie shrugged. "I don't know anything about her. But one of the other girls does."

Ulf pressed her on this. "This other girl—you mean, one of the other waitresses?"

"Yes. Kristina. She's not here tonight. She works here at weekends. She has kids, and they go to her ex-husband on Saturday. They stay overnight, which she hates. He's a brute, they say, but he has money. She's very friendly with that woman. They go back a long time, I think."

She picked up her tray. "Must go, Blommy."

Blomquist blew her a kiss. "You take care, Marie." Then, to Ulf, he said, "I could speak to that woman, Kristina, if you'd like, Varg. I could drop by on Saturday." He smiled. "I like garlic. I don't mind."

Ulf hesitated. Blomquist was looking at him, his face full of an obvious desire to be involved. He had offered to come back, but not with Ulf—by himself. Having gone out of his way to involve Blomquist in the investigation—purely because he did not want him to feel excluded—now Blomquist was proposing to do just that to him. Did the other man see that?

Ulf took a further sip of his beer. A small piece of garlic traced a fiery path across his tongue. Why put garlic in beer? Was it a deliberate act of bravado? Was it born of a desire to be unusual, to stand out from the crowd of other bars—establishments where the beer was served unadulterated?

He shot a glance at Blomquist as he raised the glass to his lips, wondering what it was like to be the other man. That was always a salutary exercise, and a useful one, to imagine yourself in the shoes of the other—of the person sitting across from you at the table; of the person driving the car next to yours in the line of cars at the road junction; of the person in the seat next to yours in the dentist's waiting room, who would be as anxious as you might be about the forthcoming submission to the dentist's probing instruments; who might, just like you, wish to be somewhere else. We could so easily forget what it was like to be the other, and yet that knowledge lay at the heart of our moral lives. Of course it did; and Ulf, now reminded of it by the drift of his thoughts, lowered his glass and smiled at Blomquist, and said, "That would be very good of you, Blomquist." Then he added—because the cautionary thought had just occurred to him—"It can't be on overtime, I'm afraid, because this enquiry is unofficial, so to speak."

"Oh, I knew that," said Blomquist. "So don't worry: your time, my time—nothing to do with the department."

Ulf was momentarily taken aback at Blomquist's appraisal of the situation. He had not spelled it out to him before this, but he now told himself that he should not be surprised. Blomquist was extraordinary. When you were engaged in his normal conversation—not that his conversation could really be described as *normal*—you could easily write him off as a crashing health bore. But writing him off like that obscured the fact that Blomquist had the ability—possibly just the luck—to move investigations forward. You had to give Blomquist credit for that, and yet nobody else in the department seemed to want to acknowledge his usefulness. That was envy, thought Ulf, and he should try to fight that in himself.

"I'm most grateful to you, Blomquist," he said. "We wouldn't have got where we are if it weren't for you." And then he added, "Once again."

Those two words—*once again*—had their effect. Blomquist seemed to grow before Ulf's eyes. He beamed with pleasure at the compliment—so much so that Ulf repeated it, and said, "You have a nose, Blomquist. You really do."

Blomquist automatically reached up to touch his nose, dropping his hand sheepishly as the metaphor came home. "That's kind of you, Varg. We all have a nose, I suppose—in our line of work."

"Yes," said Ulf. "But I must say that yours is particularly—how shall I put it?—particularly well attuned. You're a natural detective, Blomquist."

They finished their beer. Ulf felt the last few fragments of garlic sting the roof of his mouth. He would not repeat the experiment at home, he thought. Garlic was all very well, but its place was not in beer, or martinis. Garlic belonged to . . .

He turned to Blomquist. "Do you like snails in garlic butter, Blomquist?"

Blomquist did not treat this as an unusual question. He had views. "With parsley, Varg. You have to add parsley. My sister—you know, the one in Lund—she cooks snails that way. She has a book by that man we used to see on television—you know, the one with the moustache—the one who was arrested up in Stockholm for parking his car on somebody's foot. Do you remember that case? It was all over the papers. The chef didn't mean to park on this person's foot, but once he realised he had done so, he didn't move the car. He got out and locked the door."

"Strange," said Ulf.

"Yes. Very bad. They were rivals, apparently. This person—the other person, that is, the one with the foot—he was just standing there where the chef, the one who did the snails with parsley, wanted to park. But there was bad blood between them. Imagine heading towards a parking place and seeing your enemy's foot exactly where you intend to park. Imagine that, Varg. The temptation! Oh my God, the temptation!"

"I have never parked on anybody's foot," said Ulf. He realised that this sounded rather pompous—as if he were trying to claim the moral high ground. But it was true, nonetheless, and should one apologise for such a statement? Yet he added, "I can imagine how satisfying it must be—in the right circumstances."

Blomquist laughed. "It's sometimes hard to be what people expect us to be," he said. "If you see what I mean, Varg."

Ulf did. Every so often he felt a strong urge to forget that he was a detective, and a senior one at that. How comfortable it would be to be just a *person*, a member of the public, of whom so very much less was expected. But that was not open to him, in the same way in which it was not open to the King of Sweden to be an ordinary, unexceptional citizen, capable of enjoying the anonymity that went with the status of being a nobody. He thought of the King of the Netherlands, who had been a qualified airline pilot and who would from time to time fly jets of the national airline, emerging, in captain's uniform, from the flight deck, to the astonishment of passengers.

They left the bar. Ulf was pleased with the outcome of their brief assignment, but saddened too. The news that he would in due course have to convey to Anna would distress her, and he did not look forward to that—even if the thought of her ridding herself of an unfaithful husband gave him a secret frisson of joy.

They walked back towards the car. The smell of garlic was still strong in Ulf's nose, and even when he blew into his hand-kerchief, it remained there, doing its work: protecting him, he reflected, against various diseases, against vampires, and against close human contact.

Chapter Ten

ESTONIANS, TAPEWORMS, TATTOOS

Martin's vet, Dr. Håkansson, was fond of his patient.

"It's always a pleasure to see your dog, Ulf," he said. "There are some dogs whom I dread seeing—in some cases because of their owners . . ." He laughed nervously. "Not in this case, of course, as I am always happy to see you and Martin. But some . . . oh, my goodness me . . . And the interesting thing is that the dog's personality almost always reflects the owner's. Neurotic owner, neurotic dog—that's what I always say."

Ulf had taken Martin for his regular appointment with Dr. Håkansson. He was not entirely convinced that Martin needed to see the vet every six weeks, but he had gone along with the suggestion when it had first been made. Martin was being treated for depression, and the vet had advised him that it would be wise to monitor his serotonin levels regularly. "I prefer to under-prescribe," Dr. Håkansson had said, "as the consequences of over-medication can be quite serious, but we do want the drugs to have the desired effect."

Martin had become used to his trips to the clinic, and seemed to grasp that Dr. Håkansson's intentions were good, even if the vet sometimes pushed at a sensitive area of his stomach and appeared to take an inordinate interest in his teeth and gums. Now, with the physical examination over and the vet having expertly and painlessly drawn a small sample of blood from the scruff of his neck, Martin settled down on the examination table, closed his eyes, and dropped off to sleep.

"He's very secure, isn't he?" said Dr. Håkansson, as he washed his hands. "It's so good to see a dog with so few issues."

"Other than depression," said Ulf.

The vet nodded. "That's probably genetic. It's generally thought that Swedish dogs are more susceptible than others, you know."

"Our latitudes have a lot to answer for," said Ulf.

Dr. Håkansson agreed. "I have just been in Greece," he said. "My wife and I went to Ithaca. We took a small villa with her sister and her husband. And their children—two boys and a girl. Teenagers, I'm afraid."

Ulf looked sympathetic.

"You don't have any children, do you, Ulf?"

Ulf shook his head. "I lost my wife, as I think you know. And after that . . ." He shrugged. "I've thought of getting married again, but the occasion has never presented itself. I'm not sure if anybody would have me."

Dr. Håkansson shook a finger at him. "Oh, come now, Ulf. You must be a very eligible man. My receptionist is always saying how handsome she thinks you are." He paused. "Not that I see it myself, but there we are. But you've kept yourself in shape, and I'm sure there will be many ladies who would be very pleased were you to express an interest."

Ulf said he was not so sure. "She'd have to take on Martin—whoever she is. And he has his issues, as you know, what with his hearing impairment and his depression."

"Neither of which need discourage the lady," said Dr. Håkansson. "Indeed, women are often attracted by the lame and the weak. Or so I believe. They want to mother them."

Ulf smiled. He was not sure that he would describe himself in those terms; Dr. Håkansson was a very good vet, but he was somewhat lacking in diplomatic skills. "And some people say that I'm rather stuck in my ways." He shook his head, as if writing himself off. Then he looked again at Dr. Håkansson. "Were these teenagers as bad as all that?"

Dr. Håkansson had returned to his desk and was writing a note in Martin's file. "The teenagers? Oh yes, they certainly were. One of them, the older boy, insisted on appearing everywhere with his shirt off. He was obviously very pleased with himself, and he would sit at the dining-room table flexing his muscles. It was a most distasteful sight."

"Narcissus was a teenager," said Ulf. "We tend to forget that."

"Yes," said Dr. Håkansson. "And his sister was permanently plugged in to her music. If you tried to address her, she simply pointed at her headphones and shook her head."

"Tiresome," said Ulf. He remembered how, a week or so before, he had interviewed a teenager who was accused of hacking a military site and had insisted on dealing with his social media while the questioning took place. Ulf had eventually reached across the table and taken the boy's tablet from him, much to the outrage of its owner. He would have been less annoyed, thought Ulf, had he struck him a blow.

"But we were all teenagers once," said Dr. Håkansson. "And we must be tolerant."

"To a degree," said Ulf.

The vet sighed. "Yes." He closed Martin's file and slipped it into a drawer. "Now, Martin's progress . . . Is he getting enough exercise?"

Ulf replied that he thought he was. "I take him out first thing in the morning. He has a good run then. And during the day, when I am at work, my neighbour makes sure he has at least two outings. He has an active lifestyle."

The vet nodded. "Very good. All animals need exercise. In nature—before we turned up—they would have had their exercise looking for food. The danger is that once we turned up, they lost the incentive to forage or hunt. And that's when the rot set in." He looked in Martin's direction. The dog stared back at him balefully, as if to endorse the vet's vision of human intervention.

"Martin's lupine ancestors would have been kept busy scavenging for food," he said. "Wolves carry no extra weight, you know."

"I'm sure they don't," agreed Ulf.

Dr. Håkansson frowned, remembering something. "Speaking of wolves," he said, "I had an unusual client in the other day."

Ulf waited. Occasionally in the past Dr. Håkansson had drawn Ulf's attention to something that he felt merited police interest. In one case this had led to an investigation and to the arrest of a drug smuggler who had used dogs to smuggle drugs from South America. The dogs had been fed sausages in the middle of which cocaine had been planted in plastic sheaths. After the dogs had been brought to him for a purgative, he had told Ulf of his suspicions, and the information had been passed on to the drugs division. Dr. Håkansson had received an official commendation from the Commissioner himself and an invitation to the police Christmas party. The dogs, after their confiscation, had been taken into care and found a home with the man who serviced the outboard motors of the local police launches.

"Yes," said Dr. Håkansson, "somebody brought in a very impressive husky/Alsatian cross. In fact, I think there was more Belgian shepherd than Alsatian, but the husky gene was very obvious. Those eyes—you know what I'm talking about. Those blue eyes. A touch of yellow in this case. Amber, I suppose."

"They can be quite arresting," said Ulf. "They bring to mind snowy wastes. Forests, and so on."

"Yes," agreed Dr. Håkansson. "Anyway, this person who brought the dog in was not a regular client. He spoke Swedish with a fairly strong accent. Estonian or Latvian, probably. He was a big fellow with that bone structure the Slavs have. You know the sort."

Ulf shook his head. "They're not Slavs, Dr. Håkansson. They're really a sort of Finn. Linguistically, that is. And I suppose genetically too. They don't like it when people lump them in with the Russians and the Poles."

Dr. Håkansson wrinkled his nose. "They can be a bit fussy, I suppose."

Ulf did not think it fussy to deny a connection with Russia.

"Anyway," the vet continued, "our Estonian friend came in with his dog and asked me to fill in a health clearance form. It was a sort of import document from Colombia, of all places."

"He was sending the dog over to Colombia?"

The vet nodded. "Every so often I have to give a clean bill of health to dogs who are being taken overseas by their owners. You'd be surprised at how many animals travel by air these days. It's quite a business for the airlines. They charge enough, after all."

"I suppose they must," said Ulf. "Those travelling kennels you see must take up a bit of space."

"They do," agreed Dr. Håkansson. "I imagine that sooner or later somebody will introduce business class for dogs." He grinned. "Not really, of course, but it is a thought, isn't it?"

"Yes," said Ulf, smiling weakly. Dr. Håkansson's attempts at humour had always been rather feeble, but Ulf's natural politeness meant that he had to put on a show of being amused.

"It was the usual thing," the vet continued. "The Colombians seem to require pretty much what we ourselves require of any dog being brought into Sweden. Microchipping, for a start. We put a tiny transponder into the scruff of the neck. It's not difficult."

"And?" prompted Ulf.

"And then there's rabies. A dog is far more likely to encounter rabies over there than here, but they still require immunisation if the dog is more than twelve weeks old—which this one was."

"Reasonable enough," said Ulf.

"Yes, of course. And then they asked for treatment for *Echino-coccus multilocularis,* which is our old friend the tapeworm."

Ulf shuddered. If there was a specific tapeworm phobia, then he suspected that he would suffer from it. Dr. Håkansson noticed this and grinned once more. "You don't like the sound of that, do you?"

"No," said Ulf.

The vet reached for a copy of a journal that was lying on his desk. "Oddly enough, there was an article about it in the latest *Veterinary Review.* We call tapeworm infestation *cestodiasis.* You can spot it quite easily—the tapeworm breaks up into segments that look a bit like pieces of rice."

Ulf wanted to change the subject and was about to say something when Dr. Håkansson continued, "They're transmissible, you know. A dog can pass a tapeworm on to a human." He paused as this information sank in.

"Although you're just as likely to get a tapeworm from eating undercooked pork," Dr. Håkansson said. "And they can grow to quite a length."

Ulf looked out of the window. It was Sweden outside, and Sweden was not a place for tapeworms and undercooked pork.

"Yes," said Dr. Håkansson. "Quite a length. Two metres, you know. That was how long the tapeworm was that some American doctors pulled out of a man's mouth—yes, his mouth, because it had lodged in his upper intestine. So they gave it a tug and out it came, all two metres of it. This one was—"

Ulf interrupted him. "Should we dose Martin?" he asked.

"No harm," said the vet. "But there was an interesting thing . . ."

"About tapeworms?"

"No, about this dog I examined. The one I had to sign the papers for."

"Was there something wrong with him?"

The vet shook his head. "No, he was in fine form. A strapping, strong specimen, in fact. No, nothing wrong with him—it was the papers."

"The Colombian form?"

"Yes. You see, there was the main part of the form, where I had to certify that he had been given his immunisations and so on. But there was another bit of paper—one that I don't think the client had intended me to see. But I did."

"And?"

"It was a letter. I saw the heading, underlined at the top. It said 'Species: European Wolf.'"

Ulf absorbed this curious information. Then he said, "But he wasn't."

"No, he wasn't. He was a dog, but ... well, he could pass for a wolf, I suppose. Those huskies look quite like wolves. As do Alsatians and Belgian shepherds. They're probably closer to wolves genetically than many other breeds of dog."

Ulf was silent. He wondered what Dr. Håkansson might be expecting him to do. Had any offence been committed?

Dr. Håkansson now revealed why he had told the story. "I think that this Estonian is defrauding somebody. I think he's selling dogs as wolves."

"To whom?" Ulf asked.

"To a Colombian zoo. Or that's what it looks like."

Ulf sighed. "I suppose I should take note of this professionally."

Dr. Håkansson shuffled some papers on his desk. "That's up to you," he said. "All I know is this: somebody who thinks he's buying a wolf is being sold a dog."

Ulf told the vet that he would discuss the case with colleagues and let him know what their view was. "We can't deal with everything," he said.

"Triage?" asked Dr. Håkansson. "Is that what you people practise?"

"It is," said Ulf. "We assess the social harm—the personal harm too. If it seems serious enough, we'll take steps."

"Hard decisions," the vet said. "The emergency departments in the hospitals do exactly the same, don't they? On a busy night at least. They look after the serious cases while the rest have to wait, or are sent off to see their own doctors in the morning." He paused and looked at Ulf quizzically. "And is this serious enough?"

Ulf thought for a moment. There were any number of attempts at fraud every day of the year. Every second of the day, somewhere in Sweden, there would be somebody receiving an unsolicited telephone call inviting them to change bank accounts or invest in something illusory. Stemming those acts of fraud would be as futile as attempting to hold back an incoming tide. The volume of crimes was just too large. Triage was a regrettable necessity, even for the police.

Ulf addressed the question of seriousness. In one respect, what Dr. Håkansson had told him did not merit further attention. Sharp practices in salesmanship fell well below the threshold of police attention, he felt. There would usually be no intervention in cases of inflated or false commercial claims—the car salesman who failed to mention that a second-hand car had been involved in an accident, the purveyor of designer goods masquerading under a false label, the snake-oil salesman who sold natural remedies that were pharmacologically useless. And yet, thought Ulf, we are not completely powerless. We may not be able to deal with everything, but we could—even if only intermittently—pick up on something and make an example of somebody. This person, whoever he was, who was selling dogs as wolves, was taking advantage of somebody, and if, by sheer chance, his case were to come to police attention—as it just had—then there would be a certain poetic justice in his comeuppance. And then, Ulf thought, we are, after all, the Department of Sensitive Crimes, and it's our duty to look into unusual examples of criminality. Selling a bogus wolf was about as unusual a piece of criminal dealing as one could imagine; although, even as he thought this, he found himself remembering that case of involuntary tattooing that he had investigated a few years earlier, when a couple of rogue graffiti artists had terrorised a small coastal town by seizing isolated nude sunbathers and giving them small tattoos on exposed flesh. That had been so bizarre that even the Department of Sensitive Crimes had found it hard to believe that anybody would do such a thing. And yet that assumption was always to be proved false: people were capable of *anything,* Ulf had decided. There was no limit to the ingenuity of perversity—none at all.

He made his decision. "Give me the details," he said. "I'll look into this."

Dr. Håkansson looked uncertain. "I'm sorry, but I don't have any details. I should have noted his name and address, but he wanted to pay in cash, and I was busy, and . . ."

Ulf made a gesture of helplessness. "In that case—"

Dr. Håkansson interrupted him. "However, I did see something that might help."

Ulf raised an eyebrow. A clue? A piece of paper dropped by mistake? Unlikelier things had happened, in his experience—as in the case of the burglar who, on finding an open register when entering an office building, had signed himself in. That almost defied belief, and yet it had happened—a testament to the power of the impulse to obey officialdom.

"I looked out of the window when he was leaving," said Dr. Håkansson, "and I noticed that he was driving a small commercial van."

Ulf brightened. "You saw the registration number?"

"No," said Dr. Håkansson. "But I did see what was written on the side of the van. There was large lettering. It said something about vintage motorcycles. I forget the precise words, but it was definitely something to do with old bikes. There was a picture of one under the lettering."

"I see," said Ulf. "That definitely helps." There was one more thing. "Can you give me a rough description of the man in question? Age? Height? Colouring? You said he was large."

"Yes. Tall and well built. Not fat—more muscular. Slav-type . . ." His tone became apologetic. "I know they're not meant to be Slavs, but, as I said . . ."

"Yes. All right. Slav-looking. I know what you mean."

Dr. Håkansson frowned. "There was something else. Yes, now that I come to think of it, there was something else."

Ulf waited.

"He had a tattoo on his neck. A small one. Just here." The vet pointed to the side of his neck, just above the line of his collar.

"And what was it of?"

This brought a shrug. "I couldn't make it out. I remember thinking, though, that it was faded and rather indistinct. I remember thinking that perhaps he'd had it done when he was much younger. The ink sometimes runs, doesn't it?"

Ulf said that he thought it did. "But it doesn't matter that you can't remember what the tattoo was. You've given me enough to go on. A tall, well-built man, speaking accented Swedish, with Slav features and a small tattoo on his neck, and something to do with a business that deals in vintage motorcycles. I should be able to find him easily enough."

As he spoke, Ulf was thinking of just how he would set about that. He had a contact in the motorcycle world, and he would ask him.

Dr. Håkansson seemed pleased that something was to be done. "I'm glad this is going to be looked into," he said. "I didn't like that man."

"Well, your instinct was probably right."

Martin had been silent during this conversation, curled up on the examination table, catching up on sleep. Now he awoke and looked up at Ulf expectantly. Dr. Håkansson handed Ulf a small bottle of pills. "Here's a further supply of anti-depressants," he said. "Bring him back in a few weeks' time. In the meantime, lots of exercise . . ."

"Yes, of course."

"And cheerful activity. Throw sticks for him to fetch—that sort of thing."

"I'll try," said Ulf. "But he often just watches the stick and gives a sort of shrug. It's as if he's saying, 'What's the point of fetching sticks?'"

Dr. Håkansson laughed. "That's the question, isn't it? I saw a programme on the television about that—last night, I think. That professor . . ."

"Professor Holgersson?"

"Yes, that programme of his: *What You Should Think*. That's what it's called, isn't it?"

Ulf confirmed this. Professor Holgersson, a well-known Lutheran theologian, was in fact the father of his colleague Carl. His television programme explored topical moral issues and was remarkably popular.

"He was talking about whether we should bother to do anything—whether we should go on," Dr. Håkansson continued. "He discussed meaninglessness."

"And his conclusion?" asked Ulf.

"He said that we should engage with the world even if it all seems futile."

Ulf moved towards the door. "I'd go along with that," he said.

"Oh, and so would I," said Dr. Håkansson. "What's the alternative? Nihilism? Despair?"

"Precisely," said Ulf.

Dr. Håkansson remembered something. He passed another

small box of pills over to Ulf. "I think you should give Martin these too—just in case."

Ulf glanced at the label.

"For tapeworm," said Dr. Håkansson.

"Of course. Just to be on the safe side."

Martin looked up at the vet. His expression was reproachful. Did dogs contemplate pointlessness? Ulf asked himself. Did they think it was worth going on? Of course they did, because a dog would not be aware of any alternative. If you were a dog, you went on, because that was what dogs did. And wolves too. They went on, far away in their forests; they went on with their lupine existence, unaware of the fact that generations ago, their particular forebears made the wrong decision and decided to continue being wolves while others decided to evolve into dogs. That, by contrast, was a very wise decision, Ulf thought. It had brought one branch of the family a free meal ticket for life and a warm place to sleep. It was a great contract, a social contract between man and beast that wolves could only look upon with envy.

Chapter Eleven

ÅNGEST EVERYWHERE

The visit to the vet took place on a Friday evening. Over the weekend that followed, Ulf did very little. He had just received a new issue of an art magazine to which he subscribed, the *Swedish Art Quarterly,* and had set aside most of Saturday morning for the perusal of that. This he did, initially while eating a leisurely breakfast in his apartment, and then over a cup of coffee in his local coffee bar. That coffee bar, the Kafé Pom, was owned by a former Catholic priest, Klas Fransson, with whom Ulf had long been friendly. Klas, a thin, ascetic-looking man, still had about him the air of a priest—that neat, rather particular look of one who is not quite in the human fray but who nonetheless knows exactly what is going on. Klas had left the priesthood because of Leia, a nurse he had met when he was in hospital for the removal of his appendix. Leia had given up nursing to run a small market garden on the outskirts of town. There she grew organic vegetables to supply several thriving vegan restaurants in the city. An understanding bishop had ensured that Klas left the church in good standing, and he was still a regular attender at Mass and a frequent pilgrim to Rome and other Catholic destinations. Leia was not a Catholic but loyally attended church with her husband, sitting in the back row and discreetly doing sudoku puzzles.

Klas greeted Ulf warmly—or at least, in a way that was warm for him: the slightest of smiles, followed by a brief inclination of the head. Ulf did not have to order—Klas knew what he liked, and within a few minutes had delivered Ulf's preferred Saturday coffee, a large, creamy latte, to his table.

"Where's Martin?" Klas enquired.

Ulf explained that Martin was with Mrs. Högfors, who liked to take him to her Pilates session on Saturdays. "It cheers him up," she said. "And the exercise does him good."

Klas glanced at Ulf's magazine. "I've seen that on the news-stands," he said. "I've never seen anybody buy it, but I suppose they must. Arty people and so on, I imagine."

Ulf pointed to the heading of the article he was reading. "No more males," it announced. Klas read it; his expression became pained. He did not reply at first, but eventually he muttered, *"Ångest."*

It was all he needed to say. *Ångest*—angst—was everywhere. Every Swede carried it in his or her soul, people said.

"We're very burdened," said Ulf. "All this *ångest* over every-thing. Just about everyone has it." He thought, suddenly, of an exception, and said, "Except for one or two non-conformists—one or two free souls."

"Name one non-conformist," said Klas, a note of despondency in his voice.

Ulf did not hesitate. "Nils Personn-Cederström."

Klas gave a start. "The writer? That Cederström?"

"Yes. He lives right here in Malmö."

"I know that," said Klas. He looked at Ulf enquiringly. "Do you read him?"

Ulf nodded. "I haven't read everything he writes, but I've read some of the big novels—the ones that get all the attention. The one about elephant hunting in East Africa. I read that. And that other one about the bare-knuckle fighters."

"*Blood on Your Fists?*"

"Yes. I read that." Ulf paused. He was surprised that Klas, with his gentle, priestly manner, should be familiar with these visceral, masculine novels. Of course, people admired what they could never be—you had to take that into account. The scholar-poet worshipped the athlete precisely because that was what he was not. Now he expressed this surprise. "I wouldn't have thought these were your sort of book, Klas."

Klas smiled. "Oh, I enjoy them. I know that it's all invention."

Ulf waited for him to say something more, but Klas had picked up a cloth and was wiping the table next to Ulf's.

"Excuse me, Klas. Invention? Isn't all fiction invention?"

"Yes," Klas replied. "It is. But some novels are more inventive than others. Some authors make up worlds that they know nothing about. Nils Cederström is one of those, in my opinion."

Ulf pressed him. "Why? Why single him out?"

"Because the image he presents is of being a tough, hard-drinking womaniser. Because he makes out that he gets what he wants at whatever cost. Because he claims to be such a bad boy when, in reality, he's a very well-behaved Swede, suffering from *ångest* just like the rest of us—more so, probably, because writers often get a double dose of that."

Ulf laughed. "You speak as if you know him."

Klas's back had been turned as he spoke. Now he turned round to face Ulf. "But I do," he said. "He's my cousin."

Ulf could not think of much to say, so he simply said, "Oh."

"Yes."

"So you know him pretty well."

"You could say that. And I can tell you, Ulf, Nils is a really good man. In fact, he's virtuous—and I use that word advisedly. He practises the virtues—he really does."

Ulf thought about this. He was not sure whether he should ask the question he wanted to ask, but he decided to do so. "Is there anything ... any Achilles heel? Any weakness there?" There must be, he thought. *Everyone,* he told himself, had something of that sort—even if, as he was now prepared to admit, Nils was as nice a man as his cousin portrayed him to be.

Klas replied immediately: "No. And I can say that with complete assurance. You see, Ulf, I was a priest, as you know, and one thing about that training is that you become adept at reading people's character. You just develop a sixth sense about that sort of thing because you encounter all sorts and conditions of men, and you just know. Judges are the same. They develop that ability too. And I can tell you that Nils Cederström is one hundred per cent good. The persona he presents is all nonsense. It's made up by his publicists to sell books. It's as simple as that."

"But if he's such a saint, why does he go along with it? Doesn't that amount to lying?"

Klas put down the cloth with which he had been wiping the table. "I've often thought about that," he said. "And I once even asked him. I was surprised by the answer."

"Which was?"

"He needs the money."

Ulf smiled. "So he's human after all. He's as avaricious as the rest of us."

Klas shook his head. "No. He gives seventy-five per cent of his earnings to a school in northern India. He supports thirty-two boarders there. Dalit children—the lowest of the castes. He supports those kids. Food. Books. Everything." He paused. "And he does good works round here, you know. He funds that mission to skateboarders."

Ulf raised an eyebrow.

"You haven't heard of it?" asked Klas. "It takes teenagers off the street and tries to wean them from their skateboard dependence. It's the most mindless pursuit, skateboarding. It encourages young men to be thoughtless—utterly vacuous, in fact. The mission tries to get them involved in youth clubs and so on. Sports. Football, in particular. And Nils does a lot for them."

Ulf thought about this. It was an object lesson, he thought. One could jump to conclusions only too quickly, and then be shown to be completely wrong. But then he remembered his conversation with the bookseller, Torn. If Nils was not interested in young men, then was he possibly interested in young women?

He looked at Klas. "Tell me, Klas, where do you buy your books from? These Cederström books, for example?"

Klas looked puzzled. "Why?"

"I'm curious," said Ulf. "It's my job to be curious."

"A place called Jens Bokhandel, as it happens."

Ulf nodded. "Torn?"

"Yes, I know Torn."

Ulf decided to be direct. "I'm a bit suspicious of that fellow."

Klas laughed. "Why? There's nothing to be suspicious of. He doesn't actually *do* anything. He sits there writing his PhD thesis on Nabokov. He's been working on it for years."

Ulf waited.

"He's already written a book on Nabokov's style in *Lolita*. It was published in America, apparently. Now he's doing this great big study for his PhD. A complete waste of time, in my view, as nobody's going to read it. I certainly won't."

Ulf was silent. He knew that Klas was utterly truthful. He still considered himself a priest—of sorts—even if he had been released from his vow of chastity. He would not make any of this up, nor even embroider it. So that settled that: Torn and Nils did *not* share any illegal or dubious interests.

"I see," said Ulf. And then he added, "You must be proud of your cousin."

"I am," said Klas. "Immensely proud." He suddenly looked anxious. "I take it that I can rely on you to keep our conversation confidential. I wouldn't want it to get out that Nils isn't what he's made out to be." He looked at Ulf, as if assessing whether further explanation was necessary. It seemed that it was. "That could seriously reduce his earnings, you see, and that would end the support for the Dalit children. It's as simple as that. The press, you see, would have a field day, but they would never care about what happened down the line."

"I can imagine," said Ulf. He had experienced press disregard for the consequences of a disclosure. There were many journalists who were sensitive to that, but there were others for whom all that mattered was the scoop and the forty-point headline. Klas was right: if Nils were to be shown up for what he was, the disappointed readers might desert in droves, and it would be the children, those . . . what was it . . . those thirty-two Dalit children who would suffer. And the skateboarders too.

There was only one thing for Ulf to say. "Don't worry. I give you my word, Klas: I shall not say anything publicly about this."

"Thank you, Ulf," said Klas. "You, too, are a good man."

Ulf gently brushed the compliment aside. "I'm not. Not really. And be careful: you sound as if you're about to call me *my son.*"

"Old habits die hard," said Klas. "But I meant what I said."

Ulf looked away. Good men are embarrassed by being called good men. It is one of the tests of their goodness. Not that Ulf thought that, of course. He was thinking about how he might rescue Nils from the anxiety and distress that blackmail inevitably brought. Suddenly, and rather unexpectedly, this had become a case in which Ulf was emotionally invested. It had never occurred to him that he would actually like Nils Cederström, but now the feelings he had towards him were positive, even warm. He had not expected this, but the barriers, and the saliences, in life are rarely in the place where we expect them to be.

That was Saturday morning. The afternoon was given over to sport, or to the appreciation of sport, as Ulf watched two football matches on the television, one after the other. They were scrappy and inconclusive games, marred by several ill-natured arguments with the referee. That always irritated Ulf, who felt that referees should be granted powers of arrest. If the police were waiting on the lines, and offenders could be seized and marched off to the cells, then there would be none of this bad behaviour, thought Ulf. As it was, these overpaid and over-indulged sportsmen could play to the gallery, parading their egos in displays of arrogance and petulance that held up the game unnecessarily. And as for those who deliberately sought to prolong a match for strategic reasons by feigning injury, they would soon abandon that if referees were allowed to count them out on the ground, just as the umpires of boxing matches could do. They would not have to count up to ten, thought Ulf: three would probably be enough to restore these sham casualties to rude health.

He took Martin out for a walk at the end of the second football match—a draw between an Italian and a Dutch team in an inconsequential league in which Ulf took only a remote interest. "Bad football," he said to Martin, who looked up at him sharply. The dog had obviously lip-read *bad,* one of the words that was definitely in his vocabulary, but had not understood the word *football.* Martin looked dismayed, hanging his head and his tail.

"Sorry, Martin," Ulf apologised. *"Good. Good."* He articulated the word carefully, and he was sure that Martin recognised it. But still the dog looked miserable.

That changed, though, once they were outside and Martin encountered one of his friends, a scruffy terrier that belonged to one of the other tenants in Ulf's apartment block. He and Martin were on good terms, and enjoyed chasing one another for several minutes until interest in the game waned. Ulf exchanged a few words with the terrier's owner, a mild man who liked to talk about local parking issues and very little else.

Then Ulf called in at the supermarket, where he bought some frozen fish, a bag of potatoes, and some broccoli. He would cook all the potatoes, he thought, which would leave some over for lunch the following day. That was an omelette, as it always was on Sundays. I have very little life, he thought. Just this. But then he thought: others have much the same. Anna will be taking the girls to one of their swimming competitions. Her husband, she had once said, liked to talk on his ham radio set to people in other countries. They talked about the weather, for the most part, amidst a lot of static. Why did people bother to contact one another when they had so little to say, and when it was so much easier to send one another emails or messages on an internet forum? Of course people felt a very strong urge to communicate. We had to talk to people because not to do so would imprison us in ourselves.

Anna ... He thought of her so often on a Sunday for some reason, no matter how hard he tried not to do so. I should forget her. I should. And then I could go out and find somebody else, which is what any sensible person would do. I should find somebody else who did not have a husband and two girls. Who could think of me as I now think of Anna. Who could come with me to art exhibitions and then go out for dinner. Who would share something better than an omelette. Who would drive with me in the Saab, out into the country, where we would go for proper walks rather than the slouch I take around the local park. Who might like opera, or flower-arranging, or even both. Who would have a lovely laugh and a sense of humour and who would find Bergman films funny. Who would choose a new sweater for me. Who would hold my hand in bed at night and let my toes touch hers under the cover and make me happy; just that—make me happy.

That was Sunday, or what Sunday might have been in a better world. On Monday morning, Ulf made a point of going into the office early, as he had several matters to attend to, including an absurd report demanded by the head of supplies on the use of ordered items. This meant that anything ordered in the past six months had to be accounted for—either signed off as consumed, as was the case with printer paper, for example, or listed on an inventory as still in use; a USB stick, say, would fall into that category. It was entirely pointless, thought Ulf, but it was part of a new policy, introduced by the Commissioner, and described as "continuing audit." Ulf could have delegated this—it was just the sort of thing that Erik liked to do—but a specific instruction had been given that every section head should file the report personally. It would take at least five hours, Ulf thought, and so he would need to make an early start if he were to accomplish anything else that day.

Ulf had never liked Monday mornings. As a boy, waking up on Monday had always been accompanied by regret for the weekend that had just passed. The weekend represented freedom and all the possibilities that came with freedom. Monday was the opposite of that, made all the worse by the late-afternoon piano lesson that he was obliged to attend. Ulf's mother was determined that both her sons should learn the instrument. Ulf tried, but he never warmed to it and rarely practised enough. This brought sharp reprimands from the piano teacher, who kept a ruler at the end of the keyboard, and would rap his knuckles lightly when he made mistakes. Björn had a natural talent for the piano, and this made it worse for Ulf, whose playing was compared adversely with his brother's, often by Björn himself, who said, "You're really useless, Ulf. Has anybody told you that? Really useless."

In the course of his therapy, Ulf had mentioned these lessons to Dr. Svensson, who had shaken his head with disapproval.

"I can't tell you the number of times," he said, "I've had people in here, sitting right where you're sitting, who have told me about problems with a teacher. Some teachers don't realise just what power they have to discourage, to hurt. It's a very great power that they wield."

"I never practised very much," said Ulf. "And I don't know if I have much of an ear."

"That," said Dr. Svensson, "proves my point. She discouraged you. And then your brother took advantage of that and made you feel even worse."

Ulf said that it was not a great problem. "It was a long time ago," he said. "I don't think about it very much."

"You should," said Dr. Svensson. "You shouldn't bury these things."

"I don't think I've buried it." He stared at Dr. Svensson, who was looking at him in a thoughtful way, as if he was assessing the psychological damage that a ruler-wielding piano teacher might wreak.

"Have you forgiven her?" the therapist asked.

Ulf made an impatient sound. "Of course I have. As I've said, it was a long time ago."

"Well, that's something," said Dr. Svensson. "But forgiveness occurs, you know, at various levels. There's formal forgiveness, articulated as such, but possibly not indicative of real, inner forgiveness. Then there's forgiveness that comes from what we used to call the heart."

Ulf looked up. Was this some new manifestation of political correctness? Was it in some way wrong to refer to the heart? "What we *used to* call the heart? Is it called something different now?"

Dr. Svensson smiled. "No, the heart—the physical organ, that is—that's still called the heart. It's just that its metaphorical use is, I'm sure you'll agree, somewhat old-fashioned."

Ulf pondered this. "So we can't speak from the heart any longer?"

Dr. Svensson inclined his head. "Alas, no."

"Nor suffer from a broken heart?"

"That, too, is a misleading metaphor. A broken heart . . ." The psychotherapist made a gesture of helplessness. "A broken heart would not beat for long, would it?"

Ulf closed his eyes. He reminded himself that he was not paying for this—that his therapy sessions, previously a drain on his own pocket, were now being covered by the Police Benevolent Fund, a body that had discretion to provide extra support for serving members of the force. This had been at the suggestion of Dr. Svensson, who had discovered Ulf's eligibility for subsidised therapy and had encouraged him to apply. "It takes the pressure off everybody," Dr. Svensson said. "You, me—we don't feel that we have to rush anything."

Ulf was about to point out that it might take the pressure off the two of them, but it did so simply by transferring it elsewhere. But he did not; he felt a certain sympathy for Dr. Svensson, who must be aware, he thought, of just how strange it was that people like him should pay good money simply to rehearse their anxieties. Did Dr. Svensson ever make anybody actually feel *better,* or did he simply make them feel *more complicated?*

"I don't want to go on about the heart . . . ," Ulf began.

"By all means. Talk about the heart if that's what you want to talk about. Don't suppress these things."

Ulf looked up at the ceiling, which was painted in a light shade of green. Green was meant to be a restful colour, he thought, and that must be why Dr. Svensson had chosen it for his consulting-room ceiling. Presumably people looked up at his ceiling a lot, and he would want them to feel calmed. There were some ceilings that were definitely not calming, possibly because they said too much. A ceiling should not be strident, thought Ulf. The Sistine Chapel ceiling, for instance, said rather too much, beautiful though it may be in a Catholic sort of way. Ulf liked Protestant ceilings, which, as a rule, were less vocal.

"Do you think," Ulf mused, "that the Pope has an ornate bathroom? Particularly his bathroom ceiling—do you think that it has a fresco of some sort? Perhaps John the Baptist immersing people . . ."

Dr. Svensson was looking at him over the rim of his half-moon spectacles. "I don't think we should be discussing the Pope," he said. "It's infantile to speculate about the Pope's bathroom, you know."

Ulf felt a growing irritation. "And we shouldn't allow the inner infant to express himself?" I can talk the psychoanalytical talk, he thought.

Dr. Svensson made a conciliatory gesture. "Of course we should. And I shouldn't have stopped you talking about the Pope—if that's what you want to do."

But the moment had passed, and Ulf shook his head. "No," he said. "I don't." He sounded petulant, he thought, but he had nothing more to say about the Pope's bathroom.

Now, on that Monday morning, he made his way into the café opposite the office and ordered a latte. The barista was the difficult young man whom Ulf suspected of harbouring feelings for Anna. They greeted one another politely, but without warmth. As the young man heated the milk for Ulf's coffee, he turned and said, "Good weekend?"

Ulf replied politely. "Average. Nothing much happened."

Then the barista continued, "See Anna?"

Ulf frowned. Why would he ask that? Did he suspect something? He hesitated before replying, "Why would I see her over the weekend?"

The young man was still dealing with the milk and spoke to Ulf over his shoulder. "We often see our friends over the weekend, don't we?"

"She's a colleague," Ulf snapped. "It's different."

The barista turned round and flashed a smile. Ulf noticed his teeth, which were perfectly regular—like the teeth of an American who's spent his childhood wired into a brace. These were not *European* teeth. And the whiteness against the tanned skin of the young man's face . . . Ulf felt his stomach tighten. What if Anna were to have eyes for this young man because of his teeth and the regularity of his features and his ridiculously slim hips? What chance would there be for him, even if people assured him that he had weathered well and looked a good ten years younger than he really was?

"Sure, it's different," said the young man. And then, with a smile that Ulf felt could only be described as conspiratorial, he went on, "I think she likes you."

Ulf struggled to control himself. "Of course we like one another," he said, his voice even. "We work together. It would hardly be easy if we didn't like one another." He paused. "I take it that you like the people you work with."

"Yes, of course. But not like as in . . . you know, *like*."

Ulf took a deep breath. "I don't like this," he muttered. Then he leaned forward and said, "I'd prefer it if you wouldn't say that sort of thing."

The young man froze. He stared at Ulf in disbelief. Then, his voice wavering, he said, "I wasn't suggesting anything, you know. I was just trying to—"

Ulf cut him short. "Good," he said. "Because there's nothing to suggest."

He took the cup of coffee that was passed over to him. He noticed that the barista's hand was shaking. Ulf hesitated. He leaned over the counter again. "Look," he said, "I'm sorry I spoke rather sharply just now. I felt that you were straying a bit into personal affairs. That's all."

The young man looked relieved. "All right. No harm done."

"And, as I said, there's nothing there. Nothing to comment on."

"Of course not. Of course."

Ulf nodded. The conversation was over, and now he made his way to his usual table. Somebody had left a copy of the morning paper, and he settled down to read this. A large hole had opened up in a South American city and a picture of this dominated the paper's front page. Several cars had toppled over the edge and into the hole; a cluster of policemen looked down into it. It would be yet another thing for the people of that city to bear, thought Ulf; along with poverty, and floods, and bad government. There were no large holes in Sweden. We were so lucky.

His name had been uttered. Somebody was addressing him. He looked up, dragging himself away from the South American hole. Blomquist was lowering himself into the chair on the other side of the table.

"Good morning, Blomquist." Ulf tried to make himself sound as if he was pleased to see his colleague. He had wanted some quiet time—time to read the paper and to think about things over his steaming latte; that possibility was now excluded.

Blomquist launched straight into a mention of his aunt. "You may remember I told you about my aunt," he began. "The one who goes over to Florida a lot."

Ulf nodded. "I think I remember." He tried to recall what was wrong with Blomquist's aunt: Was it high glucose levels or a fungal infection of the toenails—or was that Blomquist who had complained of those conditions?

"Well, she has a place over there. A house in a place called Clearwater. You know where that is?"

Ulf tried to envisage a map of Florida. "On the left-hand side?" he said.

"Precisely," said Blomquist. "There's a place called Naples there, and Clearwater. I've never been there, although she's invited me. I'll have to go someday, but I may have to go without my wife. She hates flying. Some people do, you know. They seize up. They find it hard even to climb the steps up to the aircraft."

"That's a pity," said Ulf. "Your wife would probably like it over there."

"She would. But then she wouldn't be able to settle down to enjoy the holiday because she'd be worrying about the return flight."

"No, I don't suppose she would." Ulf was wondering where this conversation was heading. It was hard to tell with Blomquist, and it was always possible that it was heading nowhere.

He glanced at the newspaper again, and thought of the people in the *barrio* in which the hole had suddenly appeared.

Blomquist's eye followed Ulf's gaze. "I heard about that on the radio," he said. "That's a sinkhole."

Ulf looked up. "I feel sorry for those poor people."

"Yes," said Blomquist. "That's probably caused by illegal mining."

"Really?"

"Yes. People dig for gold there, they said. They're not meant to, but they do anyway."

Because they have nothing, thought Ulf. If you have nothing, and there's the faintest possibility of finding gold, then you would do anything to achieve that. That's what he would do if he were in their position—there was no doubt in his mind about it.

Blomquist was back in Florida. "That aunt of mine—I heard from her over the weekend. She wrote me a long email. She's found out how to dictate directly into her email programme and so she writes quite long messages to me now."

"Oh yes?"

"Yes. And this weekend she told me about her neighbour out there. He comes from Chicago, apparently, but he loves going down to Florida, even in the summer. Some people don't mind the heat. I do, of course, but a lot of people say that the hotter it gets, the better it is for them."

"Not me," said Ulf. "I've never liked the heat."

"No," said Blomquist. "I get this condition called prickly heat. You know about that?"

Ulf looked away.

"It's fungal, actually. Fungus likes sweaty folds of flesh. You treat it with a fungicidal cream, although you should wash and dry the relevant area first. You have to do that."

"Please, Blomquist!" Ulf protested.

"No, perhaps we shouldn't go there," said Blomquist. "Anyway, this neighbour of my aunt—the one in Florida—was attacked by an alligator, apparently. He liked to go diving, and an alligator took him. They found one of his flippers with a large chunk missing from it."

"I'm sorry to hear that," said Ulf.

"My aunt was very upset."

"I'm not surprised."

"She said you don't expect to hear that people you know have been eaten by alligators."

Ulf thought that this was probably true. Being eaten by an alligator was definitely a fate that befell other people—particularly if you were Swedish. He looked at his watch. "Look, Blomquist, I must keep an eye on the time. I like hearing about your aunt, but there's work to do."

"Of course," said Blomquist quickly. "But I must give you some information. I had a word with the waitress—not the one we spoke to, but the other one—the one who knew the doctor and his girlfriend."

Ulf waited. Blomquist did go on and on, but in spite of all that, he was essentially a very effective, methodical policeman.

"Yes," prompted Ulf. "And?"

"This other waitress," Blomquist continued, "is called Kristina. She comes from Stockholm originally, but her mother's Norwegian. Kristina wants to be a model. She works in the café to keep body and soul together. Breaking into modelling is not easy, apparently."

Ulf said that this did not surprise him. "But . . ." He tried to steer the conversation back to Jo and the young woman; however, Blomquist had more to say about modelling.

"It's the casting couch problem, you know. The agents are in a pretty powerful position when it comes to deciding who gets the shoots. And they can be sleazy, you know."

"I bet they can," said Ulf. It was best, he decided, to let Blomquist say what he wanted to say, and then gently guide the discussion back onto more productive tracks.

"My cousin knows this girl—she's just a girl, really. Seventeen, eighteen . . . and she went for an audition, and this sleazebag with a toupee said that he'd give her the job if she'd come and have dinner at his place."

Ulf sighed. He had once spent four months attached to the vice squad and he had not enjoyed it. Depravity was ubiquitous, insidious, and infinitely depressing. Sex was an itch, a constant distracting itch that complicated everything. And yet it was, he feared, the spark that drove humanity.

"You know what she did? This girl said, 'Give me the job first, and then we can have dinner after the photo shoot.' Sleaze didn't like that, but he agreed, because she winked at him as she spoke and he interpreted that as a clear sign. So he signed her up and she did the shoot—modelling clothes for some big label or other."

"And the dinner?" asked Ulf.

Blomquist smiled. "She turned up, but with her mother. She said she thought he wouldn't mind."

Ulf chuckled. "She'll go far, that girl."

"Yes, she did. Apparently, she got lots of work after that—none from Sleaze himself, but that didn't matter because her career was launched."

"A nice story," said Ulf. "But what about . . ."

"Kristina? Well, she's still hoping that something will turn up."

"You spoke to her about the doctor?"

Blomquist felt in his pocket and took out a small notebook. "Do you know these pocketbooks?" he asked. "They're called Moleskine. Funny name, but they have this elastic strap, you see, that keeps the cover in place. See? I've been using them for some time now; I like them very much."

"Yes, yes," said Ulf.

Blomquist opened his notebook. "Yes, here we are. Lovisa Andersen. That's what she's called. She's a travel agent."

"And did you find out anything else?"

Blomquist looked at his notes. "I found out where she worked. And . . ." He paused. "I found out that she and Jo are having an affair. Kristina used a very vulgar expression to describe what was going on."

"I've heard these things before," said Ulf dryly.

"That may be," Blomquist said, "but I don't like language like that. It's not Swedish."

Ulf stared at Blomquist. He was not sure whether this was a joke. Swedes swore, just as everybody else did. And yet Blomquist was unsmiling.

"We used to treat one another well in this country," Blomquist continued. "Remember?"

Ulf inclined his head. Blomquist was right. Things had changed in Sweden. "I know what you mean."

"Swearing is an act of discourtesy," Blomquist said. "It's aggressive. And Sweden is not about aggression."

Ulf nodded. "You're right, Blomquist. I don't like it. I never have."

"But most of our colleagues swear," said Blomquist. "Even the Commissioner. I heard him once. Not very loudly—under his breath, really, but he did swear."

"He must be under considerable stress," Ulf said. "Being Commissioner can't be easy." He thought: Being *anybody* could not be easy, and so that, in itself, was no excuse for intemperate language. But that was not the point. The point was that Kristina had confirmed what they had expected to be the case, and had given them the information to enable them to get further confirmation, if that were to be needed.

He wondered whether he should go to see Lovisa. What was the point of that? It occurred to him that if he were to see her, then he might have an idea of what Jo's intentions were. That was something he imagined Anna would be interested to find out. Anna might want the full, sorry story in all its details: the location of the love nest, the frequency of trysts, and so on. He wanted to find that out himself: he wanted to know the full extent of Jo's infidelity because Jo was his rival, and every bit of information he had about his disloyalty made Ulf feel better about his previously impermissible feelings towards Anna. He had to know.

But he would go to see Lovisa unaccompanied. He was grateful to Blomquist for his help, but there were some situations that were so sensitive that the presence of somebody like Blomquist would be a hindrance. Even as he thought this, he felt guilty. Blomquist was a good man—a slightly trying one, perhaps—but fundamentally well disposed. Excluding him would be the equivalent of cold-shouldering a country-bumpkin cousin out of concern as to what one's urban sophisticate friends might think of one's association with such a person. It would be disloyal.

He turned to Blomquist. "I think we should go to see this young woman."

Ulf's suggestion was well received. "Whenever you like," he said.

The travel agency in which Lovisa Andersen worked was sand-wiched between a bank and a shop that sold vitamins and other health products. It was in a quiet street, and Ulf was able to park his Saab more or less directly outside the agency's window, which proclaimed, *Escape Journeys: Your Route to the Sun.*

"I know that place," said Blomquist, nodding in the direction of the health store. "I was in it last week."

Ulf switched off the ignition. "Oh yes? You get your vitamin D there?"

"No," said Blomquist. "I buy my vitamin D in bulk, by post. There's a place in Germany that does it much more cheaply, you know." He paused. "I could give you the address, Varg."

Ulf thanked him. "Maybe later," he said.

"I get my coenzyme Q10 here," said Blomquist. "And a new saw palmetto combination. It's been getting a lot of attention recently."

Ulf suppressed an inward sigh. "Saw palmetto?"

"For the prostate. You know. Prostate issues."

Ulf sighed audibly. This brought a look of concern from Blomquist. "Do you have prostate issues?"

Ulf shook his head. "Not yet. Touch wood."

"Because so many people do sooner or later," Blomquist continued. "It usually comes on a bit later—when you're in your fifties or sixties. But some people get them way earlier. My cousin, for instance. He had prostate trouble at thirty-one."

"I'm sorry to hear that."

"Yes. He's an airline pilot and it was pretty inconvenient. He couldn't rush off to the men's room during take-off, could he?"

"No," said Ulf. "I suppose not."

"I told him about saw palmetto. I bought him some."

Ulf waited. The problem with Blomquist's stories was that you wanted to hear what happened, no matter how irrelevant or long-winded they were. This airline pilot cousin, for instance: Would he have to find another job? Could the co-pilot take over in the middle of take-off or landing?

"Is there always a co-pilot?" asked Ulf. "If your cousin has to go, can he just hand over to the co-pilot?"

Blomquist explained that it depended on the plane. A small plane—a twelve-seater, for example—could be piloted single-handed; anything larger might require a co-pilot.

"Saw palmetto really helped him," Blomquist said. "He was sceptical at first, but then he told me that after a couple of weeks he could do a whole flight without going."

Ulf said nothing.

"I don't have prostate issues myself," said Blomquist. "I had an examination, you know, where the doctor—"

Ulf interrupted him. "Yes, yes, Blomquist. I know all about that sort of thing. You don't have to tell me."

Blomquist laughed. "You aren't squeamish, are you?"

Ulf felt the back of his neck getting warm. "No, I'm not squeamish. I just think that there are some things we like to hear about, and some ... well, there are some things that are private."

Blomquist looked offended. "I know where the lines are, Ulf ..."

"Do you? Sometimes I wonder, Blomquist." Ulf paused. He should spell it out to Blomquist—it would be more honest to do so.

"You see, Blomquist," he continued, "vitamin D deficiency is one thing, but prostate issues are another."

"There's a connection between vitamin D and prostate health," interjected Blomquist. "I read about it. There's evidence."

Ulf persisted. "Blomquist, people don't want to hear about other people's bowels."

"The prostate's nothing to do with the bowels."

"I didn't say it was. It's just that anything down there tends to be private. It's just the way it is."

Blomquist spoke defensively. "But that's the problem, isn't it? If men won't talk about these issues, then they won't seek medical advice, will they? So they let symptoms go uninvestigated."

Ulf reached for the door handle. "We should go in," he said. "I don't think we should be sitting out here, talking about the prostate."

"You raised the subject."

Ulf raised his voice. "No, I did not," he replied. "You did, Blomquist. You started talking about saw palmetto."

"I was just telling you—that's all. You don't need to take my advice if you don't want to. But there's no harm in giving it to you."

Ulf sought to lower the temperature of the exchange. "I'm sorry. Let's forget it," he said. "We need to go and talk to this Lovisa Andersen."

"Are we just going to stroll in and interrogate her?" asked Blomquist. "Won't that seem a bit odd?"

Ulf pointed at the painted window. "*Escape Journeys: Your Route to the Sun.* We're potential clients." He smiled. "We might bear Icarus in mind, of course."

Blomquist frowned. "Icarus."

"He flew too close to the sun. He secured his wings with wax, and it melted." He looked apologetic. "I was just thinking out loud."

"I've heard of him," said Blomquist.

Ulf felt a pang of embarrassment, of shame. You did not flaunt your knowledge.

"He just crossed my mind," said Ulf. "That's why I mentioned him."

Blomquist nodded. He looked awkward. "What are you going to say?"

Ulf shrugged. "I'll think of something."

They entered the agency. There were two desks in the room, one occupied by a young man wearing large horn-rimmed spectacles. Lovisa sat at the other. Ulf recognised her immediately.

She looked up and smiled. "Good morning."

Ulf returned the greeting and gestured to the chairs in front of her desk. "May we?"

"Of course."

She waited until they were seated. Then she smiled again and said, "So? What may I do to help you?"

"I'm interested in getting away somewhere," said Ulf. "Somewhere warm."

Lovisa glanced at Blomquist. Ulf realised that she was assessing the relationship. "Just me," he said. "Not my friend."

"I'm staying here," Blomquist volunteered. "I never go anywhere."

Lovisa seemed uncertain as to how to react to this. Was he trying to be funny? Or did he mean it? She smiled weakly. "If everyone were like you, I'd be out of a job." She turned to Ulf. "And where in particular? Have you any views?"

Ulf shrugged. "I love Italy. Sicily, perhaps." He paused. "Haven't we met before?"

Lovisa frowned. "Have we? I'm sorry, I—"

Ulf cut her short. "With Jo? Was it with Jo?"

The effect was immediate. Lovisa had been holding a ballpoint pen, and she now put this down sharply. Ulf saw, too, that she was blushing.

"I'm not sure," she stuttered. "Possibly . . ."

"I think it was," Ulf continued. "I haven't seen him for a few weeks. How is he?"

Lovisa glanced at her colleague. The young man returned her look, and then shifted his gaze to Ulf. He looked disapproving. Ulf noticed his stare; it irritated him.

"He . . . ," Lovisa began, and then her voice faltered. "He . . ."

"He's not ill, is he?" asked Ulf.

This question was greeted with silence.

Ulf reached into his pocket and took out the earring that Anna had passed on to him. He held it lightly between thumb and forefinger. Lovisa's gaze went to it, and stayed focused on it. Then she suddenly stood up. She looked flustered. "Please excuse me," she stuttered.

Ulf raised his hands in concern. "I'm sorry," he said. "I'm sorry if I've upset you. I'm terribly sorry."

Lovisa said nothing, but swept past Ulf and Blomquist towards a door at the side of the room. She fumbled with the handle, and then retreated into a further office. The door slammed shut behind her.

The young man at the other desk had now risen to his feet. He took a few steps towards the door though which Lovisa had gone, appeared to think better of it, and turned to face Ulf.

"She's very upset," he said, his voice heavy with reproach.

Ulf felt as if he were being accused of gross insensitivity. His irritation with the young man increased. He made a protestation of innocence. "Look," he said, his voice raised. "I just asked after her boyfriend. That's all. Obviously there's something . . ."

The young man sighed. "They've split up," he said, and then added a rhetorical "Haven't they?"

Ulf snapped back at him. "How was I to know that?"

The young man continued to speak in an accusing tone. "It's over with Jo. She's taking it very badly. Everybody knows that."

Blomquist intervened. "He ended it? His wife found out?"

The young man, scarcely concealing his impatience, threw Blomquist a glance. "Yes, he ended it. Obviously."

"Not obviously," interjected Ulf.

The young man looked away. "I don't know anything about his wife. But he ended it—and that's why she's so upset. What can you expect?"

Ulf stood up. "I think we should go."

Blomquist stood up too.

"She might just be a moment," said the young man. "I'll go and check up on her."

"No," said Ulf. "I'll come back some other time. Tell her I'm very sorry."

"Yes," said Blomquist. "Me too." He threw the young man what looked like a warning glance.

Once outside, they walked in silence to the Saab. As Ulf started the car, he remarked to Blomquist, "That doesn't really change anything."

"Pain in the neck, that fellow," muttered Blomquist.

"He's young," said Ulf. "He'll learn." He thought: I was just like that.

"With his stupid glasses," Blomquist went on. "Sitting there. Pleased with himself." He coughed. "I'm developing laryngitis," he said. "I can feel it coming on. I'm going to have to take aloe vera. My immune system . . ."

"Rest your throat," said Ulf. "Don't speak for a while."

Blomquist ignored the advice. "It confirms that they were having an affair, though."

Ulf agreed. "Yes. It puts that beyond doubt, I'd say."

Blomquist looked thoughtful. "So, what are you going to do?"

"Tell her, I suppose."

Blomquist shook his head. "Why do people make life complicated for themselves—especially when it comes to sex?"

The Saab pulled out into the road. Ulf wondered how to answer Blomquist's question. The supposition behind it was not something with which he would argue. People did complicate their lives, and yes, much of this complication had to do with sex; but as to why so many people found it difficult to avoid such complications, he was not at all sure. Perhaps it was weakness—we were weak, and in the face of the dark, anarchic forces of sex, this weakness became powerlessness. Look at me, Ulf thought. I fall for people, just as everyone else does, but I fall in the wrong place. Not only were there his feelings for Anna, but from time to time he had feelings for others, and these women were usually just as unattainable.

In retrospect, he felt bad about having shown Lovisa the earring. That had been unkind; it had been unnecessary, and he felt dirtied by the act, which now seemed to him like an act of bullying. And yet, it had confirmed what needed to be confirmed, and he reminded himself that Lovisa had entered into a relationship with a married man. She had known he had a wife and a family, and presumably she had not cared. In such circumstances, she surely had no reason to complain if her feelings were upset when she was confronted with the evidence of her wrongdoing. He tried to suppress his feelings of guilt, but it was hard. Perhaps I'm just too sensitive to be in the Department of Sensitive Crimes, Ulf thought.

Chapter Twelve

RELATED TO WOLVES

U lf was back in the office shortly after eleven. He found himself
alone, as Erik was on a training course and both Anna and
Carl were at an all-day interdepartmental meeting. There were several new files on his desk, placed there by Erik, whose job it was to
receive new reports, log them into the system, and then put them
on Ulf's desk according to his assessment of their urgency. Ulf
glanced at the notes that Erik had penned on the front of each file:
*Unusual assault (biting of ear of American consular official by mem-
ber of the Swedish–American Friendship League); Theft of culturally
sensitive property from university department; Placing of stones in
windsock of regional airport.* Ulf raised an eyebrow over the last of
these; Erik had put it at the bottom of the pile, deeming it to be the
least urgent, but Ulf wondered if he understood the seriousness
of what had been done. If you interfered in that way with a windsock, it would mean that an incoming pilot might assume there
was no wind. This was potentially an act of terrorism, and those
leapfrogged over everything else in the Commissioner's eyes. But
on top of these three files was the folded page of a newspaper with
several red lines drawn down the margin. In Erik's handwriting

was the scribbled message: *I heard you talking about Cederström—have you seen this?*

Ulf picked up the newspaper. A photograph of Nils Cederström dominated the page. He was pictured sitting in a bar, a martini glass in front of him. Opposite him, a man with a large unkempt beard appeared to be arguing a point with the author. The headline, in large type, proclaimed: *Cederström, the truth behind the image.* Ulf read on.

Ever since he burst upon the Swedish literary scene ten years ago, hard-drinking author, Nils Cederström, has impressed his readers with his larger-than-life antics. Cederström recently returned from a trip to Kenya, where he was reputedly thrown out of the Muthaiga Country Club, once headquarters of the legendary Happy Valley set. Cederström was shown the door of the exclusive watering hole after he became too friendly towards the wife of a member of the committee, a prominent safari operator. Neither appreciated it, and from Cederström's side there was certainly little regret. "Do I deny any wrongdoing?" said Nils in an interview with the local paper. "Certainly not. Nothing wrong with wrongdoing!"

Readers may look forward to a frank and explosive exposure of the reality behind this literary streetfighter's colourful lifestyle. In this newspaper next week! Order your copy now!

Ulf re-read the article, dwelling on the breathless phrases. What, he wondered, was meant by "a frank and explosive exposure"? Would this reveal previously unknown episodes—more fights and arguments and episodes of hard drinking—or would it be something fundamentally new? And what might that be? He considered the possibilities. Something new about Cederström would have to be something unexpected. And what would one *not* expect about the apparently ill-behaved author? Good behaviour? That would certainly be a surprise for the readers of the newspaper. After all, nobody was ever thrown out of the Muthaiga

Country Club for behaving *well*. Or could it be that the journalist behind this article had something particularly shocking—
something that went beyond the normal litany of provocations
that seemed to form the mood music of Cederström's life? Ulf pondered this. It would be sexual, he thought: it had to be. Anything
less would just be too tame to merit the description *explosive*. Or
political, of course. What if Cederström had joined the Moderate
Extremists, or even the Extreme Moderates, a party which, in spite
of its misleading name, was known for its inflammatory extrem-
ism? He considered that possibility, but quickly dismissed it. No, it
would be something more salacious than that: it would be a story
of infidelity, weakness, or downright tawdriness. That is what the
public wanted to read about, and that, in essence, is what public
figures obligingly gave them. Nemesis must love these people, he
thought. She was watching, her radar set, sending out the signals
that would detect ordinary human weakness every bit as easily
as they would reveal lofty instances of hubris. This is what had
happened here; he was sure of it.

He put down the newspaper and was about to toss it into the
bin when he stopped himself. If he could get the journalist who'd
written the article to tell him what it was that they'd discovered . . .
He checked the column again, and saw the name: Åke Holmberg.
A man, then; although one had to be so careful these days not to
mis-gender or make general statements based on male pronouns;
he had been obliged to attend a gender awareness workshop in
which these sensitivities were laid bare. Of course, journalists were
wary about informal conversations with detectives, and he knew
that even if he managed to find out what the gravamen of the
charges against Nils were, he would not be given any information
about the source. That did not matter: if he found out about Nils's
weak point, it would be easier for him to work out who was blackmailing him over it.

He lifted up the phone and dialled the general office of the newspaper. Yes, there was an Åke Holmberg who worked on the paper. Yes, he was in the building somewhere, but he was not answering his extension.

"He's not in trouble?" asked the receptionist; Ulf had revealed that he was phoning from the police department. "Åke is a bit fragile at the moment and I don't think we'd want him put under any pressure. It's hard enough for journalists these days without any extra demands."

"It must be," said Ulf. "And no, Åke's not in any trouble."

The receptionist sounded relieved. "Good," she said, "because I told him, you know, that he was sailing a bit close to the wind. I know he needs the money, but—" She broke off, obviously realising she had already said too much. Some people were like that, thought Ulf: they blurted out the first thing that came to mind without regard to consequences. He did not like the term *motormouth,* but somehow it expressed things quite accurately.

Ulf made a mental note of this unexpected revelation. What was Åke Holmberg up to? he wondered. Increasingly it seemed to him that *everybody* was sailing a bit close to the wind. The Sweden of his youth was an upright place, stiffened by a Lutheran code, firmly committed to a vision of a society that was egalitarian and supportive. Something had happened to that, and now you could make no assumptions as to the values that people would profess. Well, they had been all but exhausted by now, and all you had to do was to shake a tree and all sorts of things would fall out of the branches, including mixed metaphors.

He decided that he might try to find out more about the journalist. "Good old Åke," he said, breaking into a laugh as he spoke. "Always on the scrounge."

"Well, I wouldn't call it that," said the voice. "He didn't run up the debts himself, remember."

"Of course not," said Ulf. And then he added, as a long—and rather wild—shot, "What was her name again?"

"Frieda. That's the new one, of course. Åke's wife was ... I forget, actually. It was so long ago."

"I never knew her," said Ulf, truthfully. He thought: This woman can't resist talking. She's a gift—a real gift.

"A real shrew. Moan, moan, moan."

Ulf felt sorry for Åke. "He put up with a lot, I hear."

"Yes. Serious stuff. You know something? There are people—and I'm not one of them, I can tell you—who think that he may have ... how shall I put it? ... not been entirely uninvolved in the accident." There was a pause, during which Ulf reflected on the fact that the woman on the other end of the line was a total stranger. They had not met, and she had no idea who he was, and yet here she was entrusting him with defamatory gossip of the worst kind. Unless, of course, it was all true, which was also possible.

"I'd never heard that," he said. "And people can say the most extraordinary things. They must have looked into the accident pretty thoroughly—they always do, don't they?"

The reply came swiftly. "Not in this case. I would have looked at the electrical connections."

Ulf struggled. Electrical connections?

"Not a nice way to go," he said.

"Awful. I can't imagine anything worse, frankly."

He thought very carefully about what he would say next. "The machine itself ... ," he began.

"The blender?"

I would never have thought of that, he said to himself, and smiled. A two-way conversation could go on for a long time before one party realised that the other knew nothing about what was being discussed. But his smile faded: it must have been a very unpleasant affair.

"Yes, the blender," Ulf said, wondering whether he had heard correctly. "Just thinking of it makes my blood run cold."

"Same here," said the receptionist. And then, "Look, there's another call coming through. Do you want to leave a message for Åke?"

"No, I'll drop by," said Ulf. "Will he be in for the next couple of hours?"

He would, she said, and Ulf made up his mind. This was the most promising lead to date, and he would make as much use of it as he could. The newspaper offices were not far away, well within walking distance, and it was a perfect afternoon for a stroll.

He met Åke Holmberg in the front office of the newspaper. The journalist appeared from a side door after Ulf had waited for no longer than a few minutes, during which he had browsed the latest copy of the newspaper, displayed, page by page, on a large noticeboard.

"Old-fashioned, isn't it?" said a voice behind him.

Ulf turned round to see a man in his mid-thirties, with hair already greying at the temples. His features were regular, though perhaps a little bony, which gave him a slightly hungry look. His clothing was functional, best described as the "smart casual" of invitations: black jeans with short turn-ups, and a shirt with a very faint green check and a button-down collar. A linen jacket, navy blue in colour, completed the look. It was an outfit that would not have disgraced an up-and-coming architect or designer, but also seemed just right for a popular columnist.

Ulf introduced himself. He pointed to the displayed pages. "Old-fashioned because it's actual print?"

Åke nodded. "It's extraordinary to think that there are still people who want to read physical media. Most people get their news electronically these days, but somehow newspapers like this survive."

"For which I, for one, am grateful," said Ulf. "But then I might be old-fashioned myself."

He noticed Åke running an eye over his clothing.

"Not necessarily," said Åke. "I know some very radical figures who still insist on reading the physical paper. A lot of them, in fact. It's to do with the tactile experience."

Ulf pointed to an article he had been reading that bore Åke Holmberg's by-line. Its subject was the rapid growth of a new biotech company. "You have a wide remit," he said. "Biotechnology, the arts, finance . . . How do you do it?"

Åke shrugged. "You get the facts. You acquire a basic knowledge of the issue. Then you write."

"And that's it?"

"More or less. It's rather like filling a car with fuel. The facts are the petrol. You fill the tank and then you use the fuel in the writing of the article. After that, it's gone, and you fill up with more facts. You forget most of what you learn."

As they spoke, Ulf became aware of Åke's barely concealed glances. He felt a slight embarrassment, as he always did when he thought he was being looked at. What was the nature of Åke's interest? It was hard to tell.

"I like your jacket."

Åke's compliment was sudden and unexpected. Most men did not compliment one another on their clothing within a few minutes of an initial meeting unless there was a reason.

Then Åke said, "I've got one exactly the same as that."

So that was why he'd said it, Ulf decided. "Good choice on your part," he remarked.

Åke smiled. "Not me. My wife chose it."

Ulf responded cautiously. "Your wife? I heard that you lost your wife. I'm so sorry about that. Your receptionist mentioned it."

Åke looked at him sharply. "Elena? She told you that?"

"Yes."

"She never draws breath, that woman."

Ulf laughed. "She was fairly chatty, I must admit."

"Yes, I did lose my wife. She was electrocuted."

Ulf winced. "I'm so sorry."

"Thank you. It was a faulty kettle."

Ulf said nothing. He could check on this anyway; there would be a police report to which he would have access. But he did not think that Åke was making anything up. It was Elena, obviously, who had things wrong.

Åke now said, "Your name, by the way: Did I hear it correctly? Ulf Varg?"

Ulf nodded. "Yes, I know," he said, and affected a sigh of resignation.

The sigh made Åke smile again. "Where did you get it? Wolf Wolf. Somewhat unusual, you must admit."

"Where does anybody get their name?" replied Ulf, and then answered his own question. "As a boy, my father used to have his leg pulled about being called Varg—or so he used to say. Then he said that he became used to it and ended up liking it. He used to say to me, 'We're related to a pack of wolves, you know.'"

"Hah!"

"And," continued Ulf, "I remember believing that. When I was a young boy, I remember I actually thought that my great-grandfather was a wolf."

Åke laughed. "How odd."

"Yes, it was. But children believe all sorts of odd things, don't they?"

"Oh, they do." Åke looked at his watch. "Look, I was about to go out to lunch. I have to be back at two-thirty for an editorial conference, but there's a place near here where we can pick up a sandwich or a salad. Something light. Would you be interested?"

Ulf said that he would, and they left the reception hall of the newspaper together. As they began to walk along the pavement, Ulf continued the conversation that they had just started. "Yes, I actually believed we had wolves somewhere in the family. I suppose I had read something about it, or I had listened to the usual stories. 'Little Red Riding Hood,' for example."

"'Peter and the Wolf,' of course. Or 'Romulus and Remus,'" said Åke. "I remember I had that story in a book I loved when I was about six. I believed they had really existed."

Ulf said, "That statue . . . Isn't there a famous statue somewhere? Of the wolf and the two infants?"

"There is," said Åke. "And I can tell you what it's called. The *Capitoline Wolf.* It's a big bronze. Etruscan. The wolf herself is pretty ancient; the figures of the two boys are a later addition." He made a self-deprecatory gesture. "That was something I had to look up the other day. We have a column in the paper that answers people's questions. My colleagues and I take it in turns to write it. It was my turn last week. I had to answer that one—about the statue—that's how I know about the addition of the two children."

"You'd think people could just look it up online," Ulf said. "The answer would be there, surely."

"They could. But they want to see their name in print, I suppose. Or they're looking for things to do . . . There are an awful lot of people, Ulf . . ." He said the name hesitantly, as if it might be booby-trapped. "There are an awful lot of people who believe in things that you and I would find just inconceivable. They believe in them even if there's no evidence for them—or, what's worse, I think, even if there's evidence to the contrary." He paused. They had reached a corner diagonally opposite a restaurant with a bright red awning over its front door. "That's the place. Rue des . . ." The letters of the name, painted on the awning, had faded and become illegible. "They just call it the Rue—everybody does."

They began to cross the street towards the restaurant. "Do you believe in astrology, Ulf?"

The question came out of nowhere, and it took Ulf a moment or two to gather his thoughts. "Astrology? Of course not. Who does?"

"Well, I write the astrology column for the paper," said Åke. "Yes, I know you'll think me feeble-minded, but I do. I don't believe in it, of course, but then journalists today have to write a lot of things we don't believe in."

"Such as?"

"Editorials praising something that we may well hate ourselves, but it's company policy to support. Don't believe everything you read about editorial independence." Åke laughed. "In fact, don't believe too much of anything these days."

Ulf felt he had to voice an objection. "But that's exactly what demagogues want you to do, isn't it? If you can persuade people that the news they read is simple invention, then they've got you where they want you."

"Yes, of course," said Åke. "Perhaps I should put it this way: Don't be surprised by insincerity."

They had reached the door of the restaurant. Above their heads, the red awning flapped gently in the wind that had sprung up from the sea. There was a smell of something on it—something burnt, Ulf thought, although he could not quite place it.

Åke was known to the woman at the door, and she quickly found them a table. She left them with a menu and went away. "That woman," said Åke, his voice lowered, "is married to a man who controls half the drug routes into this city. He bought her this restaurant for her birthday."

Ulf had vaguely heard about that, but he gave no indication of knowing. He hoped that Åke would not make a further, more specific disclosure that he would then be bound to investigate. So he said, "Does anybody who reads your astrology column actually believe in it?"

Åke caught the waiter's eye. As the man came over to their table, Åke signalled to him, and he went off into the kitchen. "I've ordered some sparkling water," he said. "Is that all right with you? I'm paying, by the way."

Ulf shook his head. "Not allowed, I'm afraid. I'm on duty. I'd have to declare your gift if you paid the bill, and that would involve filing in forms, and so on."

Åke accepted with good grace. "Dutch then? Split the bill?"

"It's always better that way."

The water arrived, and Åke poured it as they gave their order. "You didn't say why you wanted to see me," he said. "Back there in the office, when you showed me your card, you didn't say what this was about."

"Did I not?" said Ulf. He thought of something. "But if you write the astrology column, wouldn't you have already known?"

Åke grinned. "Oh, that one. You probably know the story of the editor writing to the paper's astrologist—'as you already know, you're fired.'" He paused. "Before he'd been told of his dismissal, in fact . . ."

"Yes," said Ulf. "I get the joke."

"Anyway, you were going to tell me what you wanted to talk about. I don't suppose I have to tell you about our view of sources. You must know that. We don't disclose them."

Ulf assured Åke that he was well aware of that policy. "I'm not here to ask you to do that."

"Good, because I wouldn't."

Ulf waited a few moments before saying, "Nils Cederström."

Åke opened his mouth, and then shut it. Ulf frowned. He assumed that this was a sign that any request for further information would be met with refusal. That was much as he expected it, of course: a scoop was a scoop, after all, and just as there was a company policy on not revealing sources, there was bound to be one on not breaking embargoes. But then Åke answered, "Nils who?"

"Cederström, the writer."

Åke hesitated, as if he was unsure how to respond. Eventually he said, "Oh, him. Of course."

Ulf thought this strange. Åke was preparing to publish a major disclosure about Nils and so the writer must have been on his mind. But now he appeared to be vague about him, to the point of having to be reminded as to which Nils was being talked about.

"I read your article," said Ulf.

Åke nodded but said nothing.

"It was interesting," Ulf persisted. "As far as it went." He paused. "Which was not very far, of course."

Åke stared at him.

"I'm referring to the tantalising bit," Ulf continued. "You said you were going to reveal something important about Nils next week. That's what interests me, and I wonder whether we could talk about it."

Åke suddenly seemed to relax. "Oh, that," he said. "Well, sorry to disappoint you, but I don't think we'll be running that after all."

Ulf was puzzled. "But you said—"

Åke stopped him. "We need to pique the readers' interest from time to time. Everybody does it. But we can't always deliver, and so we'll come up with something else about somebody or other. We'll throw them a bone to chew."

"So you're letting Nils off the hook?"

The metaphor appeared to disturb Åke, who looked away, avoiding Ulf's gaze. "There are decisions to be made," he said flatly. "Editorial decisions."

"You won't tell me what it was that you were proposing to reveal?"

Åke turned round sharply. He was now the toughened journalist, standing his ground against prying officialdom. "Sorry, I can't do that. But what I can say is this: we didn't have any proof to back up the allegations, and so the article was spiked by the editor. It happens, and I agree with her. She said it was too weak."

"What allegations?" asked Ulf.

"I told you: I can't say anything about them."

Ulf tried another tack. "What do you think about Nils yourself? Personally?"

Åke was now back in control of the encounter. He met this question with a thin smile. "I don't know him."

"Not at all? But you've written about him."

This struck home, and Åke became defensive. "I've met him, I believe. But that's not the same as knowing somebody."

"You must have formed an impression. You wouldn't have been indifferent to him, surely."

Åke looked thoughtful. "Yes, I did form an impression. I'd say what you get is what you read about. He's a tough cookie."

"That's all? Just a tough cookie?"

Åke nodded. "People talk about Hemingway in the same breath, although most people have forgotten who Hemingway was. But the comparison is appropriate, I'd say. He's our Swedish Hemingway."

"An oxymoron?"

Åke considered this. "Perhaps. But I'm not sure that I subscribe to the Swedish exceptionalism position. We're people, after all, and people are pretty much the same the world over. Flawed. Selfish. *Non angeli sed Sueci* ... Remember the story of Pope Gregory and the English boys? *Non Angli sed angeli?*"

Ulf shook his head.

"Oh well," said Åke. "It was a long time ago. I'm suggesting that we're not angels, but Swedes ..."

The waiter returned with the two salads they had ordered. Åke doused his in extra olive oil, and then handed the bottle to Ulf. "I can't resist olive oil," he said.

"It's good for you," Ulf agreed. "It's meant to help in—" He broke off; I'm beginning to sound like Blomquist, he thought. I must not become Blomquist.

Ulf drizzled olive oil over his salad. He broke a bread roll and applied oil to that as well, the oil turning the white bread green.

Åke was watching him. "That was a turning point," he said.

"A watershed—when people started putting olive oil on bread rather than butter. One could base one's calendar on that. The year 3 AOO—'after olive oil.'"

Ulf laughed. "Like the French revolutionaries and their new calendar."

"Exactly. Except that it never works. People retain their old dating systems, don't they?"

Ulf pointed out that BC and AD had been largely abandoned, and that appeared to work. He took a sip of his sparkling water. "Astrology," he said. "Are you utterly cynical about it?"

Åke looked surprised. "Why would you accuse me of cynicism?"

"Because you write about this astrological mumbo-jumbo … And you clearly don't believe in it."

Åke raised an eyebrow. "I might just be saying that."

Ulf held up his hands. "Who could possibly believe that what the stars are up to in their orbit has the remotest bearing on our human lives down here?"

Åke laughed. "Does it occur to you that you might be wrong?"

"On this subject, frankly, no."

"And those who doubted Copernicus," said Åke, "what about them? Did it occur to them that their views were baseless?"

It was different, thought Ulf. They were clearly wrong, whereas he was clearly right. Yet Åke had a point, he conceded: you can never really be sure of your beliefs because the paradigm on which they're based might just be proved to be fallacious, and in that case things that are self-evidently right could be shown to be quite wrong. It was possible.

"No it didn't," he said.

"Well, there you are."

"Yes," said Ulf. "There you are. It's possible that we might suddenly discover that astrologists have been right all along, but I doubt it. So that's my position: one of doubt. Would you be satisfied with that?"

"Perfectly," said Åke. He reached for a paper napkin. "Give me your date of birth," he said.

Ulf stared at him.

"No, go on," Åke went on, taking a pen out of his pocket and drawing a few lines on the napkin. "I'll cast you a quick astrological prediction."

"The twenty-fourth of August."

"Time?"

Ulf shrugged. "During the day—I think."

Åke scribbled a few words on the napkin. There were lines, too, and several arrows. Then he drew a box and wrote a few words within it before handing it to Ulf.

Ulf looked at what was written in the box: *Be very careful: you are a Virgo, but Mars and Venus are in stressful juxtaposition. Take care.*

Ulf stared at Åke. "What does this mean?" he asked.

"What it says," Åke replied. "But if you think astrology is nonsense, as you claim you do, then that will be nonsense too, and you needn't pay any attention to it."

Ulf folded the napkin and put it in his pocket. "Perhaps I should hedge my bets." He laughed, and the tension that had suddenly built up was dispelled.

They finished their salads. No more was said about Nils Cederström, or astrology, or anything much of note. They talked briefly about football, and about the performance of a team that neither of them liked. It had not been doing well—indeed, it had been humiliated—and for a brief moment they shared the pleasures of *Schadenfreude.*

At the end of the lunch they went their separate ways—Åke back to the newspaper office and Ulf to the Department of Sensitive Crimes. There he found on his desk, along with the files placed there by Erik, a note from his immediate superior in the Criminal Investigation Authority. This read: *I have been looking over the records they keep in supplies and see that you put in for a dog's lead. According to our human resources people (and for these purposes they are also canine resources) you do not have a dog in your department. Please explain soonest.*

The word *soonest* was ominous. It was used in police communications, but sparingly, and only in circumstances in which the person addressed was either in disgrace or in danger of disgrace. Ulf now sat with his head in his hands.

From the other side of the office, Erik, who had returned earlier than Ulf had expected, watched him with concern. "That memo about the lead?" he asked.

"Yes," said Ulf.

"Bring it back," said Erik. "I'll take the flak."

Ulf looked at his colleague. Dear Erik, he thought; good old, loyal Erik, with his angling magazines and his endless accounts of minor skirmishes with fish; good old Erik who is now prepared to do something not in the rule book in order to save my skin.

"What will you do, Erik?"

"I'll say that I ordered it by mistake and that I had forgotten to send it back. He'll give me a lecture about the need to return unwanted stores timeously, but it won't be the end of the world."

Ulf shook his head. "Thank you, but I must do it myself." He paused. "I suppose I could say that I ordered it because I was going to use Martin on a case and I needed it for that. I could say that."

"But then he might ask which case it was," Erik pointed out.

"He might," said Ulf. "And there's another reason not to do that. It would be a lie, and I don't feel comfortable about lying. I never have."

Erik looked at him admiringly. "I know that, Ulf. We all know that. And that's why we hold you in the high regard that we do."

Ulf looked away in embarrassment.

"No," said Erik. "I mean it."

Ulf smiled at him. "I really appreciate that, Erik. I really do."

"And I mean all of us," Erik added. "Anna included."

The room became silent. Eventually Ulf said, "Do you think she does?"

Erik reached for a piece of paper and folded it into the shape of a small paper plane. He did this, Ulf had noticed, when he was thinking hard about something. Then, letting the paper plane fall to the ground, he said, "What are you going to do about that, Ulf?"

"About what?"

"About Anna."

Ulf said nothing. He had not imagined that Erik, of all people, should know about his feelings.

"Nothing," he said. "Because Anna and I are colleagues—that's all."

He thought: Is that a lie? But he answered himself almost immediately. He had not allowed it to develop in any sense into an affair. He had done nothing wrong—nothing at all. And so he and Anna remained colleagues and no more. He had nothing to reproach himself over, even though inside his heart ached for her.

Chapter Thirteen

VAN DOG

As he drove home that evening, Ulf thought about the Nils Cederström affair. He had always found it useful, in reviewing his cases, to make a mental list of what he knew and what he did not know and had to find out. In this case, the list of what he knew had grown since he first started his investigation, but not by all that much. He had made several discoveries about Cederström's character: He had found out that those who knew him found him kind, charming, and utterly unlike the image he presented in public. He had also discovered that the author did substantial good works by stealth, supporting, as he did, a considerable number of children in India. This information had intrigued Ulf, but he was as yet unsure what use he could make of it. In order to find a blackmailer, ideally you had to know what the subject of the threat was. If you knew that, then you could find out who was likely to have that information and therefore possibly be the blackmailer. But Ulf was still in the dark as to the disclosures with which Nils was being threatened. Åke knew something, of course, and that could have led somewhere, but Ulf realised that he was never going to be able to get Åke to divulge anything, and so that was not a very promising line to pursue.

By the time he parked the Saab outside the apartment block, he was playing with the conclusion that this would be a case that would have to go unsolved. He hated deciding that about any crime, and this was especially so where the crime was as despicable as blackmail, but if the victim declined to co-operate, then what could one do? As he thought about this, he remembered a particularly distressing case in which it was exactly this that had led to a real brute of a man getting away scot-free. The brute in question was a barman in a sleazy bar popular with men looking for an easy pick-up. This barman had run a small stable of girls whom he rented out to the customers of his bar. This was pimping, and Ulf had a particular distaste for pimps and traffickers. He had helped a colleague in the vice squad with this enquiry because the squad had been short-staffed at the time, and they had got to within a whisker of an arrest. One of the girls, however, had fallen in love with the barman and had retracted her testimony. That would not have been fatal to the case had the other two girls involved stuck to their statements. It became apparent, though, that one of those girls had fallen in love with the girl who was in love with the barman, and that girl—the one in love with the barman—had exerted pressure on the girl in love with her to say nothing. The barman's girlfriend had not told the other girl that she was in love with the barman, but had pretended to reciprocate her feelings in order to ensure her co-operation. That left one statement unretracted, but this, too, was withdrawn when the barman disclosed to the third young woman that he had fallen in love with her. She already had a boyfriend but had always had a soft spot for anybody who said that he had fallen in love with her, and so in due course she withdrew as a witness. Once the prosecution had been abandoned, the barman left Sweden with an American woman a good fifteen years his senior. She was the owner of a sports fishing business on the Florida Keys. Ulf was told by his colleague on the vice squad that two years later the American woman fell off a powerboat and drowned. The only other person on the boat had been the barman, who now inherited the sports fishing business and the bar attached to it. The vice squad man had shrugged.

"There are reasons to believe in God," he said. "Even if you do not believe in him, there are reasons to do so. Otherwise . . ."

"Otherwise?" Ulf asked.

"Otherwise people get away with things. Otherwise there's nobody to punish that barman. He sits in the sun and drinks beer. He probably starts some new racket. Drugs, maybe—running them in from Central America—something like that. And without God he can just sit there and laugh."

Ulf thought of the barman, and of God, as he locked the Saab behind him. Oddly, he found himself wondering what sort of car God would drive—if he existed. One of those sleek Bentleys? An old Cadillac, perhaps, with a lot of chrome and those characteristic fins at the back? Or would he be humble and drive a smoke-belching East German Trabi, just to make a point? The Devil, of course, would go for something sleek and black, probably one of those old Soviet ZiL limousines that members of the Soviet hierarchy drove—or were driven in, as ZiL limousines were never personally driven by their owners. A car like that would suit the Devil, who would sit behind its tinted windows so that nobody could see him as he flashed past on his sinister business.

Ulf smiled. It was an absurd thought, but it momentarily cheered him up and enabled him to put the Cederström case into perspective. Nobody was being physically harmed. A good man was being subjected to psychological pressure, but appeared to be capable of bearing it. An unpleasant blackmailer was being financially enriched without having to do a stroke of work to justify it. There were worse things happening—far worse—and if he were now to stop any further investigation of this case, the world would continue to spin on its axis; Blomquist would still go on about this and that; Erik would continue to enjoy his fishing;

Anna would still drive her girls off to their swimming galas; his brother, Björn, would continue to run the Moderate Extremists; and Martin would still dream of squirrels and their capture. Nothing would change.

He looked at his watch. He was marginally late: he normally liked to arrive home by six in order to take Martin out if Mrs. Högfors had put him back in the flat or to collect him from her flat if she was still looking after him. Sometimes she kept him, if Ulf was detained and could not make it home until nine or ten. On those occasions Martin would be treated to a sleep-over, which Mrs. Högfors claimed he particularly enjoyed. "I allow him to sleep on the sofa," she explained. "What dog could pass up an offer like that? A whole night on a human sofa? Dog heaven, Mr. Varg, would you not agree?"

He decided to knock on her door first, and when he did so, Martin's barking in the hall told him that the dog was still there. As the door opened, Martin bounded out and licked joyously at Ulf's hands. Ulf looked down at him and smiled.

"He's happy to see you," said Mrs. Högfors. "He's had a very good day today. He almost caught a squirrel—it was a very close thing. And he found a half-eaten meat pie in the park. It was left on a bench. He ate it before I could get it from him, I'm afraid, but he's none the worse for it."

"Who on earth abandons half-eaten pies on a park bench?" Ulf mused.

Mrs. Högfors laughed. "Is that a rhetorical question?"

"I suppose so," Ulf answered. "It seems such an odd thing to do. I mean, on a bench? If you can't finish a pie, then wouldn't any reasonable person put it in a bin? There are plenty of those in the park. But I suppose people don't care any longer—not these days."

"But if your question was not rhetorical," Mrs. Högfors continued, "if you actually want an answer . . ."

Ulf smiled. "You saw the ... the perpetrator? And you didn't use your powers of citizen's arrest?"

"Can you?" she asked.

"For a sufficiently serious crime—I think. I doubt if you could arrest somebody who merely does something un-Swedish."

Mrs. Högfors shook her head in mock regret. "More's the pity ... But still, as it happens, I can answer your question. I saw them."

"Them?"

"Yes—the two men who were sitting on the bench. One of them was eating a pie. They were talking, and then they got up to go and the one who was eating the pie left half of it on the bench. I saw him look down at the pie, and he was obviously weighing up whether or not to find a bin. There was one, of course, but it was a bit far away, and he must have decided not to bother." She shook her head. "Typical."

Ulf laughed. "If we somehow managed to pull him in and put him in a line-up, would you be able to identify him?"

"Of course. Because I recognised him anyway. And the other one. I know who both of them were."

"Ah," said Ulf. "That man at the newsagent's? The one you don't like? And his aggressive brother-in-law?" Mrs. Högfors had often spoken of these two, retelling some slight, real or imagined, that one or other, or both, had given to one of her friends from the local Pilates class she attended.

She shook her head. "No, not them, although I can imagine them doing just that. No, it was that journalist and that writer fellow. The one who was on television the other night talking about how they were going to make a film of his new novel. Did you see him? He was on the same programme as your brother."

It took a moment or two for Ulf to realise the significance of what his neighbour had just said. But then it dawned on him. "Nils Cederström?"

"That's him," said Mrs. Högfors. "He's the one who they say drinks a lot. Shouts too. That one."

"So they say," muttered Ulf. *Alleged* Hemingway, he thought. *Reputed.* He looked earnestly at Mrs. Högfors. "Are you sure?" And then he added, when he saw her nod vigorously, "And who was with him? You say the other was a journalist. Was it—"

He did not have time to complete his question before Mrs. Högfors provided the answer. And it was precisely the answer he had been expecting. "Yes, it was that Åke Holmberg—the one who writes those articles. And you know what? I heard from my friend whose daughter works on his paper, he also writes the horoscope. He's very good at that, apparently. I've certainly found him accurate."

"Oh come now, Mrs. Högfors . . ."

"No—you may scoff, Mr. Varg; you may scoff as much as you like, but he's got an uncanny way of predicting what's going to happen. How he does it is anybody's guess, but he gets it right every time."

Ulf's expression made his scepticism apparent. "Are you sure about that? I don't want to sound like one of those people who won't believe anything, but even so . . ."

She was adamant. "No, I can tell you don't believe in these things, and I know you don't want to hear any evidence that would make you question your disbelief."

"Try me," said Ulf gamely.

"Well, about six months ago I consulted my horoscope and it said that I should be careful if I was planning to go anywhere that week. It said I could well be held up."

"And?"

"Two days later I was due to go up to Stockholm and my train was cancelled. I had to call the trip off. It was for my niece's thirtieth birthday. I missed the party."

Ulf looked thoughtful. "And what date was her birthday?"

"The twentieth of January."

Ulf smiled. "The week of the rail strike, as I recall."

"Yes, that was it. The trains were on strike."

Ulf waited for Mrs. Högfors to make the obvious connection, but she seemed to be oblivious. His neighbour was an intelligent woman—she had, he reminded himself, a degree in social anthropology, but that was a long time ago. This was detection, and it was perfectly understandable that the forensic keenness that he took for granted might simply not be there. He raised an eyebrow. "And that fact—the possibility of a strike—had been in all the newspapers for days. Doesn't that seem suspicious to you, Mrs. Högfors?"

Mrs. Högfors looked thoughtful. "Are you suggesting he already knew?"

"Well, yes," said Ulf. "I am suggesting that, I suppose. If you know there's going to be a rail strike, it seems entirely reasonable to predict the disruption of travel plans."

Mrs. Högfors pursed her lips. "Possibly," she conceded, a bit reluctantly, thought Ulf. And then she repeated, "Possibly." And then she smiled, thinly, and again reluctantly, and said, "It's harmless, though, isn't it? And who amongst us is not just the tiniest bit superstitious—sometimes."

Ulf conceded that everyone was probably superstitious about something. He thought of his colleagues. Erik always wore a particular belt when he went fishing—he had confessed to that once—and Carl would never arrest anybody on Friday the thirteenth: "They get straight out," he had explained. And as for Anna, she had a rabbit's foot key-ring—he had seen it himself—and why would anybody have a rabbit's foot key-ring unless they thought that it would somehow bring good luck? He himself . . . He paused; was he without any of these funny little beliefs? Rather to his disappointment he realised he was not. Why otherwise would he always be sure to step out of the bath and onto the bath mat well before the water drained from the bathtub? It was because he felt that something disastrous would ensue if he was still lying there when the final gurgle told him that the water had drained out. Or was it because it was cold and uncomfortable to be still lying there when the last of the water had gone? The former, if he were honest with himself.

The thought suddenly struck him: Were honest people *necessarily* honest with themselves as well as everybody else? Could you deceive yourself about a weakness, for instance, while at the same time being scrupulously truthful in all other respects? These thoughts were interrupted when he reminded himself that what he should be thinking about was what Mrs. Högfors had seen in the park: Åke Holmberg and Nils Cederström together. What, if anything, was the significance of that?

He answered the question almost immediately. Nils must have read Åke's piece about him and the announcement of the impending disclosure. Anxious about what might be coming out in the press, he would have contacted the journalist to plead with him not to publish. That would be it—that *must* be it. Of course, Åke would have told him, if he had any decency in him, that the article was not going ahead anyway, and on that note they would have parted company, leaving behind them the half-eaten pie that Martin was later to devour. But why would they have met in the park, on a park bench? Ulf pondered this. Perhaps Nils would not have wanted to be seen going into the newspaper office. His was a well-known face, and he would not want to be photographed by some passer-by going in— on his metaphorical hands and knees—to beg the paper not to publish. Hemingway would never have done that. Nor would Norman Mailer or any of the other tough guys of the literary world.

He became aware that Mrs. Högfors had said something to him.

"I'm sorry. My thoughts were elsewhere."

"I was telling you how sorry I am to have lost that nice new lead you bought for Martin. The one that says 'Made in China.' The leather one."

Ulf waved a hand. "Oh, that. Don't worry about that. It's just a lead."

"I bought a new one. Here it is." She reached for a smart new leash, red in colour, and stamped with the label "van Dog."

Ulf thanked her. He examined the lettering. "Van Dog?"

"I'm told it's a designer label for dogs," said Mrs. Högfors. "I don't go in for that sort of thing myself—you know, Gucci and so on. Those young people with their designer brands all over them—they don't realise how they're being manipulated."

Ulf nodded. "Most of it is just standard stuff. You pay for the label—pay through the nose." He sighed. "And now they're targeting dog owners."

Mrs. Högfors looked at her watch. "Would you have time for a quick coffee, Mr. Varg?"

Ulf said he would. He was tired and he needed to unwind; a few minutes listening to Mrs. Högfors would relax him. Afterwards he would prepare himself some spaghetti bolognese and he would eat this with a green salad. Blomquist said you should have salad whenever you had a large plate of carbohydrates. Blomquist said . . . He smiled. I must not develop an inner Blomquist, he told himself. It was so easily done; perhaps it came upon you by stealth, in stages, as a strange disease might do. That, presumably, was how Blomquist had become Blomquist—little by little.

Ulf sat down on Mrs. Högfors's sofa, Martin at his feet. If I had a normal life, he said to himself, this is what I would come home to each evening: the companionship of another, and of a dog. He would cook a meal for her and she for him—whoever she might be: that sensitive, supportive woman he should try to find, and whom he *could* find if only he were to start looking. Instead of which, he thought, I pine for one who cannot be mine, unless … unless … He felt a thrill of excitement. What a fool Jo was; what an unmitigated fool. There he was, a highly qualified anaesthetist, with a loving family, and he had to pursue some passing fancy, some tawdry little affair conducted in … where? In her cramped apartment, perhaps, or in a cheap hotel where no questions were asked about what went on in their soulless rooms.

His thoughts returned to Nils Cederström, and suddenly he had a strong desire to confide in Mrs. Högfors. He would not normally discuss his cases with an outsider—that was strictly against the rules—but Mrs. Högfors was different. She saw very few people in her normal day and would be unlikely to speak to anybody about it. Secrets were safe with Mrs. Högfors.

So he told her. He told her the full story of the approach by Nils Cederström's girlfriend. He told her of his visit to the bookseller and of the plaudits with which Nils had been showered by his friends. He told her of his visit to Åke and of the reluctance of the journalist to say anything about what the paper threatened to disclose. He concluded by saying that it seemed to him that he had achieved nothing and was unlikely to make any further progress in the case.

"Other than to make your arrest," said Mrs. Högfors.

Ulf frowned. "But, as I said, I haven't got the first clue as to whom to arrest. To make an arrest you first have to …" He stopped, and looked enquiringly at his neighbour. "You don't have a theory, do you?"

"Of course I have a theory. Or rather, I have a conviction."

He waited for her to continue. At his feet, Martin stirred in his sleep, his legs twitching, as a dog's legs will move in a dream of the pursuit of rabbits or squirrels. Ulf wondered whether in his dreams Martin heard everything perfectly, released from the handicap of the deafness he endured in his waking state.

"You see," said Mrs. Högfors, "it's plain as can be that your Nils Cederström is being blackmailed by Åke Holmberg." She looked at Ulf as if to satisfy herself that he had grasped this fundamental point. Then she continued, "Saying that he is about to publish something was his way of warning Nils that adverse consequences would follow any failure to pay up."

"And?" Ulf encouraged her. "Blackmailed over what?"

Mrs. Högfors laughed. "It's a complete reversal of the normal situation where the blackmailer threatens to disclose some wrong-doing on the part of the victim. In this case, it's not wrongdoing but *right*doing, if there is such a word. The threat would be that unless Nils pays up, the world will be told that he's not the tough, hard-drinking sort that his public expects him to be."

Ulf looked up at the ceiling. Of course, of course. He had been looking in quite the wrong place—a place of darkness—when he should have been looking in a place of light.

"You know, I think you're right. In fact, that's brilliant."

Mrs. Högfors took the compliment in her stride. "I was just putting two and two together."

Ulf shook his head. "But I didn't see it," he said.

"Perhaps that's because you're not a woman, Mr. Varg."

Not for the first time, Ulf wanted to say to her, "You must call me Ulf." Nobody used Mr. and Mrs. in Sweden any longer, and their use sounded almost like an affectation. But he did not: she *was* Mrs. Högfors, and he *was* Mr. Varg, no matter how much linguistic use changed.

"Is that it?" Ulf said evenly. "Oh well, at least I know my limitations."

"Are you going to go and arrest him?" asked Mrs. Högfors.

Ulf explained to her the difficulties of prosecuting when the victim would be the main witness and was unwilling to lay a complaint. "I shall speak to him," he said. "I shall warn him off. That should stop it, even if we can't bring him to justice."

Mrs. Högfors said that she understood. "Sometimes justice is delayed," she said.

"Or cancelled," muttered Ulf. He thought about that. The world was a bleak place of corruption and unfairness. It was enough to make one lose faith in justice altogether, but you could not do that. You had to carry on that battle, and he and his colleagues in the Department of Sensitive Crimes would do just that, even if there were inevitable disappointments and failures along the way. You continued. You worked away, asking questions, watching, following, uncovering. Then, if you were lucky and everything pointed in the right direction, you pounced. But sometimes you pounced on nothing, and you landed on the space where only a few minutes before a perfect villain had been standing. Then you picked yourself up, dusted yourself off, and resumed the battle.

That evening, after his meal of spaghetti bolognese, washed down with a glass of Chianti from a recorked bottle, Ulf took Martin out to the park. There were one or two other dogs being exercised by their owners, but nobody whom Ulf knew. Martin seemed indifferent to the presence of the other dogs—a sign of canine depression, Dr. Håkansson had told Ulf—but as they approached the park bench on which Mrs. Högfors had seen Nils Cederström and Åke Holmberg in conversation, he perked up. Ulf allowed the dog to approach the bench and to sniff at the place where he must previously have found the half-eaten meat pie. As he watched Martin lick the woodwork, he found himself wondering whether this, in the first instance at least, was olfactory or visual memory. Had Martin remembered the bench before he might have smelled the traces of meat pie? And did meat pies leave much of a scent on the things on which they rested? If so, the world must have rich seams of scents, Ulf thought—layer upon layer of odours, left one upon the other, telling the story of what had been where.

He eventually pulled Martin away. The dog seemed reluctant to leave the bench, perhaps hoping, thought Ulf, for some final miracle; hoping that the manna that had been left there would somehow manifest itself once again. They headed now for home, with Martin tugging at the lead. As they made their way back, Ulf went over in his mind the solution that Mrs. Högfors had proposed to the Nils Cederström affair. She was right, he thought, and that meant he could close the case after he had given Åke what he intended to be a very serious warning. He would not exclude the possibility of prosecution, even though he knew that this was unlikely. He would make him suffer for a while, which was fitting punishment for a blackmailer, whose trade was anxiety and worry.

With the Cederström affair settled, Ulf could turn his attention to two outstanding matters. One of these was official, one distinctly not so. The official matter was that of the export of fake wolves. The unofficial matter was the breaking to Anna of the news that her fears about Jo had been well founded. He was worried about that, of course. It was his duty to follow through, but he was not relishing the thought of that meeting. So rather than tackle that straight away, he would begin the following morning with an attempt to find that Estonian type who restored vintage motorcycles and passed dogs off as wolves. That would mean a chat with his biker friend, Arvid (the Professor) Forsberg, author of *The Great Nordic Biker War* and other works of a rather recondite nature. He would take Blomquist with him, he decided; he was not worried about Arvid himself, whom he knew and trusted, but he was not so sanguine about the place where he would find him, which was a shed belonging to a biker club, on the edge of an industrial area, a place known in more literate police circles as a "Dantean circle of hell." Better not to go alone, thought Ulf, even if it meant listening to Blomquist going on about whatever it was that had caught his attention the night before on his trawl of internet health sites: the pick of a new remedy for high blood pressure, the powers of a newly discovered dark green vegetable, or the latest figures on longevity in those areas of south India where extensive use is made of coconut oil. Or possibly all of these, thought Ulf.

Chapter Fourteen

THE GREAT NORDIC BIKER WAR

Blomquist was intrigued.

"This professor," he said. "He works for you?"

"Working for" somebody was code for an informer. Many detectives had one or two people "working for" them, in some cases for years. The relationship, if successfully concealed, could be a mutually productive one. The informer could expect a certain degree of immunity as long as he fed his "boss" a regular stream of information, usually about the informer's enemies in the criminal underworld. The relationship could turn sour, though, if the information passed on was false, or if the informer deliberately passed on out-of-date intelligence. It could turn even sourer, at least from the point of view of the informer, if the boss were ever to let slip the informer's identity. That was called a terminal event, and would end in retribution for the informer unless he was quick enough to escape the ire of his fellow criminals.

The Professor did not work for Ulf in the conventional sense. He was a revered figure in biking circles, a trusted confidant and biographer who was accepted as being above the normal fray. He knew everything about Scandinavian biking, and kept in his head a hundred, if not a thousand, items of biking ephemera—about who rode what, about who rode where, about who sold which bike to whom. These were all matters of profound unimportance to most people, but meat and drink to bikers in their alternative universe of throaty engine sounds, petrol fumes, and burning rubber.

"No," said Ulf in answer to Blomquist's question. "The Professor works for nobody. He's above all that."

"So you can talk to him openly?" asked Blomquist.

Ulf confirmed that this was so. "They—bikers, that is—they know that the Professor would never say anything that could get another biker into trouble with the police. He understands the code—in fact, they say that he actually *wrote* it."

Blomquist looked thoughtful. "How does he get by? Some of these people, you know, they're up to their necks in the drug trade."

Ulf shook his head. "Not the Professor. He owns three flats—legitimately. They were left to him by his father. He lives on the rents."

Blomquist shrugged. "I thought I'd ask."

"And it was a reasonable question," said Ulf. "But he really is something special, Blomquist. He's an author of biking books. Have you heard of *The Great Nordic Biker War*? You see it on railway bookstands. There's always a copy lying around. Well, he wrote that."

They were in the Saab. As Ulf parked and got out of the car, Blomquist asked, "One thing: you said that the Professor would never say anything that might get another biker into hot water with the police."

"I did."

"But isn't that exactly what you're going to do now? You want to find this man—this possible Estonian, you said—who deals in fake wolves. But that's going to get him into trouble, surely?"

Ulf hesitated. Blomquist could be right, but one never knew. In detective work, questions were bread upon the water: sometimes they produced results, sometimes they did not. He looked into the shed. He had noticed the members of the club milling about. There was a lot of leather, and a hardware store's worth of studs.

"Animals," muttered Blomquist.

"Animals might just come into it," said Ulf, his voice already lowered.

Blomquist was puzzled. "I don't see what you mean."

"You will," said Ulf.

The shed stood on a patch of wasteland beside a storage depot. It looked as if it had been used for rigging work in the past, as beside it were several piles of twisted iron cable, of the sort used by cranes. Half a crane arm, caked in rust, its struts buckled, lay between the abandoned wire and the fence. A wooden booth, its single window glassless, stood at the end of a path littered with fragmented bricks. It was a scene of neglect, of industrial abandonment.

They made their way into the shed, which was large, the size of a tennis court. There were motorcycles ranged against one wall, a jumble of machinery out of which, here and there, exaggerated handlebars protruded. Other motorcycles had been propped up on their stands in the middle of the floor. A group of bikers were gathered around one motorcycle in towards the back, peering at a mechanic in blue overalls who was tinkering with the engine.

There was a shout from the side.

"Ulf!" A tall, well-built man wearing round black-framed spectacles waved in Ulf's direction. He was seated behind a table on which several magazines were lying open. "Over here, Ulf."

Ulf crossed the floor, passing a couple, a man and a woman, who were seated on a static motorcycle, fixing the visitors with an intense stare. Ulf nodded in their direction and received a curt incline of the head from the man. The woman was impassive, chewing gum in a pointedly unfriendly way. She had piercings in her nose and eyebrows. A tattoo of Pegasus the flying horse covered her entire left upper arm.

Blomquist glanced at her and greeted her with an elaborate politeness. His greeting was ignored.

198 | THE TALENTED MR. VARG

The Professor rose to greet them. "My old friend—what brings you here? Bought a bike?"

Ulf reached out to shake the biker's hand. "I have my Saab, Prof. That's good enough for me."

He introduced Blomquist, who was greeted courteously.

"I know a Blomquist in Lund," said the Professor. "He married my aunt after my uncle died a few months ago. He snores a lot. It's driving her mad."

Blomquist frowned. "Sleep apnoea," he said. "Has he been tested for sleep apnoea?"

The Professor looked interested.

"It's very common," said Blomquist. "You wake up sometimes a hundred times a night. You stop breathing, you see, and it wakes you up. You end up being sleep-deprived."

"Well well," said the Professor. "Can they do anything?"

"Yes," said Blomquist. "They can. You can get these small devices, you see, that you put in your mouth. It keeps the airways open. Or you can get a positive-pressure mask. You sleep in that. You wear it all night."

"Very interesting," said the Professor. "I could talk to her about it. Where can I find out more about it?"

"There's a sleep clinic right here in Malmö," said Blomquist. "I could get you the details, if you like."

"Would you talk to him?" asked the Professor. "Do you think you could have a word with him about all this?"

Blomquist was willing. "Of course. Anything I can do to help. Sleep disorders cost the nation a great deal, you know. If you add up—"

"Yes, yes," said Ulf. "That's great, Blomquist. But we need to talk to the Professor here."

The Professor made a generous gesture, as if his time was completely and unconditionally at their disposal.

"I need a bit of information," Ulf said.

The Professor glanced about him. "Information? None of the boys has been up to anything, I can tell you that. These are clean boys, Ulf. One hundred per cent clean."

"Of course," said Ulf quickly. "No, it's nothing to do with the boys. It's just an enquiry about a man who repairs vintage bikes. He has a van that says that. And a tattoo—here on the neck. And he's Estonian or Latvian, I think."

The Professor's eyes narrowed. "A tattooed Estonian with a van? That's a big demographic, Ulf." Then he shook his head. "Sorry. Never heard of anybody like that."

Ulf waited a few moments. Then, his voice lowered, he said, "It's an animal cruelty case, Prof."

The effect of this was immediate. The Professor's brow now knitted into a look of disgust.

Ulf gestured to a motorcycle parked a short distance from the Professor's desk. This was an old red BSA, equipped with a matching sidecar. "How are the pugs, Prof?"

"Just fine," said the Professor. Turning his head, he put two fingers to his mouth and whistled sharply. After a few seconds, two small heads emerged from the open top of the sidecar and looked about briefly. Then two light brown pugs, each with a collar in the same shade of red as the BSA, leaped out and trotted over to the Professor.

Ulf bent down to allow the dogs to sniff at his hand. "They're smelling Martin," he said.

"How's he doing?" asked the Professor.

"He's still marginally depressed," Ulf replied. "We thought that it was seasonal affective disorder but now, well, we're not so sure."

The Professor nodded. "Dr. Håkansson's treating him?"

"Yes."

"He's the best," said the Professor. "He operated on Betsy here. She had a tumour. Fortunately it was benign. I couldn't have borne it if it had been anything more serious."

Ulf made a sympathetic noise. "They capture your heart, don't they?" He stopped; the Professor was shaking his head.

"It doesn't add up, Ulf. I've just remembered—I do know somebody who fits your description, but he's not somebody who would ever be guilty of mistreating animals. In fact, quite the opposite."

Ulf asked for a name. The Professor hesitated. "Karmo Pärn," he said at last. "But I tell you, Ulf, he wouldn't do anything like that." He paused. "Tell me: Exactly what is it he's meant to have done?"

Ulf was frank. He gave the Professor the details, adding, "Don't tell Dr. Håkansson I told you. I shouldn't really be passing this on—outside the force, that is."

The Professor started to laugh. Excited by their owner's laughter, the two pugs started to bark, jumping up on their hind legs, their paws scrabbling at the air.

Ulf waited for an explanation.

"Do you know what Karmo does?" the Professor asked. "Yes, he fixes old bikes, but he's a dog breeder. He has kennels outside town. He's a dog breeder and trainer."

Ulf exchanged glances with Blomquist.

"We have dogs here who look pretty much like wolves," said the Professor.

He waited for Ulf to react, but Ulf said nothing. He drew Ulf aside and whispered something to him. Ulf's eyebrows shot up. Blomquist strained to hear what was being said, but the volume of the Professor's voice was too low. He frowned.

Then Ulf detached himself from the Professor. He said, "Oh well," and then added, "So that's it."

"Yes," said the Professor. "So there we are."

"Now I see," said Ulf, and started to laugh. Blomquist looked at him balefully.

The Professor now offered them a cup of coffee, which Ulf accepted. The Professor looked enquiringly at Blomquist, who was tight-lipped, but who eventually nodded his head.

While the Professor went off to a battered coffee machine on a dirty sink, Blomquist looked accusingly at Ulf. "That was extremely rude," he said.

Ulf reached out to put a hand on Blomquist's shoulder. "I know, I know," he sighed. "But these people . . ." He gestured around the shed. "These people aren't exactly from the top drawer of society, Blomquist. You know how things are."

"But why did he have to whisper?"

Ulf shrugged. "Who knows?"

Blomquist was unassuaged. "I was standing there while you . . ." He spluttered at the indignity of it. "If this were a crime novel, this sort of thing would never happen."

"We are *not* in a crime novel, Blomquist. We are in the real world. Not everything is tied up neatly in the actual world, is it?"

The Professor now returned, carrying a tray on which three unhygienic-looking mugs were filled with greasy black coffee. He handed one each to Ulf and Blomquist before helping himself, blowing across the surface of the coffee to cool it.

"My friend here—Blomquist," Ulf gestured towards Blomquist. "My friend would love to hear about the Great Biker War."

"Great *Nordic* Biker War," the Professor corrected. He turned to Blomquist with a smile. "You're interested in biker history?"

Blomquist took a sip of his coffee, sulkily ignoring the question.

"Yes, he is," Ulf answered for Blomquist.

The Professor sat back in his chair, placing his feet—shod in ornate American cowboy boots—on the desk in front of him. He did not offer a chair to his guests, and so Ulf drew up a stool, brushed some cotton lint off its seat, and gestured for Blomquist to sit down. "Fire away," he encouraged. To Blomquist he said, "Imagine yourself at the University of Lund, Blomquist."

Blomquist stared into his coffee cup. He said nothing.

The Professor cleared his throat. "It all began a long time ago, back in 1980," he intoned. "That was when the first Hells

Angels chapter was established in Copenhagen. They were called United MC, as you may know. They had some good people in it but some bad too, but that's what the world is like, isn't it—good and bad. Schopenhauer and so on. Okay, so these guys had some enemies, you see, another club called The Filthy Few. They didn't like the Angels coming in on their turf, and you have to understand it from their point of view. You have to have what they call *historical perspective*. And so they went to this bar, you see, that was Angels territory. Big rumble. Big time. Those were the first casualties—the first guys to give their lives for their club."

The Professor lowered his eyes, as one commenting on a remembrance ceremony or the repatriation of fallen soldiers might look down in homage and in sadness.

"They were heroes, those guys," the Professor continued. "People say it was all about drugs, but it wasn't. It wasn't that at all. That just shows how ignorant people can be about biker history."

Ulf nodded sympathetically. "People know nothing." It was a simple proposition, and not really true, but he did not think there was much else he could say. And certainly, when it came to biker history, people should just admit it: they knew nothing.

"It was about honour, you see," the Professor went on. "Kids these days don't know what that word means, I can tell you. We get young guys coming in here—eighteen, nineteen—and I say to them 'Define honour.' And you know what? They stare at me and they can't open their mouths. They've never heard the word. Never."

Ulf shook his head. "Shocking," he muttered.

Blomquist stared straight ahead as Ulf started the Saab and began the drive back to the office.

"I know what you're thinking," Ulf said as he nosed the Saab out into the traffic.

Blomquist's tone was resentful. "Do you?"

Ulf glanced at his companion. He had begun to understand the other man better and had come to realise that he was more than usually sensitive. Behind the seemingly endless wittering on about health and dietary issues, there was a person who was easily hurt. And that person was a fundamentally good one, he thought.

"Yes," replied Ulf. "I do understand, Blomquist. You feel cut out of things."

"Well, can you blame me? Nobody wants to involve me. Nobody."

Ulf pointed out that he had gone out of his way to involve him in a number of investigations, including this one. "I'm doing what I can, Blomquist," he said. "And he was the one whispering, not me. Him. You can't blame me for that."

"I feel really excluded," sniffed Blomquist.

"Okay, I get that. But don't blame me, for heaven's sake."

Blomquist turned his head away from Ulf so that he was now staring out of the car window. "And it's not a new thing," he continued. "I've felt like that for a long, long time."

"Really?"

"Yes, I have. When I was a teenager I was a scout. I was quite keen and I learned all the knots and so on. I had a lot of badges: cookery, woodcraft, community service—the lot. But you know what happened? When we went on scout camp, we had tents that took two. We had to share. Or, rather, everybody except me had to share. I was the only one who didn't have anybody to share a tent with."

"I'm sorry to hear that, Blomquist," said Ulf. "I really am."

"Thank you. But it carried on, you know. At police training college we had to find a partner for some of the exercises. Do you think I could find one? No, I could not. They had to team me up with one of the police dogs. It was really embarrassing: everybody had somebody except me. I had a dog."

Ulf asked what the dog was called.

"Rufus," answered Blomquist.

"And was he a good dog?"

Blomquist sighed. "He was. But then he started avoiding me."

"Rufus avoided you?"

Blomquist nodded.

"And that still upsets you?"

Blomquist scratched the back of his neck. "Yes, it does."

"You could see somebody about it, you know. I see a therapist. He's been very helpful." He was not sure why he said that. He did not think that Dr. Svensson had helped him all that much, and he was not at all sure that the psychotherapist would be able to do much for Blomquist.

But Blomquist's interest had been piqued. "Can you give me his details?" he asked. He paused for a moment before adding, in a slightly anxious tone, "I take it he's not too expensive . . ."

"The department pays for most of it," said Ulf. "It's a perk of being part of the Department of Sensitive Crimes."

They continued their journey. A little later, Blomquist again raised the subject of the whispered consultation between Ulf and the Professor. "Am I to be let in on the secret?" he asked.

"Yes," said Ulf. And he told him, and at the end of the explanation Blomquist nodded and said, "Well, well." And then added, "You couldn't make it up, could you?"

To which Ulf said, "No, you couldn't, could you?"

Once back in the office, Ulf found a note on his desk from Anna. He unfolded it carefully and read, "I'm taking the afternoon off. The girls have swimming practice and the trainer wants to speak to me. I'm using some of my flexi-hours entitlement. Can you and I meet to discuss the matter we were talking about the other day? I don't want to talk about it in the office or on the phone—for obvious reasons. Could we have lunch tomorrow, do you think? There's a new Thai place that I read about. We could meet there. Look it up online. It's called the Ko Samui. We should go separately, as I don't want the others to wonder what we're up to. Love, Anna."

Ulf read and re-read the note. *Love, Anna.* She said *Love, Anna.* It was the first time she had used the word *love* and he wondered what it meant. He knew that a lot of people signed off that way, and that in many cases it was meaningless, but this could be different. He slipped the note into the pocket of his jacket, and as he did so, he felt the presence of something he had forgotten was there. It was the new lead that Mrs. Högfors had bought for Martin and that Ulf was planning to return to the supplies department and in this way forfend any of their prying enquiries.

He rose from his desk and crossed the room to where Erik was engaged in sticking labels on files. He asked Erik for a padded envelope in which to send the lead back to supplies.

"That lead we discussed," he said. "I'm going to send it back to supplies."

Erik noticed the lead in Ulf's hand. "May I?" he asked, reaching for it.

He examined it closely, subjecting the gold lettering of its label to particular scrutiny. "What's this van Dog?"

"It's a label," Ulf replied. "That's a designer dog lead, you see. Van Dog is the last word in these things, I'm told."

Erik looked doubtful. "Supplies would never provide a designer dog lead. They just wouldn't. Where's the original?"

"Lost," said Ulf.

"Well then, we should report it as such."

Ulf shook his head. "But if it's reported lost, we have to fill in a lost item report. And you may recall that the lost item form has a section in it headed 'Operational circumstance in which the item was mislaid or destroyed.' Remember that? Well, what are we to put in there? We don't have a dog in the department, as they well know."

Erik looked uncomfortable. "But what if they say, 'This isn't one of ours'? What then?"

"We just ignore their query," said Ulf. "If you ignore things, they go away. Our conscience will be clear."

Erik considered this. "I suppose so," he said at last.

Ulf smiled. "Or I suppose you could say that we're working on a lead."

Erik looked at him blankly, and then found a padded envelope that he handed to Ulf. Ulf wrote a note and slipped it into the envelope, along with the lead. *Re recent query re dog lead: ordered by mistake and now enclosed. Please inform audit department.* He decided to add *soonest* to the final sentence. It was all very well for people like the audit department to insist that others did things *soonest*, but others could use the same term if they wished.

He sealed the envelope and put it in Erik's out-tray. In his mind he had a vision of a bureaucrat somewhere receiving the note and its accompanying lead and suspecting—rightly as it happened—that somewhere there was something irregular happening, but uncertain as to what precisely it was. It was a comforting image. One could make a habit of that, he thought, doing what one could, in tiny, petty ways, to confound the ranks of bureaucrats who presided over those who actually had to do something. It was childish, of course, but then there was a time for childishness, just as there was a time for being adult. The important thing was to know which time was which.

Erik finished his labelling of files and took a fishing magazine out of the drawer of his desk. Ulf noticed a headline on the cover: *Big Trout,* it read. *More News. Record Catches.*

Erik paged through his magazine. Then, quite casually, he said, "What's Ko Samui like? Have you eaten there?"

Ulf froze as the significance of Erik's question struck home. How dare he? How dare he read notes left on his desk, folded so that prying eyes would not fall on them?

He did not answer. He glared at Erik, who looked away. Ulf stared at his hands, struggling to contain his anger. If he could not trust Erik not to read his private correspondence, then could he trust him with anything? He glanced across the room; Erik had risen to his feet and extracted Ulf's padded envelope from his out-tray. "I'm taking this down to the post room," he announced. Ulf nodded curtly.

Now Ulf was alone in the office. He waited for a minute or so before he got up and crossed the room to Erik's desk. Ulf respected the privacy of others, but he had decided that he would show Erik what it was to have one's private papers violated. Opening a drawer, he quickly browsed through its contents. There was a small box of paper clips with, written on the outside in Erik's script, the code used by supplies for such an item. There was a ballpoint pen, slightly chewed at the top; a pair of cheap, over-the-counter reading glasses that Ulf had seen Erik wear only occasionally; an advertisement for fishing-line torn from an angling magazine; there was a circular from the pensions department, several parts of it underlined by Erik in red ink.

He closed the drawer and looked in the one below. This had several fishing magazines, including the one he had seen Erik browsing earlier on. There was the cover that said *Big Trout,* and now Ulf could see, behind the text, a picture of a large trout lying next to a set of fishing scales and a measuring ruler. And then, underneath the magazines, a well-handled notebook. Ulf took this out and examined it.

This was Erik's fishing diary. It took a simple form: on the verso page was a column headed *Place and Date.* This was followed by a column headed *Species and Weight,* and finally, the recto page was given over to a single broad column headed *Observations and Conclusions.* Ulf smiled at this. What possible conclusions could one reach in relation to the unequal struggle recorded in the columns to the left? That a fish had been landed? That if you put a hook into the water with suitable bait attached you will be able, in many cases at least, to drag an unintelligent and unsuspecting fish out of its element and onto a bank? That any fish so treated will die?

He paged through the partly filled book, reaching the final entry, which was for a week earlier. And that was where he read the comment: *Nice trout today. Used one of my new flies. One took, but spat it out (bad luck!). Then a real beauty and one not so big. Should have released the not-so-big one (underweight) but lake superintendent not around so I kept him. Delicious. Conclusion: a small trout can be much tastier than a big one.*

Ulf read the entry rapidly and was about to close the book and put it back in the drawer. He stopped himself. Erik would be back any moment, but he still had time to photocopy the final page of the diary and return it to its drawer. This he did, using the photocopier kept on the table next to the main filing cabinet.

He managed to get the diary back just before Erik returned. Ulf was on his way over to his desk when Erik came in. Erik stopped in the doorway, looked at Ulf and then glanced at his desk. Ulf remained casual. He almost whistled, but did not. He had learned at police college, all those years ago, that a whistle was almost always the equivalent of an admission of guilt. Nobody whistles any longer, they had said. If somebody whistles, they're hiding something.

Ulf sat down at his desk. He did not say anything to Erik as he tucked the photocopy into his pocket. This, he thought, is how a blackmailer must feel: satisfaction at having a piece of evidence of the wrongdoing of another. And power too: it gave you power to know that somebody had broken the law—in this case the law on the permissible size of retained trout. He allowed himself to smile. He was not going to blackmail Erik, but he would nonetheless teach him to respect the privacy of others.

He watched Erik sit down. He noticed that he looked pensive, as if trying to remember something. He saw him open the top drawer and then the drawer below that. He saw him take out the diary briefly and then replace it, evidently reassured.

Ulf almost broke his silence. He almost said, "So, Erik, are illegal trout particularly tasty—not that you would know personally, of course?" But he did not. He would keep his knowledge to himself for the time being, and then, the following morning, he would make a point of arriving in the office early and put the photocopied page on Erik's desk. Later, if challenged, he would simply deny any knowledge of it. That would teach Erik.

But then he stopped and thought. How could he? How could he be so petty—and dishonest? It was a shameful thing to do—something that lowered him to the level of Åke Holmberg; something that made him a blackmailer. He felt for the photocopied page in his pocket. He took it out, stared at it briefly, and then discreetly tore it into numerous small pieces, doing so behind the cover afforded by his desk. These he tossed into his wastepaper bin. He was ashamed; he should not have done what he did, but at least he had repented in time. He felt relieved, as one does when temptation is resisted and one emerges with moral credit.

But there was a further challenge for Ulf, and that was one that he would have to face the following day at lunch. That would be when he told Anna about Jo. He was to be the messenger who brought bleak news, and he was not looking forward to it in the slightest, even though he would be in her company, in a restaurant—something that in normal circumstances would have thrilled him to the core. He thought of Ko Samui and what it would be like: there would be discreet lighting, seats with red upholstery, a water feature, with lotuses perhaps, and a prevailing smell of lemongrass; there were always such things in restaurants with names like Ko Samui. Were there Swedish restaurants in Thailand, he wondered? He rather thought not, which was a pity, as Thai people could well enjoy *smørrebrød* if they had the chance to discover it. There were various other Swedish things they might take to, he thought, even if the atmosphere of Bangkok did not strike one as being particularly Scandinavian. Bergman films though, he imagined, were unlikely to be well received in Thailand, as he thought that the Thais probably preferred slightly *noisier* films. The Indians certainly did; Ulf occasionally watched a Bollywood film and rather enjoyed the lively dance sequences that engulfed the entire cast. That was something one never saw in a Bergman film, nor indeed in any Swedish film, for that matter, although ABBA, to whom Ulf had never really warmed, came perilously close to that from time to time. Mrs. Högfors, of course, liked ABBA, and he would occasionally hear her through the wall, playing "Super Trouper" at full volume, to the accompaniment of an enthusiastic foot routine. She should be careful, he thought: ABBA was responsible for many a fall. If elderly people became too excited, they could fall over, and that would be ABBA's fault.

Ulf thought of Martin; before he had lost his hearing, he had enjoyed ABBA and had barked in time to their bouncy rhythms. Now, when ABBA was played, he simply looked puzzled, a reaction that Dr. Håkansson had put down to Martin's sensing the vibrations that came with ABBA's music. "That's how deaf musicians manage to hear music," the vet had said. "And it's the same with animals."

No, Sweden and Thailand were very different, Ulf thought, but it would still be to everyone's benefit if the Thais could become *slightly* more Swedish in their approach to life. One would never want to impose; that was a very un-Swedish approach, but one could just suggest that a city like Bangkok might be marginally more sustainable if they were to be a little bit more Swedish. Swedish tuk-tuks, at least, would be environmentally more responsible than the fume-belching vehicles that Ulf had seen featured in a recent television documentary, but he doubted if the Thais would ever take kindly to being told not to belch fumes. Most people did not, come to think of it; they regarded it as impertinent, but sooner or later they would have to listen to what others had to say about these matters.

His mind returned to the proposed trip to the restaurant and to the thought of Anna seated opposite him, perusing the menu. It would be wonderful to be knowledgeable about Thai food and to be able to explain the dishes to her, but it was likely to be the other way round. She would tell him about the menu, and he would meekly choose what she suggested. But he would be happy to do that, as he would like anything she chose—he knew he would. The picture darkened; he saw Anna waiting anxiously for his verdict, which could be only one word: *yes*. One word would end a marriage and a world. A short, single word that was normally so positive but could be so negative too. He sighed. Sometimes that was the only reaction one could muster to the world. One might intend to emit a more positive sound—a gasp of pleasure, for example—and it would come out as a sigh. That was what the world provoked in us—a sigh; for all the things we had to do that we did not want to do; for all the things that we had not done but that we would have liked to have done; for all that, and more— a sigh. *Weltschmerz*. Those German words were so useful at times, and this one seemed just right for what Ulf felt. *Weltschmerz*: this expressed in a couple of syllables a whole hinterland of regret and sorrow; as broad, in its way, as Sweden's own great northern hinterland—lonely, pristine, beyond the reach of human warmth.

Chapter Fifteen

NOT ABBA

That night Ulf had a vivid dream that was to have implications far greater than does the average nightmare. In this dream he was driving his Saab, with Martin in the seat beside him, through a pleasant stretch of rolling countryside. The air was fresh and through the open windows of the car it was making Martin's ears flap, exposing small unfamiliar hearing aids that had been inserted in each ear. Ulf felt content, as it seemed to him that he had no clear destination and no pressing need to reach it. But then the tone of the dream changed abruptly. Rounding a bend, he saw on the road ahead of him a police roadblock. Two figures stepped out from behind this roadblock and signalled to Ulf to pull over. One of these was Commissioner Ahlbörg.

Ahlbörg's manner was elaborately polite, enquiring after Ulf's health and ruffling Martin's fur in an avuncular way. But then he peered into the back seat of the car and saw the grille that Viligot Danior had given Ulf in gratitude for his support. "That," pronounced the Commissioner, "is a bribe, Varg. You're dismissed."

Ulf had protested his innocence. "I was going to report it," he said. "I was on my way."

The Commissioner was not impressed. "To where? You were on your way to where?"

Ulf's reply came quickly. "To the past," he said. "I was on my way to . . ." And there he faltered and stopped. Where was he going with the grille? He had no idea. And then Martin turned to him and said, in perfectly articulated Swedish, "This is your own fault, you know."

For a moment Ulf forgot about the presence of the Commissioner and thought only of the miracle of speech he had just witnessed. Martin had never spoken to him before, and now here he was speaking perfect, if somewhat old-fashioned, Swedish.

He woke up, the absurd dream still fresh in his mind. He opened his eyes, staring up at the ceiling above his bed. Light from the street lamps outside penetrated the louvre blinds on his window, casting a striated shadow on the ceiling. The shadow reminded him of a Saab grille.

He sat up in bed and looked at his watch. It was five in the morning, an hour and a half before his normal waking time. He thought again of the dream. The grille was still in the house, propped up against the desk in the spare room. He had been meaning to do something about it, but had been in a form of denial that had resulted in inaction, and now it was far too late. It was the same as with the lead, but infinitely more serious. If he were to be found to have accepted an unacknowledged gift, even one that he had in no sense solicited, then what had happened in the dream could happen in real life. And if he were dismissed he would lose certain pension rights. He would also find it difficult to get a job because nobody would want to employ a detective who had been dismissed for corruption. Corruption . . . it was so unfair. Ulf had kept his hands clean throughout his career; he was scrupulously honest—to the point where he found it impossible to tell even the whitest of lies. And yet, the longer he had the grille in his possession, the more difficult it would be to disencumber himself of it and the more compromised he would be if anybody were to see it. Sometimes the authorities called on police officers without any notice in order to assess their living standards. That was the way they caught corrupt officers, who would be living beyond their means; and not just corrupt officers who had accepted bribes, but those who had thoughtlessly allowed people like Viligot Danior to give them presents.

Ulf got out of bed and opened the bedroom window. He breathed in the fresh morning air and made his decision. He could not go and dump the grille anywhere because he knew, from past experience in his investigative career, that when people tried to dump a weapon they were inevitably spotted in the act. There were CCTV cameras at every turn now, and you never knew who was watching you. Then there were passers-by who had a habit of seeing things being tossed away by criminals who had no idea they were being observed. If he took the grille to the municipal dump, he would be spotted. If he jettisoned it beside a road somewhere, there was bound to be a cyclist turning the corner at the wrong moment or a woman looking out of her farmhouse window. No, he would deal with it in a completely different way.

He did not bother to have breakfast, but made himself a double dose of espresso. Thus fortified, Ulf retrieved the Saab grille from the spare room and wrapped it in sheets of the previous day's newspaper. Then he woke Martin, who was a deep sleeper in spite of his depression. He had an old lead that he was now using, having returned the new one to supplies, and this he fastened to Martin's collar. Carrying the Saab grille under his arm, he left the apartment and made his way down to the car. Martin, who had been sluggish to start with, now perked up, sniffing at the morning air with enthusiasm.

Ulf knew the changing social geography of the city as well as any member of the uniformed branch. He knew where the gangs lived; he knew where local bonds rubbed up against imported loyalties; he knew where street crime was at its most intense, and that was where he now headed. He had picked Seved because Blomquist had talked about it and its problems. "They tell us it's a particularly vulnerable area," he said. "I say that it's a particularly criminal area. But . . ." He shrugged. "I'm not a sociologist, Varg. Nor a criminologist. I'm a policeman." Then he had said something that Ulf remembered. "There's one street where, I can tell you, if anything is not nailed down, it goes. Leave something in your car for five minutes, come back, and it's gone." It was to Seved that Ulf now headed.

Once in the district, he picked his street at random, nosing the Saab into a vacant parking place by a small grocery store. The lights were on in the store and he could see people moving about—the morning in this part of the city evidently started early.

"We're going for a walk, Martin," Ulf said. "Not a long one. Half an hour, maybe."

The dog looked up at him, watching his lips. He made out *walk* and wagged his tail.

Leaving all the car's windows open, Ulf set off. He felt a bit uncomfortable in this area but told himself that none of the watching eyes would know that he was a detective. In their mind, here was just another man with a dog, a stranger who had business, perhaps, with a dealer somewhere—nobody to bother about very much.

Ulf and Martin walked for forty minutes or so. A small group of youths took an interest in them in one street, but were wary of Martin, who was a good size and would probably be capable of looking after himself. They watched, but did nothing. Ulf merely stared ahead of him, wondering what teenagers were doing being up at this hour: no respectable teenager would be up at six in the morning. These young men, he told himself, were the night shift. They would go to their beds shortly, handing over to the day shift.

He planned the walk so that his route would bring him back at the other end of the street on which he had parked. As he rounded the corner at that end, he looked down towards the Saab. It was no longer there.

Ulf stood stock-still. His plan had been simple. He would leave the car unattended for a short time and the grille would be stolen, just as Blomquist had predicted. And that, according to the original plan, would have been that. But it had gone terribly wrong. The Saab itself had obviously been stolen.

He walked briskly down the street, mentally cursing his harebrained scheme. When he reached the place where the car had been, he saw the grille lying on the ground, having been thrown out of the car by the thieves. Martin sniffed at the grille and looked up at Ulf expectantly, but Ulf had nothing he could say to Martin. He closed his eyes. He wanted to cry. He loved that car—he loved it. And now some low type, filled with antipathy towards everything that the Saab represented, would be driving around in it, abusing its gearbox, planning, no doubt, to set fire to it on some desolate piece of wasteland, once he had grown tired of it. He felt the tears of frustration and self-reproach well in his eyes. And they were tears for other things too. They were tears for what had been lost. Tears for social trust. Tears for the failed idea of community and mutual respect. Tears for the death of an ideal that he, like so many others, still wanted to believe in but that he feared would not survive.

Blomquist found him several hours later in the café opposite work. Ulf did not notice the other man for a few moments, as he was staring into his coffee cup. Looking up, he saw Blomquist looking down at him with concern.

"You all right, Varg?"

Ulf nodded, but could tell that it was an unconvincing nod.

"Tell Uncle," said Blomquist, sitting down.

Ulf winced. He had heard Blomquist use that phrase before and it grated. But this was not the time to raise the issue, and so he simply replied, "My Saab's been lifted."

Blomquist looked aghast. "That beautiful old car?"

"Yes. I took it for a drive this morning—just to get some air." He was not going to reveal his failed plan to Blomquist, even if it involved a … well, he did not want to use the word *lie,* but he was in extremis now and he might be allowed some leeway.

"Where did you report it?" asked Blomquist.

Ulf was silent.

"I take it you *did* report it?" Blomquist pressed.

Ulf shook his head. "What's the point? You know as well as I do that our friends in the car crime department can't cope. Nobody can cope." He paused. "It's all very well for us in sensitive crimes. We have oceans of time to look into these small things we look into. But when it comes to bombs and shootings and car theft and so on—how can they possibly manage?"

Rather to Ulf's surprise, Blomquist agreed. "You're right. But there must be something we can do."

"We can accept it," said Ulf.

Blomquist looked thoughtful. "You remember that fellow you told me about? The one who was assaulted by the Lutheran minister?"

Ulf made a resigned gesture. "I remember him. Yes."

"What was his name?"

"Viligot Danior," said Ulf. "He's a member of—"

"Yes, I know," said Blomquist. "I'm not sure what the correct word is these days, but he's paid up in that department. Anyway— you said that you liked him?"

Ulf took a sip of his coffee. "Yes, I did. I think those people can have a tough time. People are against them. They accuse them of everything."

Blomquist hesitated. "They don't do everything," he said. "But some of them, you must admit, at least do something. Not that I'm stereotyping them, of course."

Ulf glanced at him. "Of course."

"Give him a call," said Blomquist.

"Why?"

"Because he may be able to help. He's in the car-stealing business, I imagine. Not that I'm stereotyping anybody. Or he'll know somebody who is."

Ulf thought about this. "I don't think I should. I was involved in his case. It would be as if I was asking for a favour."

"And it would be a favour," agreed Blomquist. "Mind you, there's no reason why I shouldn't approach him. He and I have nothing in the past. I could call him and say, 'My friend—you know, the one who helped you—has lost a rather nice old Saab; you wouldn't know anything about it, would you?' I could do that."

Ulf shrugged. "I suppose you could."

"Then I'm going to do it," said Blomquist. "Can you give me his number?"

"Get it from Carl," said Ulf. "It's in the file."

Blomquist ordered a cup of coffee and a second one for Ulf. As they drank it, Blomquist said, "You know that business with the dogs?"

In spite of the loss of his car, Ulf managed a smile. "Funny, wasn't it?"

"You said that that Estonian guy—the one who exported the dogs that looked like wolves—you said that he trains the dogs to be extras in films."

"Yes. He does. He gets dogs that look like wolves, spends a lot of time training them, and then sells them to film companies that need wolves in their movies. It's a successful business, apparently. I suppose one would call it a pretty niche business."

"And all above board?"

"Of course. No harm done. It's just that my vet—the vet who

looks after Martin, Dr. Håkansson—he got the wrong end of the stick. He thought he was exporting dogs that he was selling as wolves, whereas everybody knew that they were dogs who just looked like wolves."

Blomquist fiddled with his cup. "My sister has a dog," he said. "He's a good dog—very obedient. But she thinks he could be an actor. You know, in one of those shows where the dog rescues people—something like that. She's written a screenplay about a dog who does all these brave things, you see. She had her own dog in mind . . ." He trailed off. Ulf was staring at him.

"I'll put you in touch with him," said Ulf. "You never know." He looked at his watch. "I have somebody to go and speak to, Blomquist. I'd like you to come with me as back-up. Just in case."

"I'll make that phone call before we go," said Blomquist. "Then that will be out of the way."

Ulf did not say anything. Sometimes it was better to remain silent when one was concerned about a voice trail, the equivalent of a paper trail but always less compromising, being written, as spoken words are, in smoke, on the shifting air.

Åke Holmberg," said Ulf. "This is my colleague, Blomquist. He is also in the Department of Sensitive Crimes."

Åke had come down to reception to meet them. He was holding a clipboard and looked distracted.

"This isn't a very convenient time," he said curtly.

"That's not the point," said Ulf. "And I'm afraid that we don't care in the slightest whether or not it's convenient for you."

Åke gave a start. He had not expected this robust response, and his manner changed. He opened his mouth to speak, but then closed it.

"You'll know why we're here," said Ulf. It was a classic line, used by detectives who were not sure of their ground. In many cases it worked, and people blurted out their excuses, not realising that the detective had nothing on them to begin with. Åke's response showed that in this case it was working.

"We can't talk here," said Åke, his voice barely above a whisper. "There's a canteen in the basement. We can go there."

Ulf agreed, and the journalist led the way down a corridor to a staircase descending into the basement. Somewhere, there was the sound of a printing press rolling out the late edition of the paper. There was a smell of ink.

"It's a bit noisy," said Åke, "but we can talk in private here."

They sat on either side of a small, Formica-topped table.

"I can explain," Åke began.

Ulf raised an eyebrow. It was so much easier if the criminal confessed to everything. "Go ahead," he said. "But I must warn you, Blomquist here will be noting down what you say. You are not obliged to say anything, you know."

"I want to," said Åke.

"All right," said Ulf, "but frankly I don't see how you can explain blackmail."

Åke looked surprised. "Blackmail?"

"Yes," said Ulf. "Extortion. Obtaining money from others by threats."

Åke's surprise deepened. "I don't see what that's got to do with me."

Ulf snorted. "You may not like the label, but mud's mud whichever way you look at it."

"Mud?"

"Blackmail," said Blomquist. "You know what they call it? Murder of the soul."

Åke stared at Blomquist uncomprehendingly. "Murder?"

"Of the soul," Blomquist said.

Åke shook his head. "Nils was helping me. He wasn't blackmailing me—or anybody for that matter."

Ulf laughed. "He's not the blackmailer, Holmberg—you are."

"Me?" Åke's astonishment seemed genuine enough. "Me? A blackmailer?"

Ulf could tell immediately that Åke's protestation of innocence was sincere. For a moment he wondered where this was leading. Åke wanted to explain something, but it clearly was something other than blackmail. And that just went to underline the proposition that people would incriminate themselves if they thought you knew something that you did not know at all.

"You'd best explain," said Ulf. That would do, he thought.

"I only borrowed the money," said Åke. "I promise you. I meant to pay it back. I was told that the scheme was absolutely cast-iron and that we'd get seventeen per cent, guaranteed, within six months of the original investment."

Ulf's expression was impassive. "But you didn't?"

"No, we didn't. And then I discovered that it was a—what do you call it—a Ponzi scheme. They took money from a lot of people and then used it to pay back the earlier investors. Classic Ponzi."

Blomquist was shaking his head incredulously. "Why did you fall for it? You, a journalist and all?"

"I was desperate," said Åke. "I'd got myself into a mess." He looked about him, lowering his voice. The sound of the press was still sufficiently loud to mask their conversation, and there were only one or two other people in the canteen, at the far end. "I owed money. I had payments to make to my creditors. One of them was threatening to take me to court."

Ulf groaned. He had a horror of debt and could imagine no bigger nightmare than to be burdened with an unrepayable debt. He had felt for Greece when the party came to an end and the Germans blew the whistle on them. They had asked for it, of course, but still . . .

"I borrowed the money from upstairs," Åke continued. "I was a trustee of the Journalists' Benevolent Fund."

Ulf groaned again. That was the worst sort of embezzlement, he thought—taking money from a charity.

Åke was looking down at his hands. "I regret it," he said. "I regret it more than I can say."

Blomquist glared at him. "Benevolent fund," he muttered.

"I know," said Åke. "I know. But anyway, I had to pay it back and that was where Nils came in. His partner is an old girlfriend of mine. We remained really good friends after we split up. Almost like brother and sister."

Ulf looked up. "Ebba?"

"Yes. I didn't want her to know, and so when I asked Nils whether he could help me by lending me the money, I asked him if he could keep the payments secret from her. He agreed."

Ulf felt it was now beginning to make sense. "So there's no blackmail?"

"Heavens no," said Åke. "In fact, he gave me the money rather than lending it." He paused, watching the effect of this on his visitors. "Yes, that's the sort of man he is, you know. This image he has . . ."

"That image is deceptive," said Ulf.

"Yes," said Åke. "It certainly is. But to get back to what I was telling you, I've repaid every penny of the money I borrowed." He paused. "I've felt terrible. I'm an honest man, Mr. Varg, and this is the only time I've ever done anything like this. I promise you that—the only time. And I'll never, ever do anything like that again." He paused again, and then continued, "Not that I expect you to believe me on that."

Ulf took a deep breath. One crime had been excluded, but another had been revealed. According to the book, he should now caution Åke and report him to the commercial crime squad. According to the book . . . But was the book always written with real life in mind? Did the book ever allow for the exercise of that most fundamental of human virtues—mercy? Or with an eye to forgiveness? He looked at Åke in his misery. What purpose would be served by prosecuting him now for a crime that he had rectified by paying back the money he had borrowed?

Ulf said, "Will you excuse us for a moment?" He turned to Blomquist and signalled for him to follow him to the other side of the room.

"Well?" said Ulf.

Blomquist shrugged. "He took money."

"Yes, I know, but—"

"From a benevolent fund."

"Yes, I know. So I take it you think we should turn him in?"

Blomquist hesitated before he replied. "Not necessarily."

"So we let him off with a warning?" Ulf asked. It was what he wanted to do but he was concerned that Blomquist might disapprove.

"Yes," said Blomquist. "You can't punish everybody for every-thing."

They returned to where Åke was waiting for them. "May I ask you something?" said Ulf.

"Of course."

"That article you were going to write—the one that threatened to disclose something about Nils Cederström—what was that about?"

"Nothing," said Åke. "It was his idea."

Ulf waited.

"He suggested it," Åke went on. "It's his image. You know how he likes people to think he's some sort of *enfant terrible.*"

Ulf did know that. And it all made perfect sense. He glanced at Blomquist, who nodded.

"All right," said Ulf. "I won't for a moment condone what you did. But ..."

Åke looked at him pleadingly.

"I'm going to ignore what you told us," Ulf went on. "Provided that—"

"Anything," said Åke. "Anything at all. Name it."

"Your word," said Ulf. "Give me your word that you will not do this again."

Åke was trembling. "You have that."

"Good," said Ulf. "Case closed then."

They went outside, and as they did, Blomquist's mobile phone rang. He took the call and then rang off. He turned to Ulf with a smile.

"That was Viligot Danior," he said. "He's arranged for your car to be returned. It will be left outside your apartment this evening by five."

Ulf clapped his hands together in joy. "Blomquist!" he exclaimed. "You great man! You wonderful colleague! You hero!"

Blomquist shrugged off the compliments. "Thank him, not me," he said. And then, after thinking a little bit more, he said, "Karma, Varg. Karma. Good things happen to those who do good things."

Ulf made a face. Like so many good people, he did not think of himself as good.

"No, I mean it," said Blomquist.

He arrived at Ko Samui before Anna did and was sitting at a table near the window when her car drew up outside. He saw her park, and when she got out of the car and walked towards the restaurant door, his heart gave a lurch. He closed his eyes for a moment; love was a wound in the soul—we told ourselves that it was something else, but it was simply a wound, as real and as troublesome as any real tearing of the flesh. And it came upon us at random, afflicting us without warning, occurring when we were sitting in a café or walking across a park or doing any of the other ordinary human things that filled our days: love came upon us and smote us as a biblical figure might smite an enemy. Love did that, for that was what love was: an injury. We fondly thought that it was a blessing, but it was not.

She came to the table and apologised for being late.

"But you aren't," he reassured her. "I was early."

"You're so kind, Ulf," she said as she sat down. "You always blame yourself for things, even when it's the other person's fault."

He looked away, in pain; and the pain was caused by the thought of what he must do.

"The girls have another of these big competitions coming up," she said. "The Norwegians are coming. We have to beat them."

"Norwegians? Well, well." Why did people exercise themselves over the Norwegians so much? Norwegians were simply *there,* like the weather, like the trees. You didn't have to *swim* against them all the time.

But Anna had more to say. "The Norwegians are very good at backstroke."

That was news to Ulf. Was it yet another thing to worry about? These Norwegians with their ordered society and their low crime rate and their massive sovereign wealth fund ... and now their backstroke.

"What about the breaststroke?" asked Ulf.

Anna shook her head. "I think we might win that. Certainly, the one hundred metres. No, we've got a good chance there."

"I hope so," said Ulf. His heart was filled with despair and even the thought of a victory in the one-hundred-metre breast-stroke could do little to raise his spirits. He was about to destroy a marriage. That he would benefit from that—that Anna might then be free for him—was, at that moment, little consolation.

She picked up the menu, glanced at it, and then replaced it on the table. She looked at Ulf.

"I have to ask you," she said softly. "I'm sitting here thinking about keeping this conversation going and not getting to the point. We could talk about the girls and their swimming. We could talk about Martin and his depression. We could talk about Thai food and what goes with what, and about lemongrass and so on, but all the time, all the time, it would be there with us—that question." She paused, picking up the menu again, and Ulf saw that her hand was shaking.

He made up his mind. He reached out and took her hand in his. It was the first time he had done that—ever. It was the first time that he had taken the hand of the woman he loved so much.

"Jo is *not* having an affair," he said.

He felt her hand tremble, and then it pressed tight against his. "He isn't?"

He shook his head. "You have nothing to worry about. As I said, Jo is not having an affair. Whatever made you worry is ... well, nothing to worry about."

Her eyes lit up. "You're sure? You're absolutely sure?"

He repeated his verdict. "As I told you, he is *not* seeing another woman. You can put it out of your mind."

He looked up at the ceiling. What do I expect to see up there? he asked himself. The recording angel? He had told the truth. There had been an affair, but it was no longer. Jo had obviously made his choice, and it was to stay with Anna. Ulf would give him a second chance, even if it meant that there was no chance for him.

He became aware that Anna was crying. He reached out to her again, but she was busying herself with a handkerchief.

"Sorry," she said. "It sounds corny, but I'm crying from joy."

Ulf forced himself to smile. "I'm so pleased," he said. "Now, let's choose something for lunch. I have to get back and write a report."

"Oh, reports," said Anna. "Reports, reports, reports!"

That evening, Ulf Varg, senior officer in the Department of Sensitive Crimes, graduate in criminology of the University of Lund, owner of a hearing-impaired dog called Martin—the only dog in Sweden to have been taught to lip-read—enthusiast of Scandinavian art, friend of many but still a rather private man, returned to his apartment from work by taxi. There, in front of the building, was his familiar silver-grey Saab, a beautiful piece of engineering that stood for so much—for the skill of *Homo faber*, for the idea that the useful could be beautiful, for the very concept of Sweden. He paid the taxi fare, and the driver said to him, "Nice car, that."

Ulf did not go immediately to the car. He went upstairs and knocked on Mrs. Högfors's door. She opened it to him with a smile. "I was just about to take Martin out for a walk," she said.

"Then come with me," he said. "We can both take him."

"I'd love that," she said.

Martin bounded out, licking Ulf enthusiastically.

They went outside. Martin saw the Saab and went over to investigate it. He sniffed at the wheels and at one of the doors. Then he growled.

Mrs. Högfors was puzzled. "What's Martin up to?" she asked.

Ulf frowned. He imagined that Martin was picking up the scent of the thieves.

Martin barked.

"Odd," said Mrs. Högfors. "He barked like that when he saw some Russians in the park the other day. Just like that. I call it his Russian bark."

Ulf approached the Saab. Perhaps it was just the light, but it seemed to be a slightly different shade, as if the paintwork were newer. He reached for the key in his pocket and attempted to slip it into the slot in the door handle. It did not fit.

He looked up at the sky. He thought of Viligot Danior and his family of thieves. That's what they were—thieves. And they had stolen somebody else's Saab in order to please him.

Mrs. Högfors sensed that something was wrong. "Are you all right?" she asked.

Ulf took a deep breath. This was just too complicated. "I'm fine," he said.

Martin had bounded off. "We'd better keep up with him," said Mrs. Högfors. "He's got good road sense, but I don't like him to get too far away."

"No," said Ulf. "You shouldn't let dogs get too far away." *Or anything,* he thought. *Or anything.*

They turned the corner. And there he saw another silver-grey Saab parked next to a large white van. He stopped in his tracks.

"Is that your car?" asked Mrs. Högfors. "I thought the other one . . ."

"My mistake," said Ulf with a smile.

He wanted to leap in the air. He wanted to shout out his delight to all around him. He wanted to burst into song. But he was Ulf Varg, of the Department of Sensitive Crimes, and there were things that you didn't do, even if you were very pleased with the world. After all, not everybody behaved as if they were ABBA.